I walked down the corridor, feeling like I was going to the executioner's block.

There was a receptionist for the chief's office along with the county attorney and the sheriff. I didn't recognize her, which was just as well. This visit wasn't something I wanted shared on social media.

She looked up expectantly. "Yes?"

"I need to see Chief Fowler." I was amazed that my voice was steady.

"Do you have an appointment?"

I shook my head. "He'll want to talk to me. Tell him it's Roxy Constantine."

The receptionist picked up her phone and dialed a number, turning away from me as she spoke.

Of course, I wasn't absolutely sure Fowler would want to see me. Maybe he'd be too busy. Maybe he wasn't interested. Maybe…

The receptionist glanced up at me. "Go on in. He'll see you now."

So much for hope. I opened the office door and stepped inside.

Fowler was sitting at his utilitarian, city-issued desk. He gazed up at me with that same unsmiling, inscrutable look he always seemed to wear. I wondered if he ever smiled. Probably not at people like me, people he suspected of murder.

I cleared my throat. "I have some things to tell you."

He gestured to the chair in front of his desk. "Sit down, Ms. Constantine. I've been expecting you."

The Pepper Peach Murder

by

Meg Benjamin

A Luscious Delights Mystery

The Pepper Peach Murder

Cover Art by *Tina Lynn Stout*

The Wild Rose Press, Inc.
PO Box 708
Adams Basin, NY 14410-0708
Visit us at www.thewildrosepress.com

Publishing History
First Edition, 2023
Trade Paperback ISBN 978-1-5092-4692-2
Digital ISBN 978-1-5092-4693-9

A Luscious Delights Mystery
Published in the United States of America

Dedication

As always to my long-suffering hubs, and to Carol Ann,
who's always around for a good chat.

Deb —
Great talking
with you. Good luck
with your writing!
Meg Benjamin

Prologue

The Shavano County Courthouse isn't as charming as the rest of the town. The original granite building was torn down a decade ago, and the town put up a utilitarian square made of tan-colored brick. It houses courtrooms, judicial chambers, and the county attorney's office.

Also the county sheriff and the Shavano police department. And the jail.

It is not, under any circumstances, a cheerful place, even on a bright Colorado bluebird morning. Once again, I thought about turning around and heading home.

It would be better for him to hear it from you than to discover it on his own.

Nate's voice still echoed in my ears. For a moment, I wished I'd asked him to come with me. But I had to face this on my own. It was my disaster, after all.

I climbed up the stairs to the front door, pausing for a moment to check the directory on the wall inside. The chief's office was on the first floor, right down the hall. Once I turned in that direction, there'd be no going back. I'd be committed to confessing.

I walked down the corridor, feeling like I was going to the executioner's block.

There was a receptionist for the chief's office along with the county attorney and the sheriff. I didn't recognize her, which was just as well. This visit wasn't something I wanted shared on social media.

She looked up expectantly. "Yes?"

"I need to see Chief Fowler." I was amazed that my voice was steady.

"Do you have an appointment?"

I shook my head. "He'll want to talk to me. Tell him it's Roxy Constantine."

The receptionist picked up her phone and dialed a number, turning away from me as she spoke.

Of course, I wasn't absolutely sure Fowler would want to see me. Maybe he'd be too busy. Maybe he wasn't interested. Maybe…

The receptionist glanced up at me. "Go on in. He'll see you now."

So much for hope. I opened the office door and stepped inside.

Fowler was sitting at his utilitarian, city-issued desk. He gazed up at me with that same unsmiling, inscrutable look he always seemed to wear. I wondered if he ever smiled. Probably not at people like me, people he suspected of murder.

I cleared my throat. "I have some things to tell you."

He gestured to the chair in front of his desk. "Sit down, Ms. Constantine. I've been expecting you."

Chapter 1

"Don't you dare boil over, you bastard."

Honestly, I don't normally curse that much (although my uncle Mike might snicker if he heard me make that claim). The one exception is when I'm making jam. There's something about a jam pot that can lead to lots and lots of obscenities. You need to keep the damn thing in line. Jam has a mind of its own, and you need to show it who's boss. Or at least try to.

I gave the jam pot a smoldering look. Not that smoldering looks would do anything to stop it from boiling over, but it made me feel better.

Herman stared up at me from his cushion on the other side of the cabin, trying to judge the threat level. The Great Dane part of his bloodline is into protection, particularly protection of me. The mutt part is more into napping. "It's okay, Herman," I muttered as I tried to get to the boiling pot. "Don't worry about it. I'm fine. So help me."

I let the jar I was currently pulling out of the canning kettle sink into the hot water and stretched across the stove to turn down the burner under the offending jam pot. Raspberry-colored molten goodness was still popping out of the kettle to land on the cooktop, and the smell of burning sugar filled the air.

"Crap, crap, crap, crap." Like I said, jam involves a lot of cursing, along with a lot of dexterity around very hot substances. I pulled on my heavy silicon gloves and moved the brimming kettle to the cold burner at the back. A ribbon of jewel-bright raspberry flowed across my glove as I did it, still hot even though the silicon protected me from the worst of the spill. At least I wouldn't get a burn out of it, although the heat was enough to remind me to be more careful next time.

The ding of the timer yanked me back to my original mission. "Crap, crap, crap."

Herman gave another concerned whimper as he watched me hop to the other burner. He considers himself a watch dog, but he didn't really want to get involved in what was going on. Not with me cussing up a storm. He knows when to lay low.

"Don't get upset, Herm," I reassured him. "I'm fine." I grabbed the lifter again and fastened the tongs on the top of the jar of processed jam, hoisting it carefully out of the boiling water. One down, seven to go.

One by one I lined up the glistening jars on the work table rack. They'd have to sit overnight so I could check to make sure the seals were good. Once they'd passed inspection, I'd slap on the labels and put them in a carton for the farmers market.

It was mid-May, which meant the market vendors wouldn't have a lot of fresh produce yet. Most of the products on sale this Saturday would be ready-made stuff like my jam and Bianca Jordan's baked goods and maybe some jerky or honey or hot sauce.

This week's farmers market would be my chance to hook a few customers before they got distracted by fresh peaches and sweet corn. I needed to concentrate on getting a good selection of jam ready to go before Saturday, and burning a pot of jam wouldn't help.

I really shouldn't have tried to do two things at once. It always makes me impatient, which makes the jam persnickety. Honestly, fruit knows when you're not being properly respectful. Burned jam is the punishment for losing your temper.

I turned to check the offending pot. Streaks of raspberry dappled the sides while the smell of burnt sugar lingered around the stove. I put my hands on my hips, ready to reassert my control over the raspberries. I was, after all, in charge of this kitchen. "If you're scorched, I'm going to be more than pissed."

"Talking to inanimate objects again?" Uncle Mike's voice made me jump. He stood in the kitchen doorway, grinning. He must have come in the front door of my cabin while I was fighting with the jam pot.

"Geez, give a girl some warning." I waved a hand in front of my face, waiting for my heart rate to slow.

"Where's the fun in that?" He sniffed the air, frowning in Herman's direction as he walked farther into my kitchen. "What'd she burn this time, Herman?"

Herman pushed himself to his feet, padding over to bonk his head against my uncle's thigh. It was almost enough to bowl him over, but not quite. Herman's a gentle giant who sort of belongs to both of us.

"It's not burned. Some jam got on the cooktop. I'm working to save it." I gave the kettle a quick stir, trying to see if the bottom had scorched.

"For Saturday?" Uncle Mike rested against the counter, raising an eyebrow. The knees of his jeans were stained with dirt, but the rest of him looked relatively clean. At least he wouldn't muck up my kitchen. He scratched Herman's ears absently.

"Maybe. If it sets up in time. It's raspberry. That

usually sells out."

"Using frozen berries?"

"Yeah. The ones I put up last summer."

He frowned. "Won't be as good as fresh, will it?"

"It'll be good enough." If something is just *good enough,* it usually isn't worth spit. But the jam I make with frozen fruit is actually okay. Not as great as the version I make with fresh fruit, but still good. I never put out anything less than good—my brand means something, even in the small market of Shavano, Colorado.

"What's that?" Uncle Mike gestured toward the two cartons of jars sitting near the door.

"Pepper peach." I raised my chin and gave him my best *don't mess with me* look.

The smile he returned was dry. "Still pushing it? Hope springs eternal, eh, Herman?" Herman gave him a jaundiced look before returning to his cushion in the corner.

"It moves great later in the summer when the tourists come to town. There's no reason it won't sell in the spring, too." Pepper peach was a real sore point for me. It was tasty but unusual. Tourists from Denver and the Front Range loved it. But a lot of people from Shavano thought spicy jam was weird.

"You know the people who come around the farmers market right now are locals." Uncle Mike shook his head. "They're not the most adventurous folks. Trust me—I'm the man who tried to peddle strawberry leather a few years ago."

I returned his dry smile. "The same strawberry leather that sells out at the farmers market in Boulder?"

"The very same. But college students will eat

anything. Around here, you have to ease into things."

"I'm only going to take a couple of cases of the pepper peach. If they don't move now, I can always sell them later."

Uncle Mike grinned. "If I didn't know you so well, I'd swear you'd mellowed. How'd you do in town this morning?"

I sighed. My marketing skills aren't great, although I work hard. I'd been trying to sell my jams to some of the local restaurants. But so far I hadn't had a lot of luck. "I talked to Madge Robicheaux and Lorna Griffin. I'm doing a tasting for Lorna next week. Madge's being a little hard to get." I gave the raspberry jam another vigorous stir. So far it didn't look scorched.

"Robicheaux's Café does a good breakfast business. Back in the day they did, anyway. I'd think they'd be interested in some first-rate jam to go along with their biscuits."

"They'd be more than interested if I could make it as cheap as those little packets they use now. Madge said she'd like to try it, but I need to work the numbers a little more to see if I can do a deal for them."

Uncle Mike settled against the counter. "What did you think of Robicheaux's? I haven't been there since Robert Robicheaux was cooking. Used to be a great diner when he was in the kitchen."

"Seemed busy. Lots of people at the counter. Mostly burgers and fries from what I could tell."

"I'll have to go check them out sometime. Used to make a hell of a cheeseburger. And Madge Robicheaux's a great manager." Uncle Mike rubbed a hand through his salt-and-pepper hair. "You want a ride to the market Saturday? Carmen and Donnie are taking the van for the greens."

I shook my head. "They'll probably sell out before I do. I'll take my truck." Carmen and Donnie worked with Uncle Mike year-round. They lived just down the road and would probably sell out in the first hour, given the quality of Uncle Mike's spinach and arugula.

"Okay, sweetheart. If you change your mind, just call me." He stood again, maybe a little more slowly than usual, a sign he'd been picking greens in the cold frames.

The man has been farming most of his life and has arthritis in his hands and knees that creak like the stairs in a haunted house when he stands up. He should have been supervising more than picking.

"I thought you were going to take it easy this week," I chided.

He stretched, pressing his hands to his lower back. "I did. This is me taking it easy. You just don't recognize it. You don't see it enough."

I bit my lip and kept my peace. I never like to think about Uncle Mike growing old. He's been my rock, my savior, my protector through thick and thin from the time my dad and I moved to the farm when I was three. But now I'm fully grown—more than fully grown, some would say—and I don't need a protector as much as I once did.

I leaned over to kiss his cheek. "Let Donnie pick the spinach and arugula, okay? That's why you have a crew, as I recall."

"I don't pick. I organize." He gave me a hug and turned toward the door. "See you at dinner."

"Okay." I watched him amble out toward the cold frames, probably to pick a few more pounds of early arugula. I could bitch and moan all I wanted, but Uncle

Mike would do what he thought needed to be done. And if that meant he had to take a couple of muscle relaxers before he went to bed, so be it.

When my dad had a stroke and died while running a tractor in one of the fields, Uncle Mike had been the one who drove to my high school to tell me. And he'd held me while I cried and told me he'd be there for me every day just like my dad had been.

When I'd decided to go to culinary school instead of college, he'd sighed and said that probably wasn't what my dad would have wanted, but he was okay with it. When, a couple of years out of school, I got the job as a line cook with a big time chef, at one of Denver's hippest restaurants, we'd celebrated with champagne and fresh raspberries from the canes he'd planted himself.

And when I came home from Denver, weary and heartsick and wondering if I should just give up, he'd looked me right in the eye and told me to figure out what kind of cooking I wanted to do next. Because he'd be damned if he'd let some scumbag drive his favorite niece out of the game.

And that, more than anything else, was the beginning of Luscious Delights, and my current reign as "jam queen of Shavano, Colorado" according to an article in the *Shavano County Sun*.

I owed Uncle Mike my life, and if he wanted to pick arugula, I'd let him.

I gave the raspberry jam one more stir. It looked okay. I took a tasting spoon from the jelly jar beside the stove and sampled carefully. Tasted…fine. About average. What you'd expect from frozen berries.

I sighed as I dropped the spoon in the dishwasher. *Average. Okay. Fine.* None of them were words I used

9

for my jam, and I didn't want anybody else to use them either.

I could always put this jam in jars and then sell it to Bianca Jordan at cost. Bianca could probably figure out something to use it for in her bakery. Maybe jelly doughnuts or kolaches. Something where the jelly wasn't the main player.

But I wouldn't be putting it into jars with my label on it. This jam wasn't up to the standards of Luscious Delights.

Because *okay* would never be enough for the jam queen of Shavano. I'd hold out for *good*, and hope for *extraordinary*.

Chapter 2

The Shavano farmers market is set up in River Park along the biking and jogging trail. It's a great location since tourists love strolling by the river so they can watch the kayakers and white water rafters making their way through the course that runs under the main bridge. A lot of those strollers make their way to the market, too.

But that's later in the season when the tourists begin to flood the mountains and fill Shavano's hotels and cabins and campgrounds. In mid-May the customers are mostly locals. Picky locals. Fortunately for me, these same picky locals like to buy my jam—most of it, anyway.

I try to get to the market early so I can get everything set up before the customers start to arrive. Uncle Mike designed my booth: nylon fabric with a metal frame and wooden counter. It's deep enough to give me some storage at the back so I can stow cases of jam and boxes of crackers for my samples. And it's got a roof overhead. Later in the season that roof provides shade from the killer mountain sunshine, but in mid-May the main worry is rain. And possibly snow. When you live at altitude, you get used to weird weather shifts.

It took me fifteen minutes or so to get the booth set up, and then I got going on the sample bowls. Some market vendors really hate samplers, the customers who breeze through to sample your stuff and move on. They don't bother me that much. I figure anyone who tastes my jam is going to want to buy some, if not this week then next week or the week after. I've met people who don't like pickles or mustard or hot sauce or jerky. But I have never met anyone who doesn't like jam. Maybe not mine in particular, but jam in general is always a winner.

I got ready to open, pouring a limited amount of each of my jams into the plastic bowls I had ranged along the front of the booth. I also had several bowls of crackers placed strategically alongside the jam. Good sturdy suckers, too. Believe me, there is nothing less appetizing than a bowl of jelly filled with cracker shards.

This Saturday I had my best sellers—raspberry and peach preserves—along with strawberry and apricot jam. Later in the year, I'd try some more exotics like lavender peach and tarragon apricot. But right now I was sticking with the basics. Along with pepper peach, which I was going to sell out if it killed me.

Other vendors walked by as I got everything arranged, calling out greetings and commenting on the brilliant blue sky and bright sunshine (which could become pouring rain or snow flurries in the blink of an eye—we weren't kidding ourselves). Bianca Jordan, who baked terrific bread and breakfast pastries, stopped long enough to pick up the jars of okay raspberry jam that I'd sold her wholesale.

She held one of the jars up to the sun, then shrugged. "Looks good to me, kid."

"They're good," I said, a little defensively. "They're fine. They're just not…"

"Great." Bianca sighed. "Yeah, I know how that is. They'll be good for danishes and maybe filling some kolaches." She dipped a cracker into the apricot and winked at me. "Luscious as always. See you later."

When I first decided to call my jam company Luscious Delights, I was a little embarrassed. It seemed like bragging, and I could picture some guy from New York taking a taste and sneering, "You call that Luscious?"

But in fact I do call it Luscious. That seemed to be the word I heard most frequently when I was taste-testing my early batches. There were also a lot of "Oh my Gods" and "Wows," but they didn't seem to lend themselves to a company name. So Luscious Delights it was.

Normally, I had an assistant at the market, Carmen and Donnie's daughter, Dolce. But Dolce was off doing something 4-H related this weekend, and I was on my own. No problem. I'd done the farmers market by myself before.

Annabelle Dorsey walked by, followed by her daughter, Dorothy. Annabelle does pickles and other fermented stuff as the Shavano Pickler. It's not a name I would have chosen myself, but it does tell you what she's up to. Her stuff isn't bad, provided you like ferments. Dorothy helps out in the summer, sort of. She's fifteen, and she's clearly not delighted to be spending her Saturdays pushing sauerkraut and pickled garlic. On the other hand, keeping her at the market means Annabelle doesn't need to worry about what else she could be up to. Dorothy's currently deeply into Goth and she looks more like twenty than fifteen, but I remember her when she was a sweet-faced toddler and I know how old she is.

I was just watching the first customers of the day stroll along the path when I heard muttering from the booth next door. Loud muttering.

The booth to my left was Martha Benavidez's salsa. To my right was the demo booth where the local restaurants put out samples and tried to attract customers. The muttering was definitely coming from the restaurant side.

I stepped out of my booth and peeked around the edge of the demo space. A man was standing at the rear of the booth, trying to set up his hotplate. His back was to me, and the words he was muttering outdid my cursing performance with the raspberry jam by a mile.

I took a breath. Might as well be neighborly. "Having problems?"

He turned around then, and I got my first good look. Reddish brown hair, brown eyes, strong jaw, currently dropped. He stared at me, looking a little dazed.

I get that a lot, so I'm used to it. There aren't too many women my size around Shavano. I hit six feet when I was seventeen, and the rest of me is pretty much in proportion. Plus I usually pull my hair up into a topknot to keep it out of the way, which adds a couple of inches on top where I probably don't need them. Since I'm half Greek-American, I get a lot of references to Amazons. But I figure any man who's intimidated by my size isn't worth my time.

"Problems?" I repeated, trying not to grit my teeth.

The restaurant guy managed a grin. "Oh. Yeah, a little. Do you know if there's an outlet around here where I can plug in my hotplate?"

"Back there," I said, pointing to the heavy-duty outlet on a pole about four feet away from the booth.

Restaurant guy stared where I was pointing, then grimaced. "Damn. I didn't bring an extension cord. Nobody mentioned I'd need one."

"I'll lend you mine. I'm not using it." Electrical connections are always kind of iffy at the market. Fortunately, I don't do much cooking in my booth. I located my orange extension cord. When I straightened he'd stepped beside me.

We were almost eye to eye. Given that I was wearing hiking boots with thick soles, that made him a couple of inches taller than me, give or take. And a very handsome two inches they were. I swallowed and handed him the cord.

He grinned as he took it. "Thanks. I'll bring it back as soon as my demo's over."

"Take your time." I stepped away slightly. "I won't be using it today."

"Great." He extended his hand. "I'm Nate Robicheaux. From Robicheaux's Café."

I gave his hand a quick shake. "Pleased to meet you, Nate. I'm Roxy Constantine. Luscious Delights."

His eyes widened slightly, and his ears turned pink.

"That's my jam," I added quickly. "Luscious Delights jam."

"Oh." He glanced at the counter where I had my samples laid out. "May I?"

"Sure. That's what they're for."

He took a cracker and scooped up a little apricot. It was left over from last summer, but jam doesn't go bad, and it would be a few more weeks before the first apricots of the season came in. He popped the cracker into his mouth and paused, chewing. After a moment, his lips spread in a blissful grin. "Holy crap, that's good."

I could feel my own ears getting warm. "Thanks."

He took another cracker and scooped up a little strawberry. "Oh, man. That's delicious."

"Glad you like it. When are you supposed to be doing your demo?" I'd have to come try his stuff. I really hoped it was good so I could say something nice about his food, too.

He glanced at his watch. "Hell, I'm on in ten minutes. I'd better get set up. I'll bring your extension cord when my half hour's up. Your jam's stupendous." He gave me another smile and trotted to the demo booth.

I blew out a long breath. Nate Robicheaux was a very good-looking guy. And he was my height, more or less. Most women would leap at the chance of getting something going with someone like that.

I sort of did, too, but I also sort of didn't. That was my problem, and I needed to work on it.

Once the real customers started showing up, things got a lot busier. I had the inevitable groups of kids who wanted to load up on free samples. With them I had a strictly enforced one sample per customer policy. But once the adults started crowding around too, the kids had a hard time working their way to the front.

There was a brief lull after fifteen minutes or so, and I slipped next door to grab one of Nate Robicheaux's samples. He was doing grilled cheese, cutting the sandwiches into quarters and setting them out for people to grab. It was tasty—super crunchy on the outside with a little kick to the cheese. Nate Robicheaux seemed to know what he was doing.

I lost track of time after that since I had a steady rush of customers. I'd forgotten just how tough it was to keep an eye on the samples, answer questions, and ring up sales on my own. I swore to myself I'd make sure Dolce was richly rewarded for showing up as my assistant from now on. I might even hire another assistant, given the number of people we were dealing with. Maybe Dolce had a friend who'd be willing to spend a couple of hours at the market on Saturday mornings.

I glanced up to see Dorothy Dorsey scooping up a sample from the ample bowl of pepper peach. It still wasn't selling as well as it should have been, but I didn't have time to worry about it. "Dorothy," I called. "Do you have some free time right now?"

Dorothy narrowed her eyes. "Maybe. Why do you want to know?"

"My assistant's off this weekend and I'm swamped. You want to make a quick twenty bucks?"

Her eyes stayed narrow. "Make it thirty."

"Thirty it is. If you can stay until the rush dies down."

"I can stay." She stepped around the end of the booth. "What do you want me to do?"

"Make sure the bowls stay filled and try to keep the kids from stealing all the crackers. I'll ring up the sales."

"I can do that."

We worked together for another hour or so. I felt a little guilty about stealing Dorothy away from Annabelle's booth, but I figured if Annabelle really needed her, she wouldn't have been free to wander around the market.

Once the crowds began to die down again, I took a minute to grab a bottle of water from my cooler. "Would you like some water?" I asked Dorothy.

She shook her head. "Nah, I'm good. You get a lot of customers."

"It's been a good day. How's your booth doing?"

"Okay. Not as busy as this, though." Dorothy shrugged. "It's pickles."

"Good pickles," I said quickly. I'm not a big pickle fan, but Annabelle's were tasty.

Dorothy shrugged again. "If you say so."

"Dorothy, there you are." Annabelle stood a few feet away, her hands on her hips. "Come back to the booth. You're supposed to be working for me."

Dorothy grimaced, then started to follow her mother.

I grabbed my purse. "Hang on a minute. I owe you thirty bucks."

Dorothy waited while I fished out my billfold, then jammed the bills into her pocket. "Thanks."

Annabelle gave me a fixed smile. "Poaching my assistant?"

"Dorothy helped me out when I was swamped. My own assistant's out of town this weekend." I tried looking apologetic. "Sorry if I ran you short."

Her fixed smile didn't waver. "Glad she was helpful. It's good practice. Come on, Dorothy. Martha's watching the booth right now."

Dorothy muttered something that sounded like "no loss," but she followed her mother down the path.

I refilled all the jam bowls and put out a few more crackers. The noon rush was over, and it was close to our two o'clock closing time, but I always try to have samples available. You never know who might show up, even late in the day.

And actually, somebody did show up—Nate Robicheaux. "Oh good," he said, as he rounded the corner next to my booth, "you're still here. I was afraid you'd have gone home by now." He looked like he was panting. Maybe he'd run up from the parking lot.

"I'm always here until closing, unless I sell out." I

actually had sold out on peach and strawberry. And I was close to it on raspberry and apricot. Unfortunately, I still had a healthy supply of pepper peach.

"I didn't even know when the market closed." He gave me a sheepish smile. "I'm a total beginner. I had to go to the café and cook lunch after my demo, but I forgot to give you back your extension cord." He held it out.

"Thanks, but you could have given it to me next week. I'm always here on Saturdays."

"Will there be more vendors next week? This week seemed a little thin." He turned to survey the reduced line of remaining booths.

"Most of the produce guys have packed up and left—they sell out fast this early in the season. Once the summer crops start coming in, we'll have a lot more vendors and a lot more customers." I paused. I'd just been assuming he'd be around, but there were several Robicheaux kids, as I recalled. There was no guarantee he'd be the one doing the cooking next week. "Will you be doing demos every week?"

He nodded slowly. "I think so. We haven't worked out my schedule yet. I just came to Shavano a couple of months ago."

"Where were you before that?"

"Las Vegas." His expression sort of shut down, and I didn't ask him what he'd been doing there. I'd heard something about one of the Robicheauxs, but I couldn't remember the details right then. Maybe I'd ask Uncle Mike.

"Well, welcome to Shavano." I gave him my best hometown booster smile.

"Thanks." He smiled back.

He had amazing eyes, now that I got a good look.

The color of chocolate sauce, with some hints of gold around the edge. The dark eyes were a nice contrast with his auburn hair.

I very carefully did not look at his hands. Men's hands are a major turn-on for me, particularly with a man like Nate who did interesting things with those hands. I very much did not want to be turned on by Nate Robicheaux. *Keep it friendly. Keep it remote.* That was my current motto.

"Well," he said, "thanks again for the extension cord. Next time I'll bring my own. I guess I'll see you next week."

"Right. We'll probably be side by side all summer." Which sounded a lot more like a come-on than I'd meant. "I mean our booths will be in the same place every week."

"Great, I'll look forward to that." His grin flashed white against his tan, and I felt a quick flicker of something I hadn't felt for quite a while. "See you, Roxy." He turned up the path.

"See you, Nate," I mumbled, although he was already too far to hear me. I turned to my jams and pretended they were fascinating.

Oh, watch it, Roxy. Just watch it. I needed to ignore any and all feelings that might be inspired by a flashing grin. I wasn't in the market for somebody like Nate Robicheaux, even assuming he was in the market for somebody like me.

Which, now that I thought about it, seemed unlikely. Why was I agonizing over possible relationships with good-looking strangers who hadn't indicated any particular interest in me? He was probably just a nice guy who was trying to be friendly with the booth-holder next door.

I checked my watch, and found it was two o'clock. Time to close down and load up my truck. And then to think about lunch.

Which most definitely would not be eaten at Robicheaux's Café. I needed to get some distance from that killer smile.

Chapter 3

After I packed everything into my truck, I did a quick survey of the line of restaurants on Second Street. I was always ravenous by two, and if I ate a late lunch, it could count as dinner, too. After weighing my options, I decided on Dirty Pete's. Their enchiladas were terrific, and I was in the mood for spicy. Plus I'm friends with the bartender.

Said bartender grinned when I came in. I'm not really a regular, but I do show up there now and then. And Lord knows I'm memorable. Actually, the bartender at Dirty Pete's is pretty memorable himself. His name's Harry Potter. Yes, really. He's around six five and weighs maybe two eighty. Nobody screws around at Dirty Pete's.

I found a table toward the windows in front where I could watch people walk by then gave the waitress my order. There weren't too many people in the restaurant at that time of day, but my friend Susa Sondergaard waved from a distant table where she was having lunch with some guy. Susa is always having lunch with some guy. She has a constant rotating group, all devoted.

A sudden image of Nate Robicheaux slipped into my brain, all yummy muscle and bashful grin. He might even have had a dimple, although I really hadn't looked close enough to check.

The waitress brought my plate of cheese enchiladas

with rice and beans, along with a king-size iced tea. I took a deep breath, inhaling the scent of cumin and paprika. Heaven. I used to make a mean plate of enchiladas myself back in the day. Now my culinary adventures were pretty much limited to jam, but sometimes I missed experimenting with other stuff.

As I took my first bite, the door to the bar swung open with a swish and I made the mistake of looking up. Brett Holmes gazed back, the corners of his mouth edging into a faintly predatory grin.

I quickly switched my attention to my enchiladas and beans. Maybe if I started eating, he'd take the hint and leave me alone. Of course, Brett wasn't all that good at taking hints.

"Well, well, Roxy Constantine. Should have known you'd be in town for the farmers market. This seat taken?" He raised his eyebrows as he sauntered to my table, then leaned on the chair opposite my seat.

"It is, actually. I'm expecting a friend." I gave him a smile that was closer to a grimace, since it didn't involve much beyond my teeth. It went without saying that my nonexistent friend was not Brett.

"I'll join you until he shows up." Brett pulled the chair out and dropped into it, moving a couple of inches closer to me. He gave me a smile that let me know he didn't believe the friend story anyway.

Clearly, we were going to be playing games, whether I wanted to or not. I took another bite of enchilada. "What's on your mind, Brett?"

"Just having some polite conversation. How's the jam business?"

"Fine. How's the restaurant business?"

"We're doing great. Made it into *Colorado Life* a

couple of weeks ago." He gave me a self-satisfied smile.

Brett was the head chef at one of Shavano's more upscale restaurants. They'd hired him away from a place in Denver where he claimed he'd been head chef. My guess was he'd been a line cook. That's what he'd been when I'd known him before, when we'd both worked at the same Denver restaurant.

"I saw that article. Nice coverage of the town." It had, in fact, been a guide to visiting Shavano, including a listing of almost every restaurant in the downtown area. Brett's place, High Country, had been one of them. So had Robicheaux's, as I recalled.

Brett shrugged. "Every bit helps."

"I suppose." I returned to my enchiladas, sending out heavy *go away* vibes.

Brett had no talent for reading vibes. He settled in his chair. "So what are you doing this afternoon, now that the market's over for the day?"

I gave him another phony smile. "I'm heading to the farm as soon as I finish lunch. My uncle needs my help this afternoon." Uncle Mike didn't need my help for much of anything, but I figured it was as good an excuse as any.

Brett gave me a smile that was probably supposed to be seductive. It fell short by quite a bit. "Too bad. I was hoping you might stick around for a couple of margaritas. I don't have to be in the kitchen until six or so."

"You drink before you cook?" My eyebrows went up even though I had no intention of continuing this conversation. Going into a restaurant kitchen half-buzzed was a very bad idea, given the incredible number of things that could hurt you.

Brett's smirk intensified. "Alcohol just ups the excitement. Smooths out the rough spots. Makes you work more on the edge."

It would also increase the possibility of cutting off a finger. Not that I cared. His hands did nothing for me.

"You could come by High Country tonight, let me fix you dinner. Maybe we could go someplace for a nightcap after."

"Sorry," I said flatly. "I've got to fix dinner for my uncle."

Brett leaned closer, and I fought to keep from scooting my chair farther away. I didn't want him to know he was getting to me. "I can show you a good time, Roxy. We both know what you like. Just give me a try."

I let myself go still. Ice dripped down my spine at the same time my cheeks flushed hot. Part of me wanted to push my enchiladas in his face, but mostly I wanted him to go away. I was hungry. I wanted my lunch. Of course, right then my stomach felt so tight I wasn't sure I could swallow it.

Brett apparently hadn't noticed any changes in my expression. "Come on, sweetheart, give me a chance here. Let me show you what I can do."

"Roxy, there you are." Susa's voice sounded unnaturally loud in the mostly empty restaurant.

I glanced up at her, trying to push my frozen facial muscles into a smile.

"Sorry I'm late," Susa trilled. "Glad you started without me." She stared fixedly at Brett. "Maybe you could find another place to sit. We're supposed to be having lunch."

Brett pushed himself up slowly from the table. His smirk was back in full force. "Just stopped to say hello."

Susa gave him a token smile, then dropped into the chair he'd just vacated, turning toward the waitress. "Hey, Caroline, can I get an iced tea, please?"

Fortunately, Caroline didn't ask why Susa couldn't drink the iced tea that was already at her table. Susa turned to me, ignoring Brett completely. "So how are you, kid?"

"Fine," I managed through my gritted teeth. "I'm fine. How are you?"

Brett stood for a moment longer, hands on his hips. Maybe he was hoping I'd invite him to join us. Then he shrugged. "Okay, Roxy, see you around. Think about dinner, okay?"

The only thing I thought about dinner was that it would be a lot better without Brett Holmes around. I watched him head out the door again then blew out a long breath.

"Are you okay?" Susa had lowered her voice to normal levels, her blue eyes suddenly concerned.

"Yeah, I'm good. Thanks for the save."

"You looked like you could use an intervention." Susa grimaced. "That guy didn't seem to understand the word *no*."

I almost shuddered. The last thing I needed was another asshole who didn't understand what *no* meant. "He's just a jerk."

Susa took her glass of tea from Caroline. "Who is he anyway?"

"Brett Holmes. He's the chef at High Country. Started working there a couple of months ago."

"Oh." Susa frowned. "Did you want to go out with him? I'm sorry I butted in."

"Lord, no." I took another long breath. "I don't want

anything to do with that creep."

Susa's eyes widened. "He's not the one from Denver, is he?"

I shook my head. "He worked in the same kitchen, though. He knows the story." Or anyway, he knew one version of it. Not mine.

Susa narrowed her eyes. "Is that why he was being such a jerk? He thought you really liked being manhandled?"

"Maybe." I rubbed a hand over my forehead. Talking about Denver usually gives me a headache. "Or maybe he's just a jerk in his own right."

Susa arched an eyebrow. "Should I get Leon to pay him a visit? Maybe teach him some manners?"

Leon was one of Susa's many boyfriends. The one with the tattoos. Regretfully, I shook my head. "It's not that serious. He just comes on strong. I don't want to go out with him, but he won't accept it." I took another bite of my enchilada, although my heart wasn't in it anymore.

"Like *you* said, a creep." Susa pushed herself to her feet. "You want to join us? Harry's trying out a new margarita recipe."

I glanced at Harry, who gave me a slightly devilish grin. I should probably have had him toss Brett out on his nose. Maybe next time. "Thanks anyway. I need to get home as soon as I finish lunch."

Susa gave me a searching look, but then she shrugged. "If you really don't need girlfriend time, I guess I'll go back to my table. Don't want to leave Sean on his own too long."

"Right. Who knows what ideas he might come up with." I managed another smile. "Thanks, again. We'll have to get together next week."

"Sure, just say the word."

Susa ambled along to her date while I considered the last of my enchiladas. I couldn't eat them now. I'd been looking forward to them all morning, but my appetite had disappeared along with Brett Holmes.

I did have things to do at the farm—ideas for making better frozen fruit jam and a new recipe for grapefruit marmalade, among other possibilities. And I would make supper for Uncle Mike later on. It was the only cooking I still did these days, outside of making jam and preserves, and I usually looked forward to it.

I'd do all that as soon as my hands stopped shaking and my jaw unclenched. And my heart unfroze.

But that would take a lot longer, as I knew only too well.

Chapter 4

I guess it figured that I'd be thinking about my life in Denver as I drove to the farm. When I'd first gotten the job as a line cook at one of the trendiest restaurants in town, I thought it was my Big Break. Everybody at my culinary school was envious. When foodies came through Denver on their way to the Aspen Food and Wine Classic, they always stopped off at that particular restaurant to see that particular chef.

I'd had a couple of internships and met a few chefs who knew their way around a kitchen. I'd actually been offered a job at one of the big new hotels in Denver, where the chef was a young guy just making a name for himself. But then I heard the trendy place was hiring, and I got a three-night tryout.

It was nerve-wracking and exciting and one of the most intense experiences I'd ever had. At the end of the week, the sous chef pulled me aside and told me the job was mine if I wanted it.

If I wanted it? Of course, I wanted it. I couldn't understand why he didn't seem as excited as I was, but maybe he'd seen enough young chefs come through to think it was no big deal.

The first couple of months were everything I'd hoped for. I learned a ton from the guys on the line, got used to the flow of adrenaline that came with the evening rush, saw the kitchen slide into the weeds and slide out again. I began to feel like I belonged there, like this was what I was meant to do. I was ready to buy myself a new chef's coat and beanie, so full of myself I almost burst my buttons.

It wasn't all great. There were a few jerks like Brett Holmes who made lousy cracks about the women cooks. I learned to avoid the jerks, and Brett and I didn't work that closely. But even then he made my skin crawl.

And then one night the head chef himself showed up to expedite, the guy who'd developed the restaurant to begin with.

For somebody that important, he wasn't much to look at. Stocky, dirty-blond hair slicked in a bun, slightly sketchy moustache and goatee. He sat on his stool at the expediter's spot in front, watching us with cold gray eyes.

We were all doing our best, us new line cooks. Hoping he might notice us and tell us we were good.

Yeah, we really were that naïve.

That evening seemed to go fast, much faster than usual. The kitchen was like a machine, but a machine that put out incredible food. The head chef stayed at his expediting station all night, raising his voice when he needed to but mostly just watching everything. It was one of the best experiences I'd ever had as a cook.

Well, the early part of the evening had been the best, anyway.

When things began to die down, we started cleaning up our stations, making a few muttered comments about things that had gone well and not so well. Brett wasn't there that night, which made things go a little more smoothly. I lost track of the head chef as I worked, figuring he was maybe out front. Most of the other cooks took off, leaving a few of us newbies to do the final cleanup. I'd pulled off my apron and cap, getting ready to leave.

But suddenly, the chef was right in front of me. "You," he said. "What's your name?"

I swallowed hard. "Roxy. Roxy Constantine."

"Okay, Roxy Constantine, come with me. I need your help in the pantry."

I followed him across the kitchen, trying not to look nervous. I had no idea what kind of help he needed. I only hoped I wouldn't screw it up.

The pantry was off at the rear of the kitchen, a smallish room with shelves on three sides, full of bags of flour and bottles of olive oil and big cans of tomatoes. I followed him inside, waiting to be told what to do.

He closed the door, and then he grabbed me.

I was so shocked I didn't react at first. He pushed me against the shelves and plastered his mouth to mine, all the time pulling at my clothes.

After a moment, I started to fight, pushing against his chest, trying to get him off me. But he was a big man, close to six feet and heavy. He tore the buttons off my jacket and started to pull down my pants.

I was yelling by then, telling him no, telling him to stop, to leave me alone. But he ignored me. If I couldn't get away from him, I knew what he was going to do.

I wasn't really thinking at that point. All I wanted was to get him off me and to get away. I remember patting one hand desperately on the shelf behind me until I finally grasped something, picked it up, and brought it against the side of his head with all the strength I could muster one-handed.

He stopped what he was doing and stared at me with

this really odd expression, outraged and surprised all at once. And then he staggered backward, and I saw a thin thread of blood seeping into his dirty-blond hair. I glanced at my hand and saw I was holding a twenty-eight-ounce can of tomatoes, which I promptly dropped.

I grabbed at my clothes, pulling them up as best I could, and ran for the door. I managed to get my clothes in place as I stumbled through the kitchen.

I'd escaped the chef, and I'd avoided being assaulted. But actually I'd just gotten caught up in something even worse. It took me a while to figure that out.

My hair was hanging around my face and I had to hold my chef's jacket closed because he'd torn the buttons off. My mouth was swollen, and I was pretty sure I'd have bruises on my back from where he'd shoved me into the shelves. I looked like someone who'd been attacked.

I was a mess, and I was close to hysterical.

I didn't see anybody in the kitchen at first—it was late, and most of the staff had left. But then I saw the restaurant manager. I wasn't sure what he was doing there since he usually stayed in the front of the house, but he took one look at me and put his hand on my elbow to guide me somewhere away from the kitchen.

I yanked away from him, ready to fight. At that point I wouldn't trust any man to do anything, and I didn't want anyone touching me. Smart girl, as it turned out.

"It's okay. I want to help. Let me get someone to take you home," he said quietly. "Do you have a car here?"

I shook my head. I usually took the bus, but I wasn't in any shape to catch it that night.

"Okay," he said. "I'll call you a ride-share. You can wait in my office."

I didn't wonder then why he wasn't asking me what happened and why I looked so beaten up. I was too shell shocked. Now, of course, I know why. He didn't need to ask me because he already knew. He'd seen it before.

The ride home took forever, but when we got to my apartment building it turned out the restaurant manager had prepaid. Again, I didn't pause to wonder why he'd done that. I was just glad I didn't have to try to figure out the tip. I tottered inside the apartment I shared with two other women. One of my roommates was sitting in the living room watching TV. She took one look at me and jumped to her feet to help me onto one of the overstuffed chairs. Then she grabbed the bottle of tequila we kept under the sink.

I told her what had happened, all of it, including clocking the chef with the can of tomatoes. She told me I'd absolutely done the right thing, and then she offered to drive me to the hospital to get checked out. I said no. I wasn't hurt, just shaken up. And I didn't want to talk to strangers right then. Note to anyone who ever finds herself in a situation like this in the future: go to the damn hospital. If nothing else, it gives you another set of witnesses.

Finally, I went to bed, although I didn't sleep. I kept replaying the whole thing in my head, trying to figure out if I'd missed something. Shouldn't I have known what he was up to? Shouldn't I have been able to stop it before it happened?

But the chef hadn't given off any vibes when he'd told me to come to the pantry with him. As I thought about it, I got the feeling he'd wanted me to be taken by surprise, that that was part of his game.

The next morning, I felt like crap and looked like it, too. The bruises on my back had developed into shades of black and purple. There were scratches on my arms and shoulders where I'd fought him. My head ached like I was coming down with something, but it was basically stress. I was afraid to go to work because the chef might be there. But I didn't know what else to do. One of my roommates told me I should go to the cops, but I didn't want to do that either. I just wanted the whole thing to go away.

I wanted it to be yesterday again, and I wanted all of this never to have happened.

Surprisingly enough, I got to the restaurant around the usual time. I figured I'd just go to my station and start chopping onions, which always needed to be done anyway. I'd pretend it was a normal day, and that I was doing normal work.

But the first person I saw when I walked in the kitchen was the restaurant manager, the guy who'd sent me home in the ride-share the night before. I got the feeling he'd been waiting for me.

He beckoned me over to his office. I was pretty sure nothing good was going to come from this, and I was right. He told me, flatly, that I didn't have a job anymore. I'd be paid two months' wages as severance, and he'd give me a recommendation. But all of that depended on me keeping my mouth shut. If I told anyone some wild story about being attacked in the pantry, I'd not only lose my recommendation, I'd lose any chance of being hired at a restaurant in Denver. My reputation would be ruined all over town, and I'd never work there again.

I stared at him for what seemed like the world's

longest minute, trying to make sense of what he'd just said. It sounded like gibberish.

"He attacked me," I said, finally. Surely that had been clear the night before.

The manager raised a skeptical eyebrow. And then he reminded me I'd attacked the chef, not the other way around. He told me they had a doctor's report stating the chef had a mild concussion. If I started spreading lies about him, the chef would have the medical reports to support his version.

That idea was so outrageous, I gaped at the manager. How could he even think that was true? I wasn't ready to give in yet, in part because now I was truly pissed. "He told me to come into the pantry to help him, then he jumped me. I defended myself. He wanted to rape me."

But that wasn't the chef's version. According to the manager, the chef claimed our encounter was "consensual." That I'd wanted a promotion. That I'd asked him to meet me there so we could discuss it and "get to know each other better." When he refused to give me the promotion I was angling for, I hit him with the can.

I stared at the guy. He'd seen me the night before when I came stumbling out of the pantry. He knew how dazed and upset I'd been. He'd seen the state of my clothes, my face, my hair. He couldn't believe this crap he was spouting. He *knew,* dammit!

But as I took in his blank expression, the way he wouldn't really look at me, I knew he wasn't going to back down. I wasn't the first woman he'd pressured into giving up her claims. In the food world, the chef was a giant, and I was a flea. A flea that could be flicked off.

And right then, I decided the hell with it. I could

stick around Denver and argue. I could make a police report. I could go to the press. Some people would believe me. A lot wouldn't. And after I went through the hell of reliving the attack over and over again, I was pretty sure the chef would still be a big deal in the Denver restaurant scene. And I'd still be a flea. An unemployed flea, at that.

All I wanted to do was go home. Not to my apartment—to Shavano. My real home.

I packed up all my stuff that afternoon. I almost threw away my chef's coat and beanie and my knives, but I put them in a box and sealed them up. I thought someday I might want them again, although right then I couldn't bear to look at them. I still had the old truck Uncle Mike had bought for me when I was in high school. I loaded it up and turned west.

Was it a brave thing to do? Nope. It let the chef and the restaurant off the hook, and it left him free to attack other women. I felt guilty about that then, and I still do. I wish I'd been gutsier, but at the time I just couldn't face it.

More importantly, was leaving Denver a smart thing to do? Probably not, since it meant I was giving up on my dream of being a head chef. But it was the only thing I felt up to doing. I think I was suffering from a kind of PTSD, and all I wanted to do was get to the farm and hide until I felt whole again.

Uncle Mike was shocked to see me, but he figured out pretty quickly I was in no shape to explain myself when I finally rolled in after midnight. He let me sleep for most of the next day, and then he sat me down with a cup of tea and got me to tell him the whole story.

Of course after I'd finished telling him, I had to talk

him out of heading to Denver to punch out the chef and the manager. He was also pretty upset about my not going to the police, but once he realized he couldn't convince me to fight, he left me alone for a while. Until he got tired of seeing me moping around the farm.

Then he sat me down again and told me I needed to figure out what I wanted to do next and how to go about doing it. He said I was the best cook he'd ever known, and that it was a sin and a shame to let that talent go to waste. If I didn't want to cook in a restaurant anymore, so be it. But I needed to figure out some alternatives, and then I needed to get on with it.

Fortunately, I was pretty sick of sitting around by then. What he said made a lot of sense. I experimented with a few other kinds of cooking—making cookies and salsa and even baking bread. But it wasn't until I started working with the fruit that came from Constantine Farms that I knew I'd found my niche. And thus Luscious Delights was born.

If I was a glass-half-full type, I might claim that everything worked out for the best. I've got a business I love and that I'm good at. I'm in Shavano, and I really prefer being here to being in Denver. And I'm poised to be a lot more successful here than I would have been as a line cook at a trendy restaurant.

But life doesn't really work that way, does it?

My Denver experience stole something from me—a chance to be what I'd dreamed about for years, a professional cook. What's more, the chef spread rumors about me after I left. Apparently he was still pissed at me for hitting him with that can of tomatoes. Brett Holmes wasn't the only one who'd implied I'd had sex with the chef willingly and gotten burned, although Brett was the most obnoxious about it. He'd come to Shavano a few months ago, and now he amused himself by propositioning me every chance he got.

Deep down I resented the fact that I'd been forced into my alternative career rather than finding it on my own.

So yes, I'm better at making jam than I had been at cooking on the line. But I'd have preferred to discover that myself after a couple of years of experience at restaurants and to have moved on because I wanted to, not because I had to.

Ironically, the chef himself had been taken down a few months later by some women who were braver than me. He'd attacked one woman line cook in another restaurant and she'd called the cops on him. And after she had, several other women came forward to tell stories of other assaults. He'd been forced out of his restaurant partnerships and ended up in retirement in Provence. He was supposed to be working on a cookbook. I wished him writer's block.

There was still one more after-effect I was living with. I'd been out with a few guys over the two years I'd been back in Shavano. But I hadn't gotten serious with any of them. Whenever we got close to having a physical relationship, I found myself backing away. I just wasn't ready to be touched.

Being attacked sticks with you, or anyway, it had with me. I kept telling myself I'd get over it, but I hadn't yet. And until I did, I was staying single. It seemed easier that way.

Still, it really annoyed me that the chef and his buddies had taken that away from me, too. I might not be able to go into a restaurant kitchen, but maybe I could take a few steps toward getting into a relationship again. Assuming anyone ever came along I felt like getting involved with.

Somehow it didn't seem like a coincidence that I found myself thinking about Nate Robicheaux when I considered that possibility.

Chapter 5

By the next farmers market, I'd worked up a couple of new jams. I did a few jars of the grapefruit marmalade, although it was more a novelty than something I was going to do regularly. I prefer working with fruit from somewhere in the state at least, and given my choice, I stick with Uncle Mike's produce when it's available. Still, it was fun to do something a little out of my comfort zone, and the grapefruit marmalade was definitely unique.

I also did bourbon peach preserves. I usually put some up during the summer, but I decided to try a batch with frozen peaches. It was good, but not great. I was still trying to find a way around the frozen texture.

There were a lot more customers that week. School was almost out, and we were heading toward Memorial Day, which would be the real opening of the summer tourist season and the first big weekend for the market. I planned on selling a lot of pepper peach to the tourists.

My assistant, Dolce, had returned from her 4-H adventure, which meant things weren't quite as hectic around the booth. Dolce was friendly, bouncy, and a natural charmer. Unfortunately, the teenage boys she attracted didn't buy a lot of jam, although they ate a lot of samples.

We sold out of raspberry by eleven. We also sold out of the grapefruit marmalade, but I'd expected that. There wasn't much of it, and it had the exotic factor going for it. The bourbon peach also moved well, although not as well as the straight peach and the apricot. I even sold a few jars of pepper peach, one to a guy hanging around Dolce. I suspected he was trying to impress her by buying it. Fine with me.

Around eleven thirty, I looked up to find Nate Robicheaux scooping up some bourbon peach with a cracker. "New stuff?" he asked.

"Sort of. I usually make it later in the year, but I was doing some experimenting."

"Tastes great." He licked his fingers. "Looks good, too."

He looked pretty good himself, in his low-slung jeans and black T-shirt. The sun brought out the reddish highlights in his auburn hair. "What did you demo today?"

"Sliders. Supposed to be small versions of our usual burger. I saved you one."

"Great." I hadn't had much breakfast, and hunger was catching up with me.

I told Dolce to keep track of things for five minutes, then followed him to the demo booth where Harry Potter was handing out flautas.

I gave him a quick smile. "Hey, Harry. Dirty Pete's got you cooking?"

He shrugged. "I split my time between the kitchen and the bar. They needed me out here today."

"Do you know Nate?"

Harry raised a bushy red eyebrow. "Nope."

"Nate Robicheaux, this is Harry Potter. He's the bartender at Dirty Pete's." I gave Nate a smile that was meant to suggest he not mention the name.

Nate got the hint. "Pleased to meet you, Harry."

"Likewise. I know your mom." Harry returned to his flautas.

Nate picked up a paper plate with a single slider from a table at the rear of the booth. "Here you go. Especially for you. I had to hide it."

My cheeks warmed slightly. I wasn't used to having a good-looking guy do things for me. "Thanks." I turned my attention to his burger.

After I took a bite, I could see why they'd been a hit. It was a loose meat version, like the classics you get in the Midwest. And he'd seasoned it with something spicy that I couldn't identify.

"These are great," I said.

He smiled at me in a way that made my cheeks warm again. "Glad you like it."

"What's the spice?"

"Powdered Serrano. Just a touch. I thought they needed a little kick."

"You do loose meat hamburgers at Robicheaux's?" So far as I knew, loose meats were pretty rare in Colorado.

He shook his head. "That's why I said they were 'supposed to be' small versions of our regular burgers. Small versions of the real regulars were sort of…bland. I thought loose meat worked better." He looked a little guilty when he said that, but also a little defiant.

I wasn't about to criticize him for not being ordinary. "They're delicious. And now I need to get back and relieve Dolce. It looks like we're getting another wave of customers."

He turned as I moved toward my booth. "Have lunch with me?"

I paused, my heart suddenly hammering. The last man who'd asked me to lunch had been Brett Holmes, and I was pretty sure *lunch* was a euphemism in his case. Nate wasn't Brett, but what was he asking exactly?

Some of my concern must have shown in my face. Nate shook his head quickly. "Nothing fancy. I was going to grab a sub from one of the food trucks."

Cool it. It's just lunch, for Pete's sake. "Sure, that sounds good. I'm not off until two, though."

"Okay, I'll see you at two." He gave me a cautious smile. I must have looked really freaked before because instead of flirting, he was treating me like a potential nutcase.

"Great. I'll be ready." Which probably sounded even weirder because who gets that excited about food truck subs?

The couple of hours left passed quickly. We sold out of the bourbon peach. We had strawberry, apricot, and pepper peach left and did a pretty good business in all of them. Yes, including pepper peach.

Dolce's fan club took off after she went back to the farm with her parents, who'd run Uncle Mike's booth.

Nate showed up promptly at ten before two. "I can go get the subs while you finish up if you'll tell me what you want."

"Oh, sure." I dug into my pocket for my billfold. "I usually go with a turkey club."

He held up his hand. "I'm paying. I asked you, after all."

I paused, a little embarrassed and a little wary. "Oh. Okay. Maybe I can get it next time." And then I blushed bright pink because who knew if there would even be a next time?

Nate grinned as if he was pleased we had a possible future. "Sure. I'll be back in a few."

I packed away the remaining jars of jam. There weren't many, which was a good thing, of course. I was loading the cases of jars into my truck when Nate came back. He placed the sack with the subs on the booth counter and grabbed a case. "Here, let me give you a hand."

"Thanks." After we got all the jars loaded, I started to pull off the nylon roof for the booth, then paused. "Did you want to eat here? I can leave it up if you do."

He shook his head. "Let's go down by the river. If we're having a picnic, we might as well go for scenic."

He helped me break down the booth and load the truck. And then we walked to the river at the edge of the hiking and biking trail. Shavano is in the middle of prime river rafting country, and the town has taken advantage of that fact by building a course for kayakers that runs by the River Park. In the summer, people have picnics along the banks, watching the amateur kayakers and the rafters who come to shoot the rapids farther down.

We were a little early in the year for that. The temperature was hovering in the low sixties, and the river was still pretty chilly. But the competitive kayakers were out in wet suits and helmets, running the river course with a kind of fierce determination.

Nate found a park bench along the bank, and we unwrapped our subs. Fortunately, I was too hungry to feel nervous, and we ate in silence for a few minutes, watching the kayakers take their chances.

Finally, I decided I needed to say something. "So your demo went well today?"

He nodded. "All the samples got taken, and several

people told me they like the loose meat. Of course, I've got a pretty staunch critic, too."

"Who's that?"

"A little girl named Sandy. She hated my grilled cheese, too. The only reason I know her name is that her mom usually comes with her and tries to get her to eat the sample. I think I'd just as soon she stopped trying." He gave me a rueful smile.

"Oh, that's probably Sandy Grayson. Her mom has the jerky stand. Sandy never likes anything. It's a protest. She hates having to sit in her mom's booth."

He narrowed his eyes. "Geez, do you know everybody who comes to the market?"

"No, but Sandy usually goes for my samples, too. Or anyway, she goes for part of them. If I don't keep an eye on her, she empties my cracker bowls."

"I haven't tried any jerky yet. There are a lot of interesting cooks around this market." He nodded toward Annabelle's booth. "She's got some interesting kimchi."

"You should try her pickled garlic. It curls hair."

He grinned. "Hot damn. I used to put pickled garlic on charred green beans. Now there was a dish."

"Something for the menu at Robicheaux's?"

His grin faded slightly. "Nope. I did the garlic and green beans when I worked in Vegas. Robicheaux's is traditional. Our customers are more into green beans and bacon."

"I'm fond of green beans and bacon myself." Although now he'd described it, pickled garlic and charred green beans sounded interesting. I considered asking him more about Vegas, but he didn't seem eager to discuss it. "What about those loose meat sandwiches? They were great. And I'll bet the customers at

Robicheaux's would love them."

He blew out a breath. "Except it's not our usual hamburger recipe, and I'm not sure how my brother would feel about it."

"Your brother?"

"My brother Bobby runs the kitchen. He and my mom put the menu together."

"Well, that loose meat was delicious. I'd think having a variety of hamburgers on the menu would be good for a café like Robicheaux's. Plus my guess is you could do the loose meat in advance, even freeze it, and your cost per sandwich would probably drop."

Nate took a swallow from his water bottle. "You've worked in restaurants?"

I nodded a little warily. It wasn't a subject I discussed much since it could lead to questions about where I'd worked and why I'd left. "Yeah. I used to work in Denver before I came back to Shavano."

"Good foodie town." He balled up the wrapper from his sandwich, stuffing it into the sack. "I didn't grab any dessert. Sorry. If I'd been thinking, I would have snagged some of my sister's pie this morning."

"Your sister works in the restaurant?"

"Yeah. We all do. It's a family thing."

"That sounds nice," I said slowly. "Having family around in the kitchen. Better than a bunch of strangers trying to get ahead." Or trying to run you down.

"It is and it isn't." He rested his elbows on the bench. "It's easier to get on each other's nerves sometimes. You know too much about each other—where to stick the needle if you really want to make it sting."

"I can see that. Kitchens are pressure cookers. Especially when you've got a rush to take care of." I still remembered the adrenaline hit that came with the rush hour.

"Right. We love each other, but not necessarily when we've got eight orders to get out at the same time." He flashed me a dry smile.

I smiled back. "I should come eat at Robicheaux's sometime. I like diner food."

"Let me know when. I'll fix you something special."

"Like loose meat sliders?" I raised an eyebrow.

He grimaced. "Probably not. Bobby's not big on changes. Maybe I can slip you an order of onion rings or something."

"Onion rings would rock." I gathered up my own sandwich wrapper, stuffing it into the sack. "I'd better get home. I've got stuff to do this afternoon." I wanted to keep things a little slow with Nate Robicheaux. My mind needed time to catch up with my body, which seemed to be racing ahead, if the heat generated by an hour at his side was any indication.

"Yeah, I've got a few chores myself." He pushed himself to his feet. "You'll be at the market next week?"

"Oh, yeah. Next week and every week. Until fall."

"Me, too." He gave me another of those grins that started a glow somewhere deep inside. "Maybe we can do a real lunch next time."

I started to freeze again, then gave myself a mental shake. *Pull yourself together, Roxy.* "Sounds good."

"Next week then." His teeth flashed white against his tan. "See you, Roxy."

"See you, Nate." As I walked to my booth, I found myself wondering. A good-looking, charming man with a talent like Nate Robicheaux's should have been a big success in Las Vegas. What was he doing in Shavano, besides being frustrated by his family's café?

Chapter 6

The next week was more labor intensive than I'd anticipated. The first crop of strawberries came in ahead of schedule, thanks to some warm days and Uncle Mike's cold frames. I put up five cases of jam and a couple of cases of preserves. The preserves had more fruit chunks, and I'd sell them for a higher price. But they'd go fast, based on past history.

By midweek I was doing a frozen raspberry run—I knew they'd sell, and I knew I needed a few more cases—when someone rang the doorbell. We didn't get many visitors at the ranch unless they were some of Uncle Mike's commercial customers. I checked the jam kettle to make sure it wasn't in danger of boiling over and headed for the door.

My friend Susa was on my doorstep, her bright red truck sitting in my drive. "Hey, kid," she said, giving me a quick hug, "what's shakin'?"

Herman perked up and trotted our way. He loves Susa, although he likes putting his paws on her shoulders, which she's not crazy about.

Susa is maybe five foot five or so, short enough that we look sort of comical when we walk around together. But when we walk around together, people don't seem to notice me that much anyway because Susa's gorgeous. Her hair's the color of sunshine, with a little help from Clairol, her eyes are the blue of mountain lupine, and she almost shimmers with vitality. We've been friends since we entered second grade at Horace Greeley Elementary together.

"Hi, Herman," she said, patting his head absently. He followed us through the house, pressing his forehead against Susa's hip.

Susa is a tech whiz, Shavano's resident computer expert with her own company that employed a couple of junior nerds to help her out. She was in charge of city hall's tech and taught a couple of classes at the high school, along with a lot of contract work for local businesses. She also ran my Web site and made sure Constantine Farms had up-to-date accounting software and virus protection, although we were pretty small in terms of our tech needs.

"Come on in the kitchen. I've got some jam on," I said, trotting to my jam kettle.

Susa sighed. "Of course, you've got some jam on. You've always got some jam on. Which I can't complain about because it's spectacular jam and I love it." She glanced around the kitchen. "You got any coffee, and maybe a cookie or two?"

"The pot's on the counter, along with the cookie jar. Grab yourself whatever you want." It goes without saying that Susa's at home around my place.

By the time she'd gotten her coffee, I'd pulled the raspberry jam off the burner and put a test patch into the freezer to see if it was thick enough. "What's up?" I asked. I figured Susa had probably dropped by to deliver the latest gossip, which was fine with me. I could keep working on the jam while she spilled the details.

"News." She pulled out a chair at my worktable. "Big news. Great news. News that's going to rock your world."

I paused. "Okay, you have my attention. I assume this doesn't involve any of your current flames."

She shook her head. "It's bigger than that, cupcake. Although I admit I got this piece of information originally by way of Logan Revell."

Logan was one of Susa's many escorts. He worked for the city, although I couldn't remember what he did.

"So tell me."

"*Sweet Thing*'s coming to town." Susa grinned triumphantly.

I sorted through my memory. "*Sweet Thing* the TV show?"

Susa rolled her eyes. "Of course, *Sweet Thing* the TV show. What other kind of sweet thing would be touring around Western Colorado?"

I'd seen *Sweet Thing* a few times, although I couldn't remember which of the channels carried it. The two people in charge—both bakers, as I recalled—traveled to a town, or sometimes two or three towns, and showcased dessert specialists. They toured bakeries and ice cream parlors and regular restaurants as long as they featured spectacular desserts.

"Okay, we should probably tell Bianca Jordan. Her breakfast pastries could be their first stop."

Susa sighed again, louder this time. "We can tell Bianca if you want, but I came here to tell you. Luscious Delights needs to be on that show. Everybody in town knows your stuff is the bomb."

I stared at her. It actually hadn't occurred to me that *Sweet Thing* would be interested in jam. All I'd ever seen them talk about were things like brownie sundaes and tres leches cakes. "But I don't have a store."

"You're online. And you've got a booth at the market. If they came there to film, it would give the market a boost, too. Win/win."

"Yeah," I said slowly. "The market people would probably like that."

"No *probably* about it. The market people would be delighted by that. So we need to swing into action ASAP." Susa folded her arms across her chest, a commander planning a charge.

Marketing isn't my strong point. I have a Web site where I get a few orders, but most of my sales are in the Shavano area. Which we both knew was a barrier to extending my reach beyond Shavano County. " 'Swing into action' how? How do I convince these people to check me out?"

"You need to talk to Evelyn Davidson, down at city hall. She's the liaison with film crews and television shows. Logan says the program contacted her for suggestions, although they'll probably run down some possibilities on their own after they start checking us out."

I knew who Evelyn Davidson was. She'd done presentations for the market vendors about promoting Shavano. Plus she'd bought some of my jam at the market. "Should I call her? Maybe I could set up a tasting."

Susa picked up my cell phone from the kitchen table. "Call her now. I'll back you up if you need me. I know her."

Evelyn Davidson was in her office and more than willing to taste some jam. At which point I realized I had a problem. I had newly processed strawberry jam, which would be good, but probably better later in the season. I had peach and raspberry from frozen berries. I had apricot left over from last season. And I had pepper peach.

My jam wouldn't really be at its best for another month or so. "Maybe I shouldn't do this, Susa. It's too early in the season. I don't know if my stuff is good enough right now."

Susa glared at me, blue eyes flashing. "Your stuff is terrific. Year-round. This is no time to lose confidence in what you make. You take your jars downtown now and feed her some jam. And take the damned pepper peach, too. Show her what you can do."

Everybody needs a friend like Susa.

An hour later I pulled into the parking lot at city hall. I had a selection of my jams, including, yes, pepper peach. And I could promise to show Evelyn more of my stuff as the season advanced so she could taste some of the more exotic things I did later. Plus it seemed to me the farmers market would be a great marketing ploy.

Of course, everything would probably go better if someone else was doing this instead of me. But having me do it was better than nothing. I hoisted the box of jam into my arms and hiked toward the building.

I knew the receptionist, Kitty Morales. She bought a lot of raspberry jam for her five-year-old twins. "Hey, Roxy," she said, "what's up?"

"Hi, Kitty. I'm looking for Evelyn Davidson."

"Down the hall to your left. I think it's the fifth door."

"Okay, thanks." I arrived at Evelyn's door just as it opened and a tall guy in a uniform stepped out. I thought I knew everybody on the Shavano force, but he was a stranger.

He gave me what I think of as *the look.* The one that says *Geez, you're tall for a woman.* I paused to let him walk by, but Evelyn stepped out, too.

"Oh, Roxy, you're right on time. Good to see you. Do you know Chief Fowler?"

I glanced at the guy in uniform. The town had just hired a new police chief. I didn't know much about him except he was supposed to be from someplace like Indianapolis and he came highly recommended.

Just from a glance I put his height at a little more than mine. He held himself ramrod straight, like ex-military, and he had the look of a man who seldom smiled. He definitely wasn't smiling now.

"I'm Roxy Constantine. Nice to meet you." I extended my hand, although I half expected him to ignore it.

He gave me a quick shake, but no smile.

"Roxy makes gorgeous jam," Evelyn gushed. "It's just delectable."

Fowler glanced down at the box I had in my arms, one of my cases. "Luscious," he intoned.

I blinked. "Excuse me?"

He pointed at the printing across the top. *Luscious Delights*, of course. "Oh, yeah. My brand," I muttered.

He nodded. Still no smile.

"Come on in, Roxy." Evelyn stepped aside to let me by.

I gave Fowler one last glance as he strode away. He struck me as someone I didn't want to annoy.

Evelyn sat down at her desk, gesturing for me to take the chair opposite. "I want to taste your jams, but I have to tell you, I'm already a big fan. I wait all summer for your pear and vanilla bean conserve. And your apple butter is just scrumptious."

I relaxed a little. If Evelyn was already a fan of my stuff, maybe I wouldn't need to explain about the jam getting better as more fruit came in. "So what are the details about the show?"

Evelyn's smile broadened. "They're coming here later in the summer, and they've asked us for recommendations, although I guess they're going to have some spies of their own around."

"Spies?"

"Oh, you know what I mean." Evelyn waved a hand. "Advance people who come and check the town out. Listen to what the locals are saying, do some tasting of their own. That kind of thing."

"Oh. Sure. Maybe they'll come to the farmers market." In which case they could taste my jam to their hearts' content.

"Yes, that would be great, wouldn't it?" Evelyn gave me another gleaming smile. "Now what have you brought for me?"

I lined up the jam jars with their spoons and gave Evelyn the box of crackers. As she scooped up bites, I made my pitch. The strawberry jam was made with "first crop berries," which sounded really special although in reality the later crops would no doubt be sweeter. I told her the peach and raspberry were my best sellers. The apricots came from trees right here in the valley.

And the pepper peach? I'd been thinking about the pepper peach all the way into town. The chilies, I said, were Pueblos, the Colorado chili that's only available in limited quantities. The peaches, of course, came from Constantine orchards, one hundred percent Colorado grown. I pitched the flavor as a blend of sweet and spicy, sort of like Shavano itself.

Evelyn's eyes widened a bit at that, but then she grinned. "Exactly right. Just like Shavano. Oh, I love this. All of this. You're a shoo-in, Roxy. Absolutely a shoo-in."

My cheeks warmed as I grinned back. Like I say, I'm lousy at marketing, but maybe that pitch hadn't been as cheesy as I'd feared. I just hoped the people from *Sweet Thing* were into jam.

I left Evelyn the jars of strawberry and pepper peach and went home with the rest. I probably wasn't a shoo-in, no matter what Evelyn said. But I was a contender.

I described the whole thing to Uncle Mike at dinner that night. He laid down his knife and fork, raising his eyebrows. "Of course, you'll get it. No question. Everybody in town loves your stuff. The real question is, what comes next?"

"Next?" I was barely thinking beyond this week.

"TV shows make a difference. A big difference. When that show that visits diners came to Lou's over in Salida, they had so much new business they actually had to close down so they could renovate. He was scared he wouldn't get his customers again, but the traffic's stayed heavy, too. Every time they do a rerun of that episode, Lou gets a new bunch of people traveling over the Divide just to taste his latkes."

"I don't think *Sweet Thing* is quite that big," I pointed out. Although it was big enough. I didn't watch a lot of television, but I'd seen it.

Uncle Mike shook his head. "Doesn't matter. If you're on it, you'll still get a boost. You need to be ready for it."

"Ready how?" I was already making as much jam as

I could sell, putting up extra and storing it whenever I had a lot of fruit.

"Ready by hiring some help," he said firmly.

This was an ongoing argument between the two of us. I'd been happy being a one-girl band ever since I'd started Luscious Delights. It was my baby, as well as my salvation. I hadn't brought in anyone else to work with me because I didn't want to give up my control.

"You're pretty much at capacity right now," Uncle Mike said gently. "You sell out almost every week, and then you have to scramble to make more for the next weekend. If you go on this TV show, people are going to want more of your product. And you won't be able to meet that demand."

"I can increase my production," I said stubbornly.

"How? Give up sleep?" He gave me a long look. "You're spending most of your time making jam as it is. What more can you give up?"

He had a point, but I wasn't ready to concede yet. "I just work harder in the summer because that's when the crops come in."

He shook his head. "You work hard year-round just to meet the demand you've already got. If you wanted to, you could be selling more online, but you can't increase your capacity right now. You've got a great product, but this whole scarcity appeal only goes so far."

I concentrated on twirling up a forkful of spaghetti carbonara. It didn't require my whole attention, but it gave me something to do.

"Think what more you could do with just one assistant. Somebody else could be cutting up the fruit or getting the frozen stuff ready to go while you're doing the jam. Somebody else could be filling the jars and putting them into the water baths while you develop recipes. Just adding a single person could double your production, Rox."

I sighed. "Even if I had an assistant, I'd still only have four burners."

"We could invest in a commercial stove that would double that. We could do it for less than two thousand." His lips crept up in a slightly crafty smile. "I've already priced them. And Ira Ferguson could install it. He's got experience with the restaurants around town."

Of course he'd checked prices. Uncle Mike is nothing if not thorough.

"We're building up an awful lot on hypotheticals. I'm not even sure I'm going to be on this show yet. Once the news gets out, Evelyn will probably get lots of people who want to be on. And I don't do their typical product."

He reached across the table and took my hand. "Honey, I'm willing to bet you'll be on this show. And even if you're not, you still have a growing market you need to meet. Think about the future and what's next for Luscious Delights. You've done a fantastic job so far. Don't stop now."

My eyes prickled with tears for a moment. There'd been a time when I didn't know where to go next or what I could do. Uncle Mike had stood by me, and then he'd given me a push. "Okay, you're right. If I'm going to keep going, I need to start thinking bigger. Maybe I'll see if I can find some part time help, like a mom with kids in school who's looking for something during the day."

Uncle Mike nodded. "Carmen might know somebody. I'll ask her tomorrow. And I'll email you the link to the new stove. You'll love it. You can load up the burners and cuss to your heart's content. Right, Herman?"

Herman gazed up at him sleepily. If we went commercial, I'd probably have to exile him to the main house rather than letting him rattle around the cabin. No more Herman whimpering at me from across the room when I launched into a particularly colorful string of profanity. On the other hand, I'd have a commercial size stove.

I pictured all eight burners in use, jam kettles bubbling, canners simmering, an efficient assistant loading up case after case of jars for the market and my commercial customers. Luscious Delights operating at capacity.

I'd really miss Herman, no doubt about it. But missing Herman would be a small price to pay for all that, believe me.

Chapter 7

I could hardly wait to tell Nate Robicheaux about *Sweet Thing* coming to town. I knew his sister made desserts, so I had a legitimate reason for passing on the news, but I was still riding high on the possibility my jam might get a national audience. I wanted to share my excitement with someone. No, not just *with someone.* With Nate.

I'd decided to think positive. Maybe I wouldn't get to do the show, but maybe I would. And Uncle Mike was right: win or lose, I still needed to think about the future and where I wanted to go next with Luscious Delights.

The market was booming that week. It was Memorial Day weekend, and we had our first real rush of out-of-town customers. I looked for Nate when I got there, but I didn't see him. And after that I didn't have time to look again.

Dolce and I sold jam hand over fist. We barely kept the sample bowls filled. The strawberry preserves sold out within an hour. The strawberry jam took a little longer, but it was gone by noon. Then we ran out of raspberry, leaving a lot of woebegone expressions.

Once again I began to suspect I hadn't been thinking big enough. Instead of just going from Saturday to Saturday, I should have been increasing my production to take advantage of the increased tourist traffic for the holiday. We'd most likely sell out of everything by the end of the market, but I could have sold a lot more if I'd had it on hand.

I'd had business courses in culinary school, but they were more about restaurant economics. It occurred to me that I might want to take a few more courses at the local community college, particularly where planning was concerned. This whole thing was ballooning way beyond my original ideas. That's what dreaming for the future could do for you.

Around noon, Nate leaned into my booth, and I flushed pink with embarrassment. I'd forgotten all about him in the morning rush, and we had a lunch date. "You still want to do lunch?" he asked.

"Absolutely." I handed a couple of jars of apricot jam to a woman in a Crested Butte T-shirt. "I won't be done until two, though."

"No problem. I've got to run to the restaurant to help Bobby." He handed me a paper cup with a wooden spoon. "Here's something to tide you over."

I took a quick bite as the next customer placed a couple of jars of peach jam on the counter in front of me. "That's really good. What is it?"

He gave me a rueful smile. "It's supposed to be chili, but maybe that's not coming across."

I gave the customer her change, then took another bite. "Okay, now I see it. Texas style, right? No tomatoes. Really tasty."

"Thanks. Good on you for spotting it." He checked his watch. "Now I've got to run. Don't have lunch without me, okay?"

"No, I won't, I promise." But by the time he was trotting down the path, I was selling jam and filling bowls and not thinking about lunch at all.

By one, the crush had begun to die down a little. There was an arts fair in the park, and a lot of the market customers had strolled over there to grab lunch at the food stalls. I wondered if that was where Nate wanted to go for lunch. It was a pretty day, all blue skies and warm sun, the promise of green on the aspen twigs. Strolling through the park with him would be a pleasant way to spend the afternoon.

Maybe more than pleasant. But I didn't want to get ahead of myself. Right now Nate and I were friends. That was enough.

Dolce helped me put the rest of the peach, apricot, and pepper peach jars onto the counter. If we sold out completely, I wouldn't have much to pack for the drive home. As it turned out, I sold about half of what I had left, including a lot of pepper peach. But by two the crowds had thinned down to the occasional browser.

"You need help loading your truck?" Dolce asked. She'd been casting longing glances toward the arts fair for the last hour or so, but she was conscientious.

"That's okay—I can manage on my own. Go have fun." I counted out her salary for the day from the money I'd taken in, then zipped the rest into a wallet to keep in my purse until Monday when I'd take it all to the bank. From what I could tell, we'd made a lot of money, more than I'd anticipated when I'd worked out my income and cost estimates for the month.

But that was one thing I didn't mind being wrong about.

I started to break down the booth, wrapping the pieces in the canvas tarp I used to keep them clean and dry. I had it almost loaded when I heard someone clear his throat behind me. I started, then spun around.

Brett Holmes leaned against an aspen trunk, watching me. I had a feeling he'd been there for a while, which wasn't reassuring. "Roxy Constantine. Just who I was looking for."

I straightened slowly, hoping Nate would hurry up so I wouldn't have to be alone with him. "Hi, Brett."

"Heading to the farm?" He gave me one of those mocking smiles that made me shudder. He reminded me of schoolyard bullies from middle school who thought everything you did was dumb.

"I'm done for the day, yeah." And I had no desire to stay as long as he was there.

"You might want to stick around." He grinned again. "Let me take you out for a late lunch. Or an early dinner. With margaritas."

"I'm already booked for lunch. Sorry." Thank God for Nate, although I really wished he'd get here.

Brett's smile disappeared. "Get out of it. You're going to want to hear what I have to say. And I want time to discuss it with you."

"I don't want to get out of it. What's going on, Brett?" The whole mysterioso thing was getting to be a pain.

He straightened, folding his arms across his chest. "I hear you want one of the slots on *Sweet Thing* when they come to Shavano. Is that right?"

"I talked to Evelyn Davidson about it, yeah."

The mocking smile was back. "Oh, yeah, Evelyn Davidson. Good ol' Ev."

"She's the liaison with the production company," I said through gritted teeth. "She'll be making the decision about who gets in."

Brett shook his head. "Evelyn doesn't have squat to

do with who gets in. She just thinks she does. The advance guys with the production crew are the ones who'll choose the restaurants that'll participate."

I put my hands on my hips. "And you know this because?"

"I know this because I know the guys who do the choosing. I've hung out with them. One of them emailed me last week to let me know he was coming to town. We made a date for him to grab dinner at High Country."

"Okay. Good for you. I guess you'll show off your dessert cook at the restaurant."

He shrugged. "Maybe." He took a couple of steps closer, close enough that I could smell the faint scent of beer. Apparently, he'd already started on lunch. "You're missing the point, Roxy. I can put in a good word for you. I can get you on the show. They'll listen to me."

I stared at him, my jaw tightening. I was pretty sure there was a *quid* coming in exchange for that *quo.*

"Come have lunch with me. We'll have a few drinks. We'll talk. I can tell you all you need to know." He placed his hand on my shoulder, running it down my arm to hold my hand. "All you need, believe me."

That time I did shudder, pulling my hand away from his. "Like I said, I've already got lunch plans today. And I need to be at the farm for dinner." *And I wouldn't have a meal with you if I was starving, let alone go drinking.*

He scowled, his lips drawing down. "Come on, Roxy. Don't be a bitch. I'm offering you something you need. You get the publicity. We get to be…closer. No big deal. You might even like it. We both win."

I took a deep breath, trying to calm down. "If you recommend my jams to the production staff, I'll be grateful. But I won't go out with you, and I won't have sex with you. I don't like being blackmailed. That's all I have to say about this."

I was surprised to find my hands were steady. The last time Brett had tried to pressure me into sex, I'd had a near meltdown. This time around I mostly felt pissed. I started to turn away when Brett grabbed me again, a lot harder this time, his fingers digging into my shoulders.

His face was flushed, and he was baring his teeth in a grimace. I realized I'd never seen him angry before, just sneering.

"Listen, bitch," he snarled, "you don't turn your back on me. Not when I'm doing you a favor. You want on that show, you play ball. Otherwise, you're done. I'll make sure of it. You're not only out of the show, I'll make sure you're finished in Shavano." He gave me a quick shake. "You understand me?"

I'm a big woman, but I'm not that good at self-defense when there's no can of tomatoes handy. I put my hands on his chest and shoved as hard as I could, which had no effect at all. "Let go of me. Now."

Brett hung on, shaking me again. "Don't push me, Roxy. You won't like it."

And then he was stumbling backward, away from me, going down on one knee as he lost his footing on the gravel.

Nate stood in front of me. "What the hell are you doing? Get your hands off her, asshole. Didn't you hear what she said?"

Brett staggered to his feet, snarling. "Who the fuck are you, Captain America? Get out of my way."

Nate shook his head. "No. I don't think so. You okay, Roxy?"

I managed to nod, caught between gratitude for his

being there and anger at myself for not having taken care of Brett on my own.

He looked at Brett again. "It's time for you to move on. Unless you want a lot more trouble than you've already got." He gestured toward the path behind Brett where several booths were still up. Bianca Jordan had walked several feet toward us, frowning. Annabelle Dorsey was leaning out of her booth. Dorothy stood behind her, eyes wide. And Harry Potter, bless his soul, was trotting our way, rolling up his sleeves, eyebrows bristling.

The fact that they were all coming to my rescue because they were worried about me almost brought tears to my eyes, but my main concern right then was Brett Holmes and what would happen next if he decided to make some kind of idiotic move.

He straightened, breathing hard, then fixed me with what was probably supposed to be a menacing stare. "You made your choice, Roxy. Just remember that. You decided to go this way." Then he turned and stalked off, heading toward the parking lot.

I noticed that he very carefully didn't walk near Harry.

Harry himself came to my side, brow furrowing. "You okay, Roxy?"

"Yeah. Thanks for asking, Harry. And thanks for coming up here."

He glanced at Nate, as if weighing whether he needed to step in on that front, too. But he must have decided he didn't. "Okay, then." He turned toward Dirty Pete's.

Nate stared after Brett. "Who was that guy? What was he doing here?"

"Brett Holmes." I sighed, not entirely sure how to explain all of this. "He's the chef at High Country, and he's been after me to go out with him. I don't want to. He isn't taking it well."

Nate glanced at me, brow still furrowed. "Yeah, I got that. You want to report him to the cops? You probably should."

I shook my head. "I just want this to be over. I don't want to think about it anymore." I took a breath, re-centering myself. It was still a beautiful afternoon, and we still had a lunch date. "Do you want to get some lunch at the arts fair? The food stalls are open."

He paused for a moment, studying the crowds flowing around the artists' booths at the fair, then shook his head. "I'd like to cook lunch for you if you'll let me."

"Cook lunch?" A dim alarm bell began ringing in my brain. Brett had wanted to cook for me. Only *cook* had meant a lot more. Was Nate thinking along the same lines? Cooking lunch in his apartment? "Whereabouts?"

He shrugged. "How about Robicheaux's? The kitchen's roomier than mine, and I need some of the equipment we've got. They were just finishing up with service when I left, so we should be able to find a table that's free."

He flashed a quick grin, and I relaxed a little. It didn't sound like a set-up. And it went without saying that Nate wasn't Brett. "Okay. That sounds good."

Actually, now that I had a chance to think, it sounded terrific. I was more than ready to get away from the farmers market area and the lingering memory of Brett Holmes and his threats.

"Let's do it, then." Nate gathered up the last of my booth and loaded it into my truck.

67

I pulled down the cover and locked it in place. "You want a lift?"

He shook his head. "It's an easy walk from here, if you don't mind carrying a couple of totes." He gestured toward a small pile of tote bags he'd dropped when he'd come to rescue me from Brett.

I raised my eyebrows. "Is all of that for lunch?"

"A lot of it." He gathered a couple of bags, handing me a third. "I go a little nuts at farmers markets. It's the only chance I get to cook something out of the ordinary."

"You realize, I'm now expecting a lot from lunch." I took the tote bag, which was surprisingly light considering how much seemed to be stuffed inside it.

He grinned. "I'm expecting quite a bit myself." He turned toward Second Street, a.k.a. Restaurant Row in Shavano.

But as I followed him down the path, I found myself wondering again: why was a chef from Las Vegas flipping burgers at a diner in Shavano, Colorado?

Still, considering that he was ready to cook me a custom lunch, I figured that was a question for some other time.

Chapter 8

Lunch at Robicheaux's was terrific, although probably not what Nate had planned originally. I helped him fix soup with some fresh sorrel from the market. He'd grabbed a loaf of bread from Blanca Jordan that was close to fresh out of the oven.

Nate's older brother Bobby was doing prep work in the kitchen when we got there. He didn't seem delighted that we were cooking on his stove, but other than a few grunts he didn't say much. Nate's sister Coco stayed to kibitz, and his mom joined us after she'd closed down the restaurant. Nate might have thought he was just going to be feeding me, but it was clear his mom and sister expected a bowl of soup, too.

His brother, on the other hand, didn't even look up when we carried everything out to the dining room.

We had a great time sharing restaurant gossip and critiquing the sorrel soup. Madge wanted to put it on the menu, but Nate didn't think it would scale. Coco said they should start a farmers market special as long as the market was running, and Madge agreed. That led to discussions of what was available—mainly arugula and spinach—which naturally led to Madge asking about Uncle Mike's crop.

I promised I'd talk to him about becoming their arugula supplier, and Coco seemed delighted.

Of course they'd still have to convince Bobby, but

it would three against one—and my money was on the three.

After we finished eating, I helped Nate clean up, carrying the plates to the dishwasher as we talked about the possibilities for the market specials, depending on what was available.

"I'll find out how much arugula Coco thinks we'd need for a salad. Then I can talk to your uncle." Nate followed me to the kitchen, holding the door to let me walk through.

The room was dark and empty. It looked like all the other Robicheaux family members had taken off. I put the soup bowls on the counter, then turned toward the door. Nate stood beside me, so close I could feel the warmth of his skin.

For a moment, I had the feeling he might kiss me. What would I do if he did? Punch him? Yell for help?

Enjoy it?

I didn't know. But the fact that I might actually enjoy being kissed by Nate Robicheaux counted as a revelation in my book.

Which meant it was time to move on before things got more complicated.

I turned toward the door. "Thanks for lunch, Nate. It was delicious. Let me know when you want to come out to the farm for the arugula."

I stepped forward, then turned for a last look.

Nate stayed where he was, watching me. "Yeah. I'll do that. See you next week. Have a good one, Roxy."

I walked outside, trying to decide if I was relieved or disappointed that he hadn't followed me. I hiked up Second Street toward River Park, planning out the rest of the afternoon. I had enough time to check out the strawberries that had been picked today before I started getting dinner ready. Meatloaf sounded good.

I rounded the last curve in the path, heading toward the parking lot. And stopped cold.

My truck, which had previously been cleanish if not immaculate, was now caked in mud. It looked like someone had taken handfuls from the nearby riverbank and thrown it full force at the truck's sides. There were clumps on the doors, the windows, the fenders, and all along the locking cover over the back. If it hadn't been for the cover, the booth I'd left in the truck bed would have been splattered, too. I didn't want to think about how hard that would have been to clean up.

But the pièce de résistance was the word smeared across the windshield: *slut.* Done in shades of grayish black. My stomach clenched tight as I stared, and my mind tried to make sense of what I was seeing.

Who? Who did this? The words kept echoing through my mind. Did people in town really think I was a slut? What had I done to make them think that?

Nothing. I took a deep breath, pulling myself together. This hadn't been done by the citizens of Shavano, who probably had no particular opinions about my sex life, given that I didn't have one. This was done by somebody with a grudge. And the most obvious person in that category was Brett Holmes.

Most likely Brett had decided to take out his frustration on my blameless truck, maybe after a couple more beers and time to let his anger simmer for a while, since that seemed to be his Saturday routine. It was kind of an immature thing to do, but Brett didn't strike me as the mature type.

The other question I had to consider—besides the

who and why—was what to do now. Did I confront Brett? Call him out? Turn him in to the cops? That last possibility sounded satisfying. I could picture Chief Fowler giving Brett the same cold stare he'd given me. Maybe it would be enough to make him sweat.

But what would I tell the chief if I tried to turn Brett in? That we'd had a fight and he seemed like the logical person to have vandalized my truck? Brett would probably say I was just a crazy broad trying to get him in trouble.

If I went after Brett, he'd likely return the favor, maybe even passing on some rumors about my time in Denver. And then I'd be right where I'd been when I left, trying to counter sleaze spread by a scumbag.

I checked around the parking lot, looking for anyone who might have seen what happened. I'd parked the truck at the far side of the lot, leaving room for customers as the market management asked us to do. I wasn't close to any of the places people normally congregated. I didn't see anybody around now, although that didn't mean they hadn't been there earlier.

I decided I'd ask the people who'd still been at the market when I'd left with Nate—Bianca, Annabelle and Dorothy, and maybe Harry, although I thought he'd gone back to Dirty Pete's after my argument with Brett was over. If any of them had seen something, I'd go to the cops. But if I couldn't find anyone who'd been around when it happened, I'd just let it go.

Letting it go had a lot of appeal right then. I wouldn't have to explain my life to anyone. I dug out my cell phone and took a series of pictures, careful to get all the angles. I didn't think the truck had been damaged, but I still wanted the evidence, just in case. Then I threw my cell phone back in my purse and grabbed a water bottle from behind the driver's seat. I needed to get the truck washed, but first I had to see to drive.

Plus I didn't want to maneuver around town with *slut* smeared across my windshield.

It took a lot of river water, but I finally had the windshield clean enough to drive to the nearest car wash. The guy in the next bay frowned when he saw me. "Been up in the back country?" he asked.

"Something like that," I muttered.

It took me around twenty minutes of scrubbing, but I finally got the truck cleaned up enough to drive home. I really didn't want to have to explain all of this to Uncle Mike. I was still trying to explain it to myself, after all.

As it turned out, though, I didn't have much choice. He was standing in the front door of the main house, waiting for me, when I drove up.

"What the hell, Roxy?" he said as I climbed out of my truck.

I took a breath. "Which *what the hell* moment are you asking about?"

"What's his name? You know, that cook. Brett something."

"Holmes," I supplied, unlocking the truck cover.

"Yeah, him. I got a call from Bianca. She said he was yelling at you. Got physical. Somebody else had to push him off you."

At least he hadn't heard about the truck getting slimed. But hearing about Brett was bad enough. "Nate Robicheaux pushed him off. Brett got the drop on me, or I would have pushed him off myself."

"What was his problem? Why was he bothering you?" Uncle Mike folded his arms across his chest. "Has he done this before? Do I need to pay him a visit?"

"No, you most definitely do not. He's been trying to get me to go out with him, but I don't want to. This time he was trying to bribe me by saying he could get me onto *Sweet Thing* because he knows the producer. I told him no again, and he got mad. Nate pushed him away. That's all there was to it."

More or less. It was certainly all I felt like talking about right then.

Uncle Mike drew himself up. "What kind of man yells at a woman because she won't go out with him?"

"The stupid kind." I pulled open the cover and started lifting out the booth. Uncle Mike moved to help me, which provided a distraction.

Once we got everything into the storage shed where I kept the booth, I dusted my hands and tried for a smile. "How are the strawberries coming along? I sold out of some jam and preserves today. Maybe I'll double up on quantities next week, although we probably won't have as many tourists then. What with the holiday and all."

Uncle Mike was clearly not impressed. "We're not done talking about the stupid guy, Roxanne."

I sighed. "I don't know what else we can say, Uncle Mike. He's an obnoxious jerk, but I don't think he'll try anything else. He got put down pretty thoroughly today. Maybe he finally got the idea I won't go out with him." Or at least I really hoped he had.

"Which shows how much you know about jerks." Uncle Mike grimaced. "He's likely to come at you again because now he's got something to prove. He got trounced in public. He'll want to show you who's boss."

Well, hell. I took another in a series of deep breaths. Too bad Uncle Mike was so insightful. "He's already done that, for what it's worth. I went to lunch at Robicheaux's. When I came back somebody had thrown a bunch of mud at my truck."

I decided to omit references to the whole *slut* thing.

Uncle Mike raised an eyebrow. "You think it was Holmes?"

"It makes sense. He was mad at me."

"Is he really that much of an idiot? It sounds like something a ten-year-old would do."

"I haven't pissed off any ten-year-olds that I know of. But I did piss off Brett." I paused. He had a point. The thing with the truck seemed pretty immature. But Brett wasn't what I'd call a really mature adult. Particularly if he'd been drinking.

"Okay, maybe I'll go with you to the market next week," Uncle Mike said.

I shook my head. "You don't have to do that."

I really didn't want him to. When he joined me in my booth, Uncle Mike became the jam bowl cop. He kept track of anyone who took more than one sample of jam and gave them murderous looks until they slunk away, totally embarrassed. I estimated that my sales dropped by at least ten percent every time Uncle Mike accompanied me to the market.

His eyes were troubled. "Roxanne, this man is a predator. I don't want you there unprotected. I could send Donnie over, but he takes up a lot of space."

Donnie was almost as wide as he was tall, a very big man in other words. "Donnie needs to run the Constantine Farms booth with Carmen. And I don't need a guardian. Honest."

"Herman. You can take Herman. Nobody would bother you with Herman around."

I could just picture Herman in the booth, having a nice snack out of one of the jam bowls. "I am absolutely not taking Herman. It's probably against Health Department rules anyway. I'll be okay, honestly. I won't let Brett come within a mile of the booth. Now I need to go fix dinner."

It was kind of early to be cooking, but I figured it was one way to get Uncle Mike off my case. I wasn't worried about Brett, although maybe I should have been. I was pissed about him. And I intended to ask Bianca if she'd seen him hanging around my truck. But I'd make damn sure he never got within grabbing distance of me again.

Uncle Mike didn't look convinced, but he walked along beside me in silence for a moment. "How was Robicheaux's?"

"We didn't eat off the menu. Nate fixed soup with some sorrel he bought from Marguerite today. It was terrific." I kept my gaze straight ahead because I knew what was coming.

"Nate Robicheaux fixed lunch for you? After he drove off Brett Holmes?" I could hear the smile in Uncle Mike's voice. He's always trying to get me hooked up with a suitable Shavano male.

"Nate fixed lunch for everybody. His sister and his mom ate with us, too."

"You had lunch with Madge?" Uncle Mike's voice had a note that sounded a little like hope.

"I did. She's thinking of starting some farmers market specials. Using local produce, including ours." I glanced at him.

His face was faintly flushed. If I hadn't known better, I'd have thought he was blushing. "Tell her to

The Pepper Peach Murder

drop by sometime. I'll work out a price for her."

"It'll probably be Nate. I already asked him to drop by."

Uncle Mike's smile faded a bit. "Oh. Okay, I'll be glad to talk to him. Just let me know when."

"I will." But I was already wondering if there was any way I could get Madge to drop by, too. That hopeful note in Uncle Mike's voice needed encouragement.

Chapter 9

The next farmers market was almost as busy as Memorial Day weekend had been. The strawberry crop had started coming in strong, so I had a lot to work with. Along with the usual strawberry jam and preserves, I tried one of my exotics: strawberry basil jam. The secret ingredient here is grated apple, believe it or not. And I add the chopped basil at the end, after the jam is cooked, so it keeps its fresh flavor. The jam is sort of sweet and sort of savory all at once, and it's usually a big seller.

At the last minute, Uncle Mike had insisted I take Herman along, just in case. I really didn't think Brett Holmes would come back, particularly if he'd been the one who'd thrown mud at my truck. He'd accomplished what he wanted, showing me he was more powerful than I was. Coming after me again would just mean another rejection, only louder this time.

Herman was surprisingly docile when we got there. I'd brought along his crate, just in case I needed to keep him away from the food. But he'd had enough experience with me bouncing around my kitchen to know he needed to stay out of my way. He curled up beside the booth, resting his chin on his paws, and became an immediate kid magnet. Fortunately, he likes kids and he likes being petted, so there was a certain amount of natural synergy going on.

And their parents bought jam.

I was doing a big business in strawberry products, but so was everybody else. Lots of the produce stands had berries for sale, and one of the food trucks was selling strawberries and whipped cream on biscuits. The sight of all those people walking along with bowls of strawberries topped with clouds of white was enough to start anybody's mouth watering.

As I considered the possibilities for strawberries and cream, I suddenly realized I hadn't made any lunch plans with Nate yet. My shoulders tensed. I hoped he was still interested in getting together with me. I really wanted to see him again.

What are you *interested in, Roxy?* That was the question, really. Did I want something beyond just a Saturday friendship at the market? Was I ready to dive into the dating pool?

Of course, Nate might not be interested in the whole dating thing himself. He was a friendly guy. Maybe he was just being friendly with me, and I was reading more into it than I should. That idea was so depressing I decided not to think about it for the time being.

Around eleven, Nate himself leaned into the booth, smiling. "Hey, Roxy. How's it going?"

"Busy," I said, smiling back. "How about you? What are you demo-ing today?"

"Roast beef hash. Using some of our pot roast." He handed me a paper cup and wooden spoon. "I saved you one. Hide this away. They went really fast."

"Oh, that's great. That people were grabbing your stuff, I mean. It's great that you're so popular."

I shut up after all that babbling. And I kept from sliding into an idiot grin, fortunately.

"You free for lunch?" He cocked an eyebrow at me.

"Sure. Absolutely. After two, though."

"Right. I need to help Bobby with the noon rush, then I'll come pick you up if that works."

I nodded a little more vigorously than I needed to. "Sure. It works."

"Okay, see you." He gave me a quick grin and was gone. I took a bite of his roast beef hash. It was terrific, of course.

"Who was that?" Dolce asked as she refilled the strawberry preserves bowl.

"Nate Robicheaux. He's a chef at Robicheaux's Café."

"Oh." Dolce turned to the cracker bowls. "He's cute."

Nate wasn't exactly cute, but he was very easy on the eyes. He had what I thought of as chef's muscles— well-developed biceps from lifting heavy pans, mostly. And there were those hands. Those squarish, capable hands that started a warm feeling in my gut.

Focus, Roxanne. Right. I had jam to sell and around three hours still to go.

Bianca Jordan breezed by around noon, her silver hair jutting out from beneath her ball cap. "How's it going, kid?" she asked.

"Good. How about you?"

"Decent. I sold out of sticky buns and four-grain. I've still got pumpernickel and cookies. And focaccia. I may have made more than necessary." Bianca dipped a cracker into the strawberry basil. "Mmmm. I love this stuff."

"Thanks. It's selling well." I was trying to decide how to ask Bianca if she'd seen Brett around my truck last week, although I should have asked her a few days ago. I'd gotten caught up in making strawberry jam.

And I didn't really want to know, to tell the truth. If she'd seen Brett mudding my truck, I'd have to go to Chief Fowler.

Bianca beat me to the punch. "Any sign of that pissant from High Country?"

I shook my head. "Nope. Maybe he's learned his lesson."

Bianca grimaced. "Doubt it."

"Me, too." I took a breath. "Did you see him or anybody else hanging around my truck last Saturday? Somebody threw a bunch of mud at it while I was off having lunch."

Bianca frowned. "No, but I left pretty soon after you and Nate did. If it happened after three or so, nobody would have been around."

I sighed. "Okay, that's what I figured. At least there wasn't any serious damage."

"If that pissant messed with your truck, he's got some serious problems with attitude. More serious than I would have figured, anyway. You might want to talk to Fowler about it." She picked up a couple of jars of strawberry basil. "I'll take these. It'll be great on English muffins."

I took her money and sent her off, more worried than I'd been when she first came. I didn't have any evidence that Brett was behind the mud, and Fowler might wonder why I was wasting his time. On the other hand, Bianca had a point. A man who was mad enough to throw mud at a truck might have some serious anger management problems.

Of course, I had Herman, currently fast asleep and snoring faintly.

The crowds began to die down around one. We'd sold out of peach and strawberry, and we were on the last jars of raspberry. I still had some strawberry basil left, although not much. I'd probably make some more for next week, or possibly mixed berry with strawberries and raspberries. I was considering other variations, maybe involving rhubarb or alcohol, when someone called my name and I turned to see Evelyn Davidson.

She was wearing jeans and a silk shirt, not nearly the flawless city employee she'd been when I'd last seen her. Of course the jeans looked like they'd been pressed, but at least she'd made a gesture at market casual.

"Hi, how are you today?" she trilled. I hadn't remembered her being quite that peppy, but maybe she was inspired by the market.

"I'm fine. Lovely day for the market, isn't it?"

"Yes, it certainly is." She turned to my row of sample bowls, still dimpling. "Oh, what's this? Strawberry basil. Sounds interesting." She grabbed a cracker and dipped up some jam. "Why, it's delicious. Absolutely scrumptious."

All this cheer was beginning to get on my nerves a little, but maybe she was just being friendly. "Thanks. The new strawberry crop is coming in now, and I'm taking advantage of it."

"Oh, good for you." She moved down the line, dipping another cracker into the apricot. "I love this, too."

I watched her work her way through the samples, my spidey senses tingling. Something felt off. "Anything new about *Sweet Thing*, Evelyn?"

"*Sweet Thing?*" Her eyebrows rose almost to her hairline. "No, not really. We're still evaluating our locals, trying to decide who we should recommend for the show." She gave me a sunny smile that chilled me to the bone.

"Who all is in the running?"

"Oh, I couldn't tell you that." She gave me a wide-eyed look. "That's strictly confidential, you know. I mean, if I told you, everybody else would want to know, too."

I decided to cut to the point. Subtlety wasn't getting me anywhere. "Am I still being considered, Evelyn? My jams, that is?"

"Oh." Evelyn's smile faltered slightly, and she licked her lips. "Well, I don't know if I can…"

"Just tell me. I won't make trouble." I was already pretty sure I knew the answer, but I wanted it spelled out.

"All right." Evelyn paused, staring at the apricot jam. "It's not that your jams aren't terrific, Roxy. They absolutely are. I mean, I'm here today buying your jam because I love it."

I put my hands on my hips. "But?"

"But. The whole deal with *Sweet Thing* coming here is to get good publicity for the town. To convince people that we're a foodie destination."

"Right."

"So we really don't want anything to get in the way of that impression. We don't want distractions from the focus on the town. Shavano needs to be the star. No other competing stories."

I tried to make some sense of this. What did Shavano's star position have to do with me and my jam? "Okay, so how do I come into that?"

"Well, there was some concern…" She bit her lip. "I don't know how to put this politely, Roxy, so I'll just come out and say it. We were afraid that maybe your reputation might get in the way. News stories might concentrate on you and your past rather than on Shavano. You'd be the story, not the town. If you see what I mean."

I managed not to snarl. "The only reputation I've got in Shavano is as a jam maker. And my past is basically growing up in the valley. I guess Constantine Farms has a reputation, but I don't know why anyone would want to write about that necessarily. Were you thinking about my relationship with the farm?"

Evelyn's cheeks flushed, and she looked like she desperately wished she was anywhere except my booth. "Well, it's not your reputation in Shavano that's the problem. It's the Denver thing we were worried about."

"The Denver thing." Something cold slid down my backbone.

"Yes, you know. All the stuff about you and that chef in Denver. We just can't take the chance that rumors might start circulating. It would be too distracting." The smile she gave me then wasn't really a smile. More like her lips just stretched for a moment before returning to their normal position.

I closed my eyes and took a deep breath, willing myself not to scream at her or cry. That wouldn't solve anything. "Could I ask who told you about me having a reputation problem?"

"Oh, I can't reveal my sources. People tell me things in confidence, and I can't…"

"Brett Holmes," I said flatly. "Brett Holmes told you I had a bad reputation, didn't he?"

Evelyn blew out a breath. "I can't confirm that."

"You don't have to. No one else in town would say

that." And she hadn't bothered to ask me for my side of the story, which told me a lot about Brett's probable standing with Evelyn. "I don't suppose you're interested in my version of things?"

Evelyn sighed. "Roxy, I'm sorry. We're going in another direction. Probably bakeries. Maybe some ice cream. I really have to go." She turned on her heel and walked briskly up the path toward town without looking back.

She hadn't taken the jam she'd picked out. On the other hand, I wasn't sure I wanted to sell her anything. My jam deserved a better home.

Dolce glanced at me from the far side of the booth. "Are you okay?" she asked a little hesitantly.

I shook my head. "Not really. But we've only got a few minutes left."

We sold a couple more jars of raspberry and a strawberry basil, but then it was two o'clock. Sometimes I stay open longer if it looks like there might be more customers, but this time I started putting the jars in the boxes as soon as I had the last customer's money in the till. I didn't throw the jars in the boxes, but it took a lot of effort.

I gave Dolce her money and I'm pretty sure I thanked her, although I can't swear to it. All I wanted was to go home and hide.

Herman woke up and got to his feet as I started breaking down the booth. He gave me a concerned whimper and bonked his head against my hip. I scratched his ears but didn't stop what I was doing.

"Well, damn," someone said, and I turned to see Susa standing on the path. "I know I'm late, but I hoped you might still have some of your strawberry jam. I've

85

been longing for it all week."

Herman walked over to have his ears scratched as I reached into one of the boxes for a jar of strawberry basil. "Here you go. Enjoy."

Susa stared at me. "That was the least enthusiastic reading of *enjoy* I've ever heard."

"Sorry. I'll work on it." I went to the booth. Right then I didn't want to talk to anyone, not even Susa.

But Susa's my friend, and she refused to let me get away with it. She stepped in front of me, so that I had to look at her. "What's wrong? What's happened? Tell me."

I took a deep breath, ready to tell her to go away and leave me alone. But then I deflated. Snarling at Susa wouldn't help anything, and it would make me feel worse. "Evelyn Davidson was here. I'm out of the competition for *Sweet Thing*."

"Oh, honey. Who did they choose? Bianca?"

I shook my head. "I don't know. I don't think they've made their choice yet."

There was a beat of silence while Susa stared at me. "What aren't you telling me?"

"Evelyn said they wouldn't choose me because I had a bad reputation. 'All that stuff about you and the chef in Denver,' is the way she put it. She said I'd be a distraction when they wanted the show to concentrate on Shavano. I'm guessing she got it from Brett. His revenge."

Susa's jaw dropped, and she went silent for a moment. Then she let loose with one of the most inventive strings of obscenities I'd ever heard, ending by consigning both Evelyn and Brett to perdition.

"What are you going to do about this?" she

demanded.

"Nothing. If I make trouble, more people are going to hear Brett's lies. I'd just as soon not have everybody in town think I'm some kind of kitchen slut." Tears prickled my eyes, but I ignored them. I absolutely was *not* going to let Brett Holmes make me cry.

"If he tried telling people that, everybody in town would think Brett Holmes was a lying asshole, which would be no more than the truth. You can't let him get away with this, Roxy. If he wins this time, what's to stop him from doing it again? I'll go over to Evelyn's office with you. We'll tell her the truth. She'll have to listen."

The thought of telling the whole story to Evelyn made me slightly dizzy. "Let me think about it. She wouldn't be there today anyway. It's Saturday. The office is closed."

"Then let's go to that damned restaurant and tell Brett Holmes he's a lying bastard." Susa bristled with indignation. "Somebody needs to teach him some manners. He can't go around lying about people just to get his way."

If the thought of talking to Evelyn made me dizzy, the thought of confronting Brett Holmes in front of his kitchen staff and probably a dining room full of customers made me nauseous. "You're right. Someone needs to teach him some manners. But it won't be me. And it shouldn't be you either. Right now, I just want to go home." I pulled down the last bit of the booth and put it into the truck bed, ready to climb in and leave.

"Roxy?"

Nate was walking up the path toward me, frowning slightly. Hard to believe, but I'd actually forgotten we had a date for lunch.

"Hi." I ran a hand across the back of my neck and realized most of my hair had come down as I'd struggled with the booth. I probably looked more like a Fury than an Amazon. "I'm sorry. I can't do lunch. I'm…upset."

He stared at me for a moment, then reached out to brush a lock of hair away from my cheek. "Is there anything I can do to help?"

The warmth of his hand on my cheek was almost enough to make me burst into tears right there. *Do* not *lose it in front of him.* I took a deep breath and steadied myself. "Thanks, but no. I need to deal with this myself."

Nate looked stricken. Susa looked furious. I probably looked like I needed a keeper, but I couldn't worry about that. "I'm sorry, Nate, I'll see you next week." And I turned toward the truck.

Chapter 10

Susa grabbed my arm before I got very far. "Aren't you forgetting something?"

Herman was standing where the booth had been, whimpering.

"Oh, my God, Herman." I turned quickly, dropping to my knees beside him. "I'm so sorry, Herm. I would never have forgotten you, honest." But of course I had. For one stupid moment I'd been so caught up in my own misery I'd forgotten my best friend.

I rubbed a hand over his head, telling myself he wasn't really tearful. His eyes were always that wet.

"Who's this?" Nate asked politely.

"This is Herman." I pressed my head against his shoulder. "He's big but friendly. And I'm an idiot."

Nate knelt down next to me, holding out his hand for Herman to sniff. "Hi, Herman."

And that did it. I'd been fighting off tears ever since Evelyn left, and I'd been more or less successful. But the sight of Nate petting Herman so gently when I'd almost driven off and left both of them behind reduced me to a puddle of guilt. I sat down hard, fumbling in my purse as the tears started sliding down my cheeks.

Susa knelt on my other side, handing me a tissue. "Go on, kid. You've earned it." She extended her hand to Nate. "Hi. I'm Susa Sondergaard, Roxy's best friend even when she's being dumb."

"Nate Robicheaux." He shook her hand. "Glad to meet you, Susa. Would somebody tell me what's going on here?"

"I think that would be a really good idea and I think Roxy should do it and I'm leaving now so she'll have to." Susa pushed herself to her feet. "Talk to him, Roxy. You'll feel better. And maybe he can convince you to fight. God knows, I'm not having much luck myself." She turned and ambled up the path, turning once to do the "call me" gesture.

I sat on the ground next to Herman, wiping my cheeks and feeling like a fool. "I'm sorry. This day has just gotten away from me."

"Would a beer help?" Nate asked.

I thought about it. I was going to have to drive to the farm, but a beer might help settle my nerves before I had to explain things to Uncle Mike. "Okay. Where do you want to go? I've got Herman, remember."

"How could I forget." Nate reached up to scratch Herman's ears again. "Actually, I was thinking of my place, only my apartment's really small so we'd probably end up in my yard."

I wondered what kind of small apartment came with a yard. "Okay. Why not? Will it be okay for Herman to be there?"

"Herman will be great." Nate stood, extending his hand to me. "I can even give him a couple of hot dogs if that's okay."

"He'll probably love it." I stood for a moment wiping my cheeks. Herman gave a concerned *woof.*

"Can I get a ride?" Nate asked, probably as a way to get me moving.

"Sure."

We drove across town to the older part of Shavano, up on the lower flanks of Mount Oxford. Nate directed me through a maze of streets to a comfortable-looking brown brick house, a nineteen twenties style bungalow.

"You can pull up in the drive." Nate directed me around the side of the house.

"Do you have an apartment inside?" I asked.

He shook his head. "I'm up there." He pointed to a window at the eave of the garage, and I realized there was another floor upstairs.

"Oh." It looked like a big room, but I doubted there was more than one.

Nate grinned. "Full disclosure. That house is where I grew up. My mom still lives there, although Bobby and Coco both have their own places. I moved in over the garage temporarily when I came back, but *temporarily* has stretched out a bit longer than I thought it would."

I wasn't about to judge him for living in the family house since I was living on the family farm. "Looks roomy."

"It's okay. But it's a steep staircase to get up there. I'm not sure how Herman would do on it."

"No, he's not much on stairs. We'll stay down here." That took care of several problems, not least of them Herman's reaction to being in a strange house. He didn't often venture off the Constantine property.

"I'll be right back." He gestured toward the yard. "There's a picnic table there where we can sit."

"Got it." Herman trotted dutifully toward the yard while I dug through my purse for a brush. I figured I might as well take my hair all the way down. It couldn't look any worse than it did already.

The yard was spacious, lined with pines and a few

cottonwood trees. The lawn ran down a slight slope, and Herman found a tennis ball to chase.

Nate was back a few minutes later, carrying a couple of bottles of Fat Tire and what looked like a plate of nachos. "Sorry I don't have any craft beer, but at least I know it's good."

"That's fine. I don't need craft."

He put the plate on the table, then sat down beside me as Herman galloped around. I suddenly felt a little self-conscious—he seemed to be staring at me. I wondered if I should ask to go inside and wash my face.

"I've never seen you with your hair down," he said finally.

"Oh." I reached up to touch my curls. They go every which way if I don't pin them back, but I didn't feel up to it at the moment. "It came down when I was putting the booth away."

"It's beautiful." He stared at me for a moment longer, then turned to Herman again.

For a moment, I was absolutely speechless. That was the last thing I'd expected him to say about my mop. "Thank you," I managed without squeaking.

"Have some nachos. It's not a gourmet lunch, but it's filling."

I took him up on it, piling some nachos on a paper plate. They were, of course, delicious.

"Are you ready to tell me what's going on?" he said finally.

Oh, my. Where to start? "Okay. You remember I told you I worked in Denver for a while?"

I started in on the story, stumbling a bit when I got to the part about the chef grabbing me in the pantry.

Beside me, Nate went very still, staring straight

ahead. I willed him not to ask me anything yet.

"I grabbed a can of tomatoes and hit him with it, and then I ran out."

Nate's lips quirked up. "Good for you."

"Yeah, well, not exactly. The next day I got fired. And the manager said if I told anybody what happened, they'd say it was consensual."

Nate grimaced. "Bastard."

"Yep. I came back here and started a jam business. Only apparently the chef told some people that I'd come on to him and gotten mad when he didn't give me a promotion."

"Like Brett Holmes?"

"Yeah. Brett was in the same kitchen. That's why he was after me to go out with him. And got mad when I wouldn't. And now he's spreading rumors about me. He told Evelyn Davidson I had a bad reputation in Denver, and she dropped me from the *Sweet Thing* competition."

Nate held up a hand. "Wait, what?"

I sighed. Of course he didn't know what I was talking about. "The TV show, *Sweet Thing.* It's coming to town, and Evelyn Davidson is the liaison for the city. She was supposed to recommend some local people for them to include, and I was one of the ones she was considering. Only now she won't because Brett talked to her."

Nate shook his head. "That makes no sense. Even if the rumors were true, which they aren't, it has nothing to do with your jam."

I took another swallow of beer. The conversation with Nate was actually making me feel better, although it wasn't getting me any closer to figuring out what to do next. "Brett might pass on the rumors to the production people at the show. I know he's the one who told her about me."

"Maybe he's got something on her, too," Nate said darkly.

I paused. That honestly hadn't occurred to me. "In that case, she's a victim, in a way."

"No, she's someone who didn't have the *cojones* to tell Holmes to take a hike like you did." Nate gave me a dry smile as he raised his beer bottle. "Don't ask me to feel sorry for her. That's not going to happen."

"Yeah, I don't want to feel sorry for her either. I'm still trying to figure out a strategy for dealing with this."

"What have you thought of?"

Good question. "She's pretty much shut me out of the whole *Sweet Thing* competition. I don't think talking to her again will make any difference. But I don't like the idea of Brett spreading lies about me around town. I mean, I've lived here all my life, and most people would know better than to believe anything he might tell them. But they might wonder about it. And they might talk about it. It's still sort of a small town, and there's a lot of gossip. Whatever happens, it wouldn't be good for me or my business."

"So you need to get him to knock it off?"

"Ideally. But that may not be possible. I think I need to figure out how to do damage control from my end."

"I guess you could go the legal route and threaten to sue for slander," Nate said slowly.

"I probably can't afford that. And lawsuits take a while. I'd rather do something that would be more immediate."

"Hire a hitman?" Nate grinned.

"That would be immediate, but also probably too

expensive." I grinned back. "I was thinking more of doing things around town to create a positive image for Luscious Delights. Maybe do some jam-making classes at the kitchen store downtown or help with the judging for the county fair. I've already been asked to do those things, but now I can follow through and get scheduled." I might need all the positive publicity I could get if Brett really tried to poison my reputation in Shavano.

"That would probably work. And it would make Holmes look like even more of a jerk if he tries to spread rumors about you."

"True." Actually, I'd heard that Brett had done some cooking demos at the local high school himself, so he might be a little ahead of me in public relations. But I'd make major catch-up efforts.

Nate rested his elbows on the table. "This whole thing sucks, Roxy. And it pisses me off that I can't do anything to help. Unless you want me to punch out Brett Holmes. I'd enjoy that."

"No hitting. I don't want you punching Brett. I don't want Uncle Mike punching Brett. I don't want anybody punching anybody. I want to beat him by showing everyone I'm a better person than he is. Besides, you need to save your hands for cooking." I glanced down at his hands and was reminded once again that he was a very hot guy.

Nate grinned. "Thanks. I'm not doing much that requires dexterity these days, but maybe I'll put something new on the menu. Not that Robicheaux's has ever been the kind of place that went for new stuff."

He took another swallow of beer, and my curiosity flared again. "Why did you come to Robicheaux's, Nate? Did you miss Shavano?"

He grimaced, setting his beer on the table. "Not so much. I had some health problems in Vegas. Mom convinced me to come here to recuperate."

Which meant he might not be staying around once he was healthy. On the other hand, he looked pretty healthy to me already.

Steady. My heart gave a couple of hard thumps. "Are you doing okay?" I asked, a little timidly.

Nate's grin flashed in the dimming afternoon light. "I'm fine, Roxy. I'm just taking it easy. I like Shavano, and I like being back. I even like cooking at the café, most of the time."

"Still bumping heads with Bobby?"

"I don't think there's any way around that. Bobby's been in control of the kitchen for a few years now, and he worked beside my dad. Power sharing isn't something he's cool with."

"What does your mom think?"

"Mom really wants me to stick around here. She's afraid to let me out of her sight, so she's trying to find ways to make us co-equal in the kitchen. She's got me running the kitchen for breakfast and Bobby at lunch, but Bobby expedites and works the counter when I'm in the kitchen, so it's not like there's much space between us." He tipped up his beer again.

I wondered just what his health problems had been if his mom was afraid to let him go. But it wasn't something I thought I should ask him right then. If he wanted me to know, he'd tell me.

I leaned beside him, setting my empty bottle on the ground at my feet. Herman was working his way around the yard, sniffing at each tree he came to. A budding arborist, except that he also peed on each one. "Did you go to culinary school, or did you learn from your dad?"

Nate shrugged. "Bobby learned at Dad's elbow, which may be why he resists changing anything. I did culinary school in LA. Coco worked a couple of years at a bakery in Aspen, until my dad got sick."

"Did you like culinary school?"

"Well enough. Did you?"

I'd liked it until I graduated and ended up in the wrong kitchen. "Yeah. It was fun."

"And now here we are."

"Here we are."

He reached out, running his fingers along my cheek. My heart gave a quick thump, while my gut promptly clenched tight. Was I ready to move ahead?

To what, Roxy? You think he's going to jump on you in his parents' yard? You think you're some kind of femme fatale?

Nate leaned forward slowly, giving me all the time in the world to run. And I admit that part of me really did think about running. But I stayed where I was because one awful night was not going to decide the rest of my life.

He came so close I could feel the warmth of his skin. "Okay?"

I nodded.

His lips were smooth on mine, moving slightly, tongue against teeth. My heart was thundering now. I put my hands on his chest and felt his heart thumping against my fingertips. Maybe I wasn't the only nervous one.

After another moment, he pulled back, studying me. "Is this too soon?"

"I'm…" I tried to figure out how to explain without sounding like a loon. "I'm really out of practice. And I'm nervous. But I like this. I do."

He broke into a grin, brushing my hair from my forehead. "That's one of the nicest testimonials I've ever had. Does that mean you haven't done anything since…?"

I nodded quickly. It was a little embarrassing to admit, but it was the truth, much as I might like it not to be.

"Well, damn," he said slowly. "I guess I'll leave this up to you then. You set the pace. If you feel like I'm rushing you, tell me. I'll stop."

That was such a nice thing to say I almost burst into tears again. This had been one of the teariest days I'd spent since Uncle Mike had nudged me into getting to work.

"Thank you," I whispered.

"No. Thank you. For trusting me with your story. I won't let you down, Rox. I promise."

I reached up to touch his cheek, and then I leaned forward and kissed him. I hadn't thought about it or planned it—if I had, it probably wouldn't have worked. But because I'd just gone ahead and done it, I didn't feel frightened or nervous. Just warm all over and a little restless. Like I wanted to grab hold of him and push against the picnic table a little harder.

My heart was pounding, but it wasn't fear this time. Maybe I'd moved forward a few steps, after all.

Herman whimpered beside me, pushing his cold nose against my arm, and I pulled back again.

Nate reached out and stroked Herman's head. "Jealous, boy?"

Herman gave me a slightly reproachful look, and I decided it was time to go. I had dinner to cook after all.

"I need to get him home. Thanks for the beer. And the conversation. I feel a lot better."

"Any time." He paused. "I mean that, Rox. Any time you want to talk or hang out or…anything. Give me a call."

"I will." I leaned over quickly and kissed his cheek. Then I headed to the truck with Herman trotting along at my side.

All in all it had been one great attitude adjustment.

Chapter 11

I'd been dreading telling Uncle Mike about Brett and Evelyn, but it turned out I didn't have to. He had a big order to finish, and he was off helping Donnie and Carmen and their crew pack up the strawberries they'd picked earlier. He stepped in for a few minutes to grab some supper, but I told myself we really didn't have time to talk since he had so much to do.

That was my story, and I was sticking to it.

After supper, I spent a couple of hours digging through the vintage cookbooks I'd picked up at garage sales and second hand stores. I'm always looking for old jam recipes that I can try or revise to fit a contemporary market. Around nine thirty, I got Herman into the utility room where he sleeps—since there's no way a woman my size can share a bed with a dog his size—made sure he had enough food and water, and stumbled off to bed myself. I was worn out. Some nights you just tell yourself you'll get a better start tomorrow.

The next day was Sunday, usually a quiet day around the farm unless there's something that absolutely has to be picked. I decided to try an experimental batch of jam with some early rhubarb. Because I knew it would be too tart for much of anything, I planned to combine it with some strawberries and a lot of sugar. I had just finished chopping when the phone rang.

I checked the code and saw it was Susa, which made

me groan. I really wasn't up to another round of arguments over how to get Brett Holmes to be less of a jerk.

"Hey," I said quickly, "what's up? I'm knee-deep in rhubarb at the moment."

"So you're home?" Susa's voice sounded strange, excited but also upset.

"I'm home. Do you want to come out?"

I could almost hear her shake her head. "No. But there's something going on here you need to know about."

"Going on where? Are you in Shavano?"

"I'm on Second Street at Dirty Pete's. Something's happening across the street at High Country. There are cop cars all around, and I think the place is closed. Don't they usually do brunch on Sunday?"

"Maybe. I'm not sure."

"Well, they're definitely closed now. And there are definitely at least two cop cars outside."

I sighed. "Maybe there was a robbery. It's a high-end restaurant." Although robbing a restaurant seemed a little weird. There were too many people around and not necessarily a lot of cash.

"Maybe you need to come to town." Susa still sounded edgy. "It might involve Brett. Maybe Harry can find out."

I glanced at the pile of chopped rhubarb. I could put it in a plastic bag and save it for later. But once I started the whole jam-making process I couldn't stop until I was done. If I was going anywhere, it had to be now. "Okay, I'll meet you at Dirty Pete's. Give me a half hour or so."

I pulled into the parking lot twenty minutes later. Dirty Pete's didn't do anything as high class as brunch.

But they had great coffee, and they had Harry, who was second to none when it came to Bloody Marys and intelligence gathering.

Not this time, though. "I don't know what's going on," Harry said darkly. "That new chief, Fowler, can keep a tight lid on things when he wants to."

"But if it was a robbery, you guys might need to worry, too," I pointed out.

"Don't know. But even if it is, we don't need to worry." He gave me a dry grin. "We don't draw the same crowd as High Country."

I turned to stare out the front window of Dirty Pete's. A crowd had gathered outside High Country, although it was hard to say why since there was nothing much to see. Two police cars were still parked outside the front door.

Maybe the cops were inside having coffee. Or a beer. But I didn't think so.

"That's not good," Harry said suddenly.

I started to ask him what he meant, but then I saw for myself. An ambulance was circling the block to come in at the back of the restaurant. "Somebody's hurt?"

Susa leaned forward. "I think it's more serious than that. If somebody was hurt, they would have sent for the ambulance right away. If they waited this long, that means something a lot worse. And they're not running the siren."

We shifted to the side windows and watched as two ambulance attendants pulled a gurney out, getting the wheels set up before they rolled it toward the door of the building. They didn't seem to be hurrying. I was inclined to agree with Susa—it didn't look like they had an urgent care case inside.

Caroline, the waitress, stepped beside me. "You think somebody's dead?" It was what we were all thinking, but nobody had wanted to say it out loud.

Harry shrugged and went to his bar, where he started stacking glasses with a lot more vigor than usual.

Susa turned to me, biting her lip. "Who do you suppose it is?"

There was no way I was going to speculate about who might be in dire straits inside High Country. Especially since I had a personal interest in one such person, Brett Holmes. I shook my head. "Don't know. Can't know."

Don't want to know. And I really didn't.

Susa returned her concentration to the street.

I wondered if there was any future in walking over to High Country and joining the crowd outside, but I figured not. In that moment, I felt superstitious. As long as I didn't know what had happened, it had nothing to do with me. And yes, I knew that was a crazy attitude.

Finally, the ambulance attendants opened the back of the ambulance. I couldn't see who or what was on the gurney at the side, but I had a feeling it wasn't anybody lively.

"Shit," Susa whispered.

I think until that moment, we'd all been able to pretend that whatever had happened at High Country wasn't that bad. But once that ominous gurney had rolled up next to the ambulance, there was no more pretending.

This was bad. Maybe very bad.

"When did you see Brett last?" Susa asked suddenly.

I thought about it. He hadn't been at the market the day before. "Not for a few days. Maybe not since last Saturday. How about you?"

She blew out a breath. "I saw him at the Merchants Association meeting on Monday, I think. He was bitching about something." She bit her lip as if she suddenly didn't want to say anything negative about Brett Holmes.

Brett Holmes. Whom we'd been damning to hell only yesterday. Now we were both worrying that something really bad might actually have happened.

"Somebody's coming out," Harry said, and we turned our attention to the front entrance of High Country. The door swung open, and a group of men in uniform filed out. Most of them were city cops, but I thought I saw a couple of state police uniforms, too.

Chief Fowler was at the rear of the group, talking to a couple of his men. Suddenly one of them gestured toward Dirty Pete's, and Fowler turned his gaze in our direction. There was no way he could actually see us. The front window had tinted glass to keep the sunlight in check. But as he stared at the restaurant, I had the uncomfortable feeling he knew exactly who was there and what we were thinking.

After another moment, he started walking in our direction.

"Hell," I muttered. Was it too late for me to duck out the door and head to my truck without being seen? Of course it was. I had no idea why I was suddenly so nervous about his seeing me, but I really didn't want to be there when he came inside.

Susa looked like she was thinking something similar. "Harry, do you have a back door?"

"Through the kitchen, but you'll be too late. He'll see you trying to leave if you go."

He was right. Fowler was already climbing the front

steps at Dirty Pete's. I took a breath and practiced looking innocent.

Why do you have to look innocent? You are *innocent.*

Clearly this whole thing had me spooked. Me and Susa and Harry all three.

Fowler paused inside the doorway, studying the room with his usual cold stare. "You still serving lunch?"

So he was just there for food. We could all relax. Of course, none of us did.

"Sure," Harry said. "Grab a table." He handed the chief a menu, then sent Caroline over after he'd taken a seat.

"We could ask him who died," Susa murmured. "And how."

"That would be a very bad idea," I murmured back. But I had to admit, I really wanted to know the answers to both those questions.

And because I really wanted to ask the chief who died, and because I knew that would be a very bad idea, I decided it was time to go home. Let Susa listen to the gossip around town. I wanted to get down to making rhubarb jam.

I got about halfway to the door before I heard "Ms. Constantine?"

I stopped. I'd forgotten just how deep Fowler's voice was. The entire restaurant seemed to go still. Susa stared at me. I turned to look at him. "Chief Fowler."

"Can I buy you a sandwich?" He gave me an almost smile that might have passed for one with a little more effort on his part.

I hadn't had lunch yet, and I was hungry. Plus I was curious about why he wanted to buy me lunch right then.

I was fairly sure it wasn't because he enjoyed my company. "Sure. Thanks." I pulled out the chair opposite him at the table and sat.

Susa took a seat at the bar while Harry returned to stacking. And watching us.

I ordered a burger while Fowler went with a chicken sandwich. So far, so normal. He leaned back in his chair as Caroline disappeared in the kitchen with our orders. "Having a nice weekend?"

"Tolerable. I need to get home and make some more jam."

"Jam. Right." He stared out the front window, as if he was considering the details of my jam-making career. "I understand you had a disagreement with Brett Holmes at the market last weekend."

My heart promptly dropped to my toes. I hadn't expected him to start the interrogation quite this soon or this publicly. "We argued, yes."

"What about?"

"He wanted me to go out with him. I didn't want to. He didn't take it well." I could be terse if I had to be.

Fowler nodded, as if this confirmed something he already knew. "Was this the first time he'd asked you out?"

I shook my head. "He'd asked before. I told him no then, too."

"I understand you and Mr. Holmes had a physical altercation."

I stiffened. That sounded a lot worse than it had been. "He grabbed me. A friend of mine pushed him away."

"I see. And was this friend there for the whole argument?"

"No. He came up part way through." If he wanted to know Nate's name, he could ask me. I didn't feel like volunteering anything right then.

"And that's all this fight was about? You not accepting Mr. Holmes's invitation?"

When you put it that way, it sounded stupid. "That's what it was about. Yes."

Fowler sighed, staring out the window again. Then he turned to me. "Have you seen Mr. Holmes since last weekend?"

I paused. I'd already been through this with Susa, but I really didn't want to make a mistake with Fowler. "I don't think so. We might have seen each other on the street, but even if we did, we didn't speak. And I don't remember seeing him."

Fowler looked as if he was going to ask me another question, but I beat him to the punch. "Has something happened to Brett?"

Fowler's eyebrows we up. "Why would you ask that?"

Because I saw them wheel that gurney into High Country. "Brett works at High Country, and something has obviously happened there."

"What was the name of your friend who pushed Mr. Holmes away?"

No way was I going to involve Nate in this if I didn't have to. "Has Brett been hurt?"

Silence spread between us, but I had no intention of breaking it. Finally, Fowler sighed. "According to what I've been told, Nathan Robicheaux and Brett Holmes fought over you. Is that accurate?"

I shook my head. "No, it's not. Brett grabbed hold of my shoulders. He was shaking me. Nate pushed him away, and Brett staggered so he ended up on his knees. There was no fight over me. There was no fight, period." And Nate hadn't been the only one who'd come my way.

One of Fowler's eyebrows raised again, and his lips edged up. "Some people might see that differently."

"I can't help what some people saw or didn't see. That's what happened." I folded my arms across my chest, partly because I was afraid my hands might be shaking.

"What did Mr. Holmes have to say after Mr. Robicheaux pushed him away?"

"I honestly don't remember. Probably something angry. He left right after that."

"And you didn't have any contact with him after he left?"

"No." I couldn't prove Brett had anything to do with the mud on my truck, and what had happened with Evelyn hadn't been contact with Brett. I'd been planning to confront Brett at some point, but I hadn't gotten around to it.

Before Fowler could ask me anything more, Caroline arrived at our table with my burger and the chief's chicken. I looked down at the glistening bun and realized I had absolutely no appetite. "Could you maybe box this up for me, Caroline? I need it to-go."

"Sure thing." Caroline picked up my plate and headed for the kitchen.

I turned to Fowler again. This time both his eyebrows were up. I didn't care. "Do you have any other questions for me?"

He shrugged. "Did you tell anyone else about Mr. Holmes's efforts to get you to go out with him?"

"I told my friend Susa." I gestured toward where

Susa was sitting at the bar, watching us with undisguised curiosity. "And several people at the market saw what happened, including Annabelle Dorsey, Bianca Jordan, and Harry Potter."

Fowler's eyes widened. I figured he thought I was either making fun of him or possibly that I was a nutcase.

"Harry's the bartender over there. That's his real name. And he's probably heard every joke you could possibly make about it."

Fowler smiled again, a little more genuinely this time. "We'll check out how other people remember the altercation between Mr. Holmes and Mr. Robicheaux, including Mr. Potter."

Caroline brought my take-out box, and I pushed to my feet. "Any other questions?"

Fowler was pouring a pool of ketchup on his plate for his fries. "Where were you last night after ten?"

It felt like my shoulders were clamped together, but I raised my chin. "I was at the farm. I went to bed early, around nine thirty."

Fowler dipped a fry into his ketchup. "Can anyone confirm that?"

"I saw my uncle at dinner, but he was working most of the evening. And I live in my own cabin at the ranch."

Fowler nodded, as if he hadn't expected anything different. "We'll check with your uncle, see what he remembers. Thanks for your time."

"Thanks for lunch." Because I had no intention of paying the bill myself. He'd asked me, after all.

But as I walked to my truck, I glanced over at High Country again. By now there was crime scene tape in place across the front entrance and a single cop on duty near the door.

Something bad had happened there. I was absolutely sure of that. Something bad that most likely involved Brett Holmes. And given the way Fowler had avoided any hint about what was going on, I had to assume that that bad thing had happened to Brett.

And like it or not, I was going to be involved.

Chapter 12

I needed to get to the farm and talk to Uncle Mike, but I felt like I needed to talk to Nate first. From what Fowler had said, Nate had become a suspect in whatever had happened to Brett by virtue of his rescuing me. That, of course, made me feel like crap since Nate had just been there by chance and had been trying to help.

I parked beside Robicheaux's. There were still a few cars in the parking lot, maybe people who'd come for Sunday brunch. But it was almost two, and I figured the rush was probably over.

Madge was at her hostess stand when I walked in and smiled when she saw me. "Hi, Roxy. What would you like? It's too late for anything off the stove, but I can check to see what Coco has in the cooler."

I thought a little guiltily of the untouched burger sitting on my front seat. "That's okay. I've had lunch. Is Nate around?"

"He's in the kitchen. Let me go get him for you." Madge beamed at me, and I felt even guiltier. I wasn't there out of romantic interest but to warn Nate he might be a suspect in a murder.

Assuming Brett Holmes had been murdered, which was beginning to seem more and more likely.

Madge and Nate were back a few moments later, with Madge ducking away immediately to "check on something in the kitchen." Nate smiled at me, but then the smile faded. "What's up? You look…unhappy."

"Some weird stuff is happening. Can we take a walk?"

His smile was completely gone now. "Sure. Let's go outside."

We started up Second Street, in the opposite direction from High Country and Dirty Pete's. "I just had a really strange lunch with the chief of police," I said.

Nate gave me a dubious look. "Is he somebody you know that well?"

"I don't know him at all, really. I was in Dirty Pete's with Susa and Harry, and something was going on across the street at High Country. There were cops all around and an ambulance. Then the chief came into the restaurant and asked me to have lunch with him. Only it wasn't an invitation. More like he was ordering me to his table."

I knew I wasn't making much sense, but I figured it was more important to get all the information out than to do an enticing narrative right then.

"Okay," Nate said. "You've got my attention. So then what happened?"

"He started asking me about last weekend at the market. You know, when Brett got physical and you had to step in and stop him." I took a breath. "He knows about that. Or anyway, he knows a version of it. He thought you and Brett had a fight. I explained it wasn't a fight and told him what was going on. But I don't think he believed me."

Nate stopped in the middle of the sidewalk, staring up the street. "Why was that important? Did something happen to Holmes?"

"I don't know. I tried to get Chief Fowler to tell me,

but he wouldn't. Yeah, I think something happened to Brett. Fowler wouldn't have been asking me all those questions if someone else had gotten hurt."

"And he thinks I had something to do with it? I just met Holmes at the market last week. I didn't even know his name at the time."

"I know, I know. It doesn't make any sense. And there must be a lot of people who didn't like Brett around town. He wasn't what you'd call a likeable person." I closed my eyes for a moment. "I'm sorry, Nate."

Nate frowned. "What are you sorry for?"

"For getting you into this. I mean, I didn't intend to get you into my situation with Brett. It just happened. But if you hadn't pushed him away…"

"Stop it," Nate said flatly. "Just stop it. Brett Holmes created his own problems. You're not responsible for what he did. And I wanted to get involved. Somebody needed to push that jerk off you. If it hadn't been me, it would probably have been Harry. If the chief talks to me, I'll tell him what happened. I hadn't seen Brett Holmes before, and I haven't seen him since."

He took hold of my hand and pulled me down next to him on one of the park benches that lined Second Street. "You don't need to take on a load of guilt for everything that happens around you, Rox."

"I know. This just has me unsettled."

"What else did he ask?"

"Not a lot. He wanted to know if Brett had asked me out before that, and I said he had and that I'd turned him down then, too. And he asked who all knew about Brett being a jerk to me, although that's not how he put it. I didn't tell him everything. But I have the feeling that won't be the only time I have to talk to him."

"Probably not." Nate blew out a breath. "Do you think Holmes is dead?"

I closed my eyes for a moment. That was one of the main questions I'd been mulling over. "Yeah, I think he is. If he was just injured, I think they'd get the details of whatever happened from him. And none of the cops followed the ambulance when it left the restaurant, like they might have if they'd been taking him to the hospital."

Because Brett wouldn't be giving them details. I was pretty certain of that.

"Will the local news have the story? When does the paper come out here anyway?"

"Wednesdays and Fridays. But it may be on their Web site before that." I pulled my phone out of my purse and entered the URL for the *Shavano County Sun*. At the moment their front page still had a story about last winter's avalanche damage on Highway 91. "They haven't put it up yet. I don't know how quickly they can do updates. Let me check the internet."

I did a quick Google search on *Shavano* and *attack,* which yielded quite a few articles about an attack by renegade Confederates in the year 1862. I tried again with *Shavano* and *assault.* This yielded a one-paragraph story from one of the Denver TV stations about a possible burglary at a Shavano restaurant and bar which resulted in a casualty. It had been posted an hour ago, datelined Shavano, which probably meant the police hadn't told anybody the name of said casualty or his current status.

Nate read over my shoulder, shaking his head. "If they really think this was a burglary, they don't know much about the restaurant business. There wouldn't have been that much cash on the premises, and the valuable stuff in the kitchen would have required a very specialized buyer who was in the market for something like an industrial-sized food processor."

"It doesn't sound right to me either. Maybe that's why they're checking into Brett's personal life. I wonder how long it'll be before they release the real story."

"If Holmes is dead, my guess is they'll want to notify his next of kin before they make any formal announcements."

That stopped me in my tracks. Up until then, I hadn't considered the possibility that Brett had a family, too. And that family might be grieving for him. I promptly felt like a thorough creep myself. "Yeah, they probably won't say anything public until then."

"Do you know where he was from?"

"He worked at the same restaurant I did in Denver. That's all I know."

"Fowler will probably find that out." Nate paused for a long moment.

"No." I shook my head. "I'm not telling Fowler about what happened to me in Denver. It's not relevant."

"But Holmes knew about it. And he tried to use it to blackmail you. Plus he told the woman who was in charge of that TV series a version of what happened."

"It doesn't have anything to do with Brett's death," I said stubbornly. I didn't know for sure that Brett was dead. Still, the odds that he was seemed to be pretty high.

"It probably doesn't. But if Brett told other people in the kitchen at High Country, and if they thought he was having an affair with you because of it…"

My stomach clenched tight. It hadn't occurred to me that Brett would tell people besides Evelyn about my

Denver reputation. But that would be his style. He'd want the people in the kitchen to believe he had inside knowledge. And he'd want them to believe he could pressure me into sex because of what he knew.

I closed my eyes again, rolling my hands into fists. The more we talked about the possibilities, the worse everything became. "I'll think about it. I don't want to tell Fowler, but that may be the best plan."

"It would be better for him to hear it from you than to discover it on his own. It shows what a scumbag Brett Holmes was."

"But it might also give me a good motive to kill him." I rubbed a hand across my face.

Nate placed his hand over mine. "The guy was sleaze personified. A lot of us had reason to dislike him and dislike him a lot. But that's not the same as wanting to kill him. You had every reason to hate him but no reason to kill him."

I blew out a long breath. That was the truth, and I'd been worrying so much about appearances that I'd overlooked it. I turned my hand so that I was palm to palm with his, then gazed up into those dark velvet eyes. "Thanks. I needed to hear that."

"Any time. We both need to take a step back so we can see what's really going on."

A vehicle pulled to the curb near our park bench, and I glanced over to see a Shavano police car come to a stop a few feet away. My heart promptly went into overdrive. Had they come to arrest me? Why? How?

The driver's side door opened, and Chief Fowler stepped out. He narrowed his eyes, studying Nate. "Mr. Robicheaux?"

Nate nodded stiffly. "I'm Nate Robicheaux."

"I thought you might be." Fowler gave him one of those half smiles that didn't really qualify as anything in the smile department. "I'm Ethan Fowler. And I've got a few questions for you."

I laced my fingers through Nate's, pressing my hand against his, willing him to remember the advice he'd just given me.

Nate drew himself up. "Okay. Ask away."

Fowler turned those cold blue eyes toward me. "Ms. Constantine, maybe you can find somewhere else to be."

Nate's jaw tightened. I had a feeling if he refused to have his meeting with Fowler without me, Fowler might take him to the police station for questioning, the ultimate unfairness. I pushed myself to my feet. "I'll talk to you later, Nate."

He stared up at me for a moment. "You don't have to go."

I glanced at Fowler again. "I think I do."

Nate blew out a long breath. "I'll call you."

"Okay." I turned down the street toward Robicheaux's where my truck was parked. I didn't look back, not because I didn't want to but because I was a little afraid of what I'd see. Nate and Fowler didn't strike me as guys who might become best buds.

The next hurdle would be telling Uncle Mike what was going on. But I thought I'd make a little jam first. Cooking usually helped me relax, and I needed to chill out. Rhubarb strawberry jam is another one where I use a little apple for natural pectin. I got the cut up rhubarb out of the refrigerator, along with a flat of strawberries and a couple of Granny Smith apples. I have to mash the strawberries up in the kettle before I add everything else, and I was wielding my potato masher with a lot of energy when I heard Uncle Mike coming in the front door of the cabin, Herman clicking at his heels.

In fact, I heard him because he was bellowing. "Roxanne," he called. "Why the hell does the chief of police need to talk to me at my earliest convenience? Do you know anything about this?"

Busted! It hadn't occurred to me that Fowler would get in touch with Uncle Mike so quickly. So far as I knew he was just checking up on my alibi for last night, which Uncle Mike couldn't really confirm since we hadn't seen each other after dinner.

He stepped into the kitchen, looking slightly sunburned and very annoyed. "What's going on, Roxy? What does Fowler want?"

I took one last swing at the strawberries, then stepped away from the bowl. "Let's go sit down. This takes some explaining, and I'll have to start back a couple of days."

"That sounds ominous. I was hoping it was an overdue parking ticket or something."

I shook my head. "Unfortunately, no."

I hadn't filled him in about Brett Holmes and Evelyn Davidson yet—maybe I was hoping I wouldn't have to, which was clearly not realistic. When I'd finished that part of the story, Uncle Mike held up his hand, his expression grim. "This son of a bitch tried to ruin your chances just because you wouldn't go out with him?"

"Pretty much. He may have been mad about Nate pushing him down in front of all those people. That probably stung." At least I hoped it did. Which wasn't a very charitable point of view since Brett was most likely dead.

"Remind me to shake Nate Robicheaux's hand the

next time I see him. And I'll be looking in on Mr. Holmes to have a little talk, maybe tonight after we finish work." His jaw firmed. My uncle the protector was on the job.

"You can't do that," I started.

Uncle Mike raised his hand again. "I know what you're going to say. I know you don't want me getting in a fight and calling attention to the whole thing, but Roxy…"

I shook my head. "Actually, that's not what I was going to say. I was going to tell you that you couldn't talk to Brett because I'm pretty sure he's dead."

Uncle Mike stared at me, his jaw dropping. After a long moment, he scooted back in his chair. "Okay. I need a few more details here."

I gave them to him as efficiently as I could. When I'd finished, Uncle Mike was staring at me again. "So you don't know for sure that this Holmes guy is dead?"

"No, but it seems like a very good bet. If he isn't dead, he's seriously injured—so seriously that they haven't been able to question him. I don't think Chief Fowler would be traveling around interviewing everybody if it was just a minor incident."

"And why does he want to talk to me? I wouldn't know Holmes if I tripped over him."

"I think he's checking up on me. I told him I fixed you dinner last night, so he'll probably want to confirm that you saw me. I have no idea if that gives me an alibi or not because I have no idea when Brett was attacked. Always assuming he *was* attacked, of course."

Uncle Mike looked confused and slightly anxious. "Why would you need an alibi, Roxy? Surely he doesn't suspect you of doing anything to Holmes. You're not the type."

"I don't think I'm the type and you don't think I'm the type, but Fowler doesn't know me. He probably thinks I'm this big, strapping woman who could defend herself or get a little revenge on somebody who'd treated her badly." I paused, staring down at my hands. There were times when I wished I really was that type of woman. Maybe I would have beaten up the chef the way he deserved to be beaten up instead of braining him with a can of tomatoes.

My uncle reached over to grasp my hand. "Come on, Rox. You're not to blame for this, any more than you were to blame for what happened to you in Denver. And since you didn't have anything to do with this, they should clear you pretty quick. At least they'd better, since whoever did it is still out there."

I shivered at that. If Brett had been murdered, that meant the person who did it might still be in town, maybe even planning something else. Until we knew who or what was behind this, we'd all be on edge.

"You should probably call Fowler back. The sooner you get this over with, the better it'll be for all of us."

Uncle Mike pushed himself to his feet. "All right. I'll give him a call. Will you be okay here by yourself after this? Maybe you should come over to the main house for a few nights."

I shook my head. "No need. I've got Herman. I'll be fine."

But deep inside I wasn't entirely sure about that. My cozy cabin felt a lot more isolated all of a sudden. And I didn't even know for sure Brett Holmes was dead.

Herman came to stand next to me, pressing his cold nose against my hand. He wasn't the world's greatest watch dog, but he was very reassuring. Particularly when

I contemplated the long mountain nights ahead with no clear idea of what we were up against.

Chapter 13

The next day, Monday, the police department held a news conference and finally confirmed everybody's suspicions. Brett Holmes was dead, killed by an unknown intruder in "the kitchen area" at High Country at some time after the restaurant closed for the night on Saturday. High Country closed at ten. The police theorized that Brett had stumbled upon a burglary in progress and been killed by the burglar.

Like Nate, I had a hard time believing the burglar angle since there were lots of better targets for burglary in downtown Shavano. But I didn't know if the police actually believed Brett had been killed during a robbery or if this was what they were telling the public while they kept their options open.

There were a lot of other questions, too. What had Brett been doing at High Country after the restaurant had closed? I'd have expected him to be out the door as soon as the customers left, heading to the nearest bar for a round of tequila shots. How had the robber overpowered him? And, maybe most important, how had he been killed? We still didn't know, and the police were being cagey about releasing any other information.

While I worked on the strawberry rhubarb jam, I thought about Nate's conversation with Fowler. He'd called after he'd finished with the chief and confirmed what I'd already assumed, that Fowler was mainly interested in hearing his version of the struggle with Brett last week. In fact, according to Nate, Fowler had seemed more interested in what Nate knew about me than what he knew about Brett.

That started a whole series of unpleasant possibilities dancing in my mind. I kept thinking about Nate's advice to tell Fowler about what had happened to me in Denver. *It would be better if he heard it from you.* Most likely it would. Originally, only a handful of people knew about me and the chef—Uncle Mike and Susa mostly. But now a cross-section of the Shavano population might have heard something. It was inevitable that Fowler would hear about it eventually, and Nate was probably right. It would be better if I was the one who told him.

I went downtown on Monday after I'd gotten the strawberry rhubarb jam into jars and before I started another round of strawberry preserves. I figured I'd see if Fowler was around at the police station, and if he wasn't, I'd at least have tried to talk to him.

Needless to say, I really hoped he wasn't in his office.

The Shavano County Courthouse isn't as charming as the rest of the town. The original granite building was torn down a decade ago, and the town put up a utilitarian square made of tan-colored brick. It houses courtrooms, judicial chambers, and the county attorney's office.

Also the county sheriff and the Shavano police department. And the jail.

It is not, under any circumstances, a cheerful place, even on a bright Colorado bluebird morning. Once again, I thought about turning around and heading home.

It would be better for him to hear it from you than to

discover it on his own.

Nate's voice still echoed in my ears. For a moment, I wished I'd asked him to come with me. But I had to face this on my own. It was my disaster, after all.

I climbed up the stairs to the front door, pausing for a moment to check the directory on the wall inside. The chief's office was on the first floor, right down the hall. Once I turned in that direction, there'd be no going back. I'd be committed to confessing.

I walked down the hall, feeling like I was going to the executioner's block.

There was a receptionist for the chief's office along with the county attorney and the sheriff. I didn't recognize her, which was just as well. This visit wasn't something I wanted shared on social media.

She looked up expectantly. "Yes?"

"I need to see Chief Fowler." I was amazed that my voice was steady.

"Do you have an appointment?"

I shook my head. "He'll want to talk to me. Tell him it's Roxy Constantine."

The receptionist picked up her phone and dialed a number, turning away from me as she spoke.

Of course, I wasn't absolutely sure Fowler would want to see me. Maybe he'd be too busy. Maybe he wasn't interested. Maybe…

The receptionist glanced up at me. "Go on in. He'll see you now."

So much for hope. I opened the office door and stepped inside.

Fowler was sitting at his utilitarian, city-issued desk. He gazed up at me with that same unsmiling, inscrutable look he always seemed to wear. I wondered if he ever smiled. Probably not at people like me, people he suspected of murder.

I cleared my throat. "I have some things to tell you."

He gestured to the chair in front of his desk. "Sit down, Ms. Constantine. I've been expecting you."

That speech wasn't reassuring at all. Did that mean he'd had his suspicions confirmed by other people? Was he expecting me to confess? I dropped into the chair, clutching my purse in my lap.

I wasn't sure how to start, but getting to the point seemed like a good idea. "Brett Holmes was blackmailing me. Well, sort of. He was trying. He hadn't actually succeeded." I bit my lip.

Fowler had picked up his pen to take notes on a legal pad, but he put it down again. "What was he blackmailing you over?"

"We worked in the same restaurant in Denver a couple of years ago. It was a pretty famous place." I gave him the name and paused, but Fowler shook his head. He didn't look impressed.

"Oh, well, it's been on TV. Anyway, I worked there for about six months. One night I was working late, and the chef who owned the place was there, too. He told me to help him out in the pantry, and when I got there he…" I ran through all the euphemisms I usually used: *attacked, assaulted, jumped.* Screw it. I was talking to a cop. "He tried to rape me. I managed to grab a can of tomatoes and I hit him in the head. It kind of stunned him, and I got out before he could pull himself together."

Fowler had stopped writing for a moment. He stared at me. "Go on."

I took a breath. I'd gotten through the toughest part. "The next day, the manager fired me. And he said the chef would say I'd gone with him willingly, and that I'd gotten pissed when he wouldn't give me a promotion in exchange for sex. I think that was to keep me from going to the cops."

Fowler paused again. "Did you go to the cops anyway?"

I shook my head. "I came home to Shavano. I was done with Denver. And Denver was done with me, pretty much."

Fowler folded his hand on the desk. "Okay, so how does this affect Holmes? Was he there that night?"

"No. After I left Denver, the chef told his version of the story to a lot of different people, just to make sure nobody was going to believe me, I guess. He told everybody in the kitchen."

I remembered the sick feeling in my gut when I heard about the story having been deliberately spread after I left. I'd thought if I was gone, the chef would shrug it off. But apparently he'd wanted to make sure I'd never have any credibility if I tried to claim he was a predator.

Fowler wrote a quick note on his legal pad. "And this is where Holmes comes in?"

"I guess so. He heard the rumors somewhere and he remembered them when he took the job at High Country and found out I lived here. He asked me out a couple of times, and he made some references to Denver when he did—how much better he was in the sack than the chef, that kind of thing. That creeped me out, so I avoided him from then on."

"So the blackmail was he'd tell other people about you and this chef?"

"He might have implied that, but I think he'd

already told people what he'd heard about me, so that wouldn't have been much of a threat. What he did was different." I paused, sorting through what I hadn't told him yet to figure out what I wanted to say.

Fowler gave me a non-smile. "I'm all ears."

"Okay, you remember the day I ran into you going into Evelyn Davidson's office?" I certainly remembered it myself, but who knew how memorable it had been to Fowler?

"You had the cardboard box with the jam."

"Right. That was because Evelyn's working with this television show, *Sweet Thing*. They travel around the country checking out desserts, and they're due to come to Shavano this summer."

Fowler nodded, as if he was following me so far.

"I brought my jam for Evelyn to taste, and she was impressed. She said she'd already bought my stuff and liked it. I thought I had a good chance to be on the show. Then on that Saturday two weeks ago, Brett came to my booth at the farmers market. He told me he was friends with the producer of the show and that he could get me on whether Evelyn liked my stuff or not. If I'd have sex with him."

I blew out a breath, taking a moment for my pulse to slow down. It still pissed me off to think of Brett making that offer, as if I ought to be eager to go to bed with him since it would get me on TV.

Fowler looked up at me again. "This was the weekend when you had the fight with Holmes?"

"I told him I wouldn't go out with him. And I wouldn't have sex with him, even for a spot on a national TV show. He didn't take it well. We started yelling at each other and he grabbed me. He was shaking me when

Nate pulled him off."

"Did Robicheaux know about this situation in Denver?"

I shook my head. "Not then. I told him later."

Fowler paused for a long moment. "So there's more to this story, right?"

"Yeah." I cleared my throat. Spilling my guts was thirsty work. "I talked to Evelyn at the farmers market on Saturday. She said I wasn't in the running for the TV show any more. When I asked her why, she hemmed and hawed about problems with my reputation. I finally got her to admit it was about what had happened in Denver. She said my bad reputation might be a distraction from the focus on the town, so she wouldn't recommend me for the show."

Fowler stopped taking notes again. "Holmes got to her?"

"She wouldn't admit it, but I'm pretty sure he did. Not many people in Shavano knew what happened. Brett must have spun quite a story for her." I couldn't keep the bitterness out of my voice on that last bit. It still annoyed me that Brett had gone to so much trouble to get back at me. And that Evelyn had let him.

"So this was Holmes's idea of revenge?"

"Probably. I think he wanted to make me sorry I'd turned him down. And maybe he was miffed about losing a shoving match with Nate." Which made Nate sound like another target of Brett's wrath. "Nate didn't know who he was," I said hastily. "And I doubt that Brett knew Nate, either."

Fowler gave me another of those dry nonsmiles, as if he knew I was trying to keep Nate out of this. He wrote another note on his pad, then he paused again. "Anything else?"

I shook my head. "That's all of it. I don't know if it has anything to do with what happened to Brett, but I figured it would be better if you heard it from me instead of from somebody else."

Fowler looked like he was weighing that statement. "Probably true."

"I guess if that's all…" I started to stand up, but Fowler held up his hand.

"Hang on a minute."

I sat down. What now?

"This chef you clocked in Denver, was there any police report on that?"

I shook my head. "I didn't file one. And since I never heard anything from the Denver cops, I assume the chef didn't file one either."

"Right." Fowler looked down at his notes again, then at me. "Where did you hit him?"

"Where… I told you—in the pantry." *Keep up, Chief.*

"Where on his body," he said patiently.

"Oh." I paused, trying to remember. I hadn't been aiming. "On the side of the head, I think. I mean, he was on top of me and I was just, you know, trying to get him off." I stopped, taking a deep breath. My heart was racing. Flashback time.

Fowler gave me a glance that might have been sympathetic, although it was hard to say. Sympathy didn't seem to come naturally to him. "With a can of tomatoes, you said?"

"I grabbed it off the shelf behind me. I didn't know what it was at the time, just that it was heavy."

"Right." He wrote down something else, then

glanced up at me. "Okay, thanks."

I stared at him. That was it? That was *so* not it. "Why did you want to know?"

"Know what?" Fowler's expression was inscrutable again.

"Know where I hit him. Why is that something you were interested in?"

There was a long moment of silence while we stared at each other. I had the feeling Fowler was debating with himself whether he wanted to answer me or not. Finally he sighed.

"Brett Holmes was killed in his restaurant on Saturday night around eleven."

"Yes, I know." I hadn't known the time, but I'd known the rest. The hairs on the back of my neck were beginning to stand on end.

"He was attacked from behind. Someone struck him on the back of his head with a heavy object. It fractured his skull. He died very soon after that."

My face felt warm, but the rest of me felt very cold. "Do you know what the weapon was?"

"We have an idea." Fowler's lips moved into another of those humorless smiles he seemed to specialize in, but he didn't say anything else.

I pushed myself to my feet. At that moment, I really wanted to be out of there. "I guess that's all, then."

He nodded, still with the smile. "For now. If I need more information, I know where to find you."

"Right." I turned and slunk out the office door. I should probably have told him goodbye, but I just couldn't bring myself to do it.

It's better he hears it from you. Oh yeah, right. It's always better when the suspect incriminates herself rather than making the cop do it.

Because, of course, that's what I'd done. Along with providing myself with a very good motive for killing Brett, I'd also given Fowler a run-down of my previous criminal history, including the fact I'd once brained another chef with a can of tomatoes late in the evening in the chef's own kitchen.

I hadn't killed him, but maybe that just counted as a practice session before I got down to the business of giving Brett Holmes a skull fracture.

Means, motive, opportunity, and a history of violence. I'd just put myself in the prime suspect category. *Nice going, Roxy.*

Chapter 14

I drove to the farm in a daze. I didn't want to talk to anybody, not even Uncle Mike. The task of explaining that I might be arrested—and it would be because I'd stupidly put myself in the crosshairs—was more than I could face right then. So I decided to do what I usually do when I'm upset about something. I exiled Herman to the main house, and I started cooking.

I was all set to make more strawberry preserves. I had a couple of flats from Uncle Mike, along with two more I'd bought from one of our neighbors who grew more berries than we did. I never claimed to make all my jams with Constantine fruit, but I did use Colorado fruit for everything I could.

Once I got the jars sterilized and the kettle going for the preserves, I started working on the rest of the strawberries, washing and hulling and chopping and sometimes mashing, depending on what I planned to do with them. I set some of the chopped berries aside for dinner and took a time out to stir up some biscuits for short cake. I got them into the oven around the time the first kettle of preserves was ready to be processed, so I filled the jars and loaded up the water bath canner. Shavano and environs are around eight thousand feet in altitude, which means I have to let the jars process ten minutes or so longer than people canning at sea level. That extra time allowed me to set one jam kettle to soak while I got another load of strawberry jam going, more strawberry basil this time.

In the midst of all of this, I got the biscuits out of the oven and began contemplating what I'd make for dinner. Preferably something that required most of the afternoon and some intricate preparation so that I'd be concentrating on getting it right rather than on what I'd done wrong.

All this activity was supposed to numb my mind into blankness so my brain wouldn't have any space for worry. As it turned out, though, my brain was perfectly capable of handling two batches of jam, a couple of sheets of biscuits, and some spinach lasagna while still considering the very real possibility that I'd be sent to the slammer for a murder I didn't commit.

Whenever I let myself dwell on the possibilities, panic welled up in my gut and I had to fight tears. I spent a lot of time talking myself out of that panic, telling myself that Fowler must realize I wasn't some kind of master criminal, providing the police with incriminating information just so that I could thumb my nose as I walked away.

But maybe he thought I was too dumb to realize how incriminating the information had been. He didn't know me well, after all. I could be a genius criminal or a spectacularly stupid criminal, and in this case the result would be the same.

You should have kept your mouth shut. That seemed obvious. If I hadn't told Fowler about my life in Denver, he'd have had no reason to assume I was a suspect other than the scuffle at the farmers market.

But what if he'd found out about Denver on his own? There was always the chance that he might have been able to do that. Evelyn had to know some of what had happened, although she might not know I'd hit the chef on the head. Who knew what Brett had told his fellow cooks? Who knew what rumors he'd been spreading about me, particularly after I'd pissed him off?

Fowler would probably have heard stories about it eventually. If he'd heard them from someone else, he might have had a *Eureka!* moment where he deduced I had a grudge against Brett and a history of violence.

But for all I knew, he'd had a *Eureka!* moment when I'd told him about the chef. Maybe behind that impassive expression he was dancing with glee, having found himself a first class suspect at last.

I'd just pulled a set of jars out of the canner and was ready to begin the whole process again with the next batch when someone knocked on my cabin door. This was a fairly rare occurrence since only a few people knew I lived in the cabin rather than the main house. I figured it was probably Susa, since Uncle Mike would just have walked in (and I was very glad he hadn't done that yet).

I threw the door open without taking the time to check myself in the mirror because Susa had seen me in various states of disrepair through the years we've known each other. Me looking decrepit would be nothing new.

Only it was Nate Robicheaux standing on my doorstep, looking gorgeous in his jeans and a Robicheaux's Café T-shirt. At the moment, he also looked worried.

I blinked. "Nate? What are you doing here?"

"Checking on you. Or I thought I was. When I got your voice mail three times in a row, I got nervous." He still looked concerned and slightly wary. I must have been showing a little more disrepair than usual.

I closed my eyes for a moment, cursing inwardly. Maybe I'd have a chance to run a brush through my hair later. "I must have forgotten to turn my phone on. Come on in. I've got to dash." One of my many timers had gone off, but I wasn't sure which one.

Nate trailed behind me as I pulled the jam kettle off its burner. The jars were lined up waiting. He watched me as I inserted the funnel and filled each one, leaving the mandatory quarter inch of headspace.

"You eyeball that?" he said finally.

"You do it long enough, you know what a quarter inch looks like."

"Right." He leaned on the kitchen counter. "How can I help?"

I started to tell him that he didn't need to. But then I thought about how much I'd done and how much I had left to do.

And how tired I suddenly felt.

"How are you on lasagna?"

"Cooking or eating?"

"Both, I guess. But cooking for now. I chopped up some spinach and boiled the noodles, but I haven't gone much beyond that." I gestured toward the fixings on the counter. I'd meant to get back to them, but events were slipping away from me. That happened when I had too many things on my mind. And right then, my mind was overwhelmed.

Nate grinned, stepping to the sink to wash his hands. "My lasagna has been known to bring strong men to their knees. You've got stuff like onions and cottage cheese and mozzarella, right?"

"And marinara sauce. And parmesan. And pretty much anything else you could want. Just ask. How long will it need to bake?"

"Around an hour."

He rolled up his sleeves, and I checked the clock. Amazingly enough, it was after four and I was famished. I hadn't eaten anything since breakfast when I'd been almost too nervous to chew. I grabbed a biscuit and returned to my jam. At least we'd have something decent for dinner.

Nate and I worked side-by-side, happily enough. He figured out the kitchen layout pretty quickly, and after that he didn't bother to ask me questions like where I kept the oregano. I stopped worrying about just how bad I looked and concentrated on the jam, although I took a quick bio break and pulled the scrunchie out of my hair.

By the end of the afternoon I'd used up two flats of strawberries and I had about three dozen jars of jam to show for it. That meant I'd have a good supply to sell at the farmers market on Saturday.

Assuming I wasn't in a cell at the county lockup by then.

That thought was almost enough to make me drop the jars I was lifting out of the canner, but I got them to the counter before I stood still, taking a few deep breaths.

"Roxy?" Nate asked from behind me. "Are you okay?"

"I'm hanging in." I rested my hands on the counter for a moment.

"You want to talk about it?"

"In a little while, maybe." I figured I really needed to finish my jam-a-thon. Then I'd probably crash, preferably with a few servings of lasagna in my belly.

Nate got the lasagna he'd been working on into the oven as I finished up with the last jars of jam. He paused, looking around the kitchen. "Got any alcohol?"

"Rubbing, medicinal, or drinking?"

He grinned. "What do you think?"

"I've got beer and I've got wine. Beer's in the refrigerator. Wine's in the rack. Which do you prefer?"

"With lasagna? Wine. Where's your rack?"

I gestured toward the armoire on the other side of the dining room where I kept my limited supply of wine, mostly from the Colorado wineries near Grand Junction. Nate pulled out a bottle of syrah and the corkscrew. "I'll open this. You grab a couple of glasses."

Technically, we should have waited for Uncle Mike since the lasagna was also meant for him. But right then I really wanted a glass of wine. Preferably more than one.

Nate poured two glasses, then picked them up and headed for the front door. "Let's go outside. I hate to waste a nice evening like this."

The sun was beginning to dip toward the west, but the air was still warm, temperature probably in the seventies. I sank onto the top step of the cabin's front porch. "How did you know where to find me?" I asked. "Did I mention I lived in the cabin at some point?"

He shook his head. "Your uncle Mike told me where to go. He said to tell you he'd find his own dinner. Unless you really wanted him to share the food."

My cheeks flushed hot. Uncle Mike probably thought he was being a matchmaker, but in fact I was really glad I didn't have to tell him about Fowler until tomorrow. "More lasagna for us then," I mumbled.

Nate took a swallow of his wine. "Now, tell me what's up. Something's happened. You're really upset, and I need to know what's going on."

I told him. He was already up to speed on all the relevant details of my interactions with Brett and Evelyn. The details about Brett's murder were new, though.

"Somebody hit him in the head? Hard enough to kill him? Doesn't that mean it's a man?"

I'd mulled that question over during my jam-making extravaganza. "I guess it depends on what kind of weapon they used. If it was something big enough, a woman might be able to do it, assuming she could lift it."

A moment of silence stretched between us. I lifted a lot of things in my kitchen.

Then Nate shook his head. "Fowler can't suspect you. What kind of murderer would tell the police a bunch of details that would make her look guilty? There may be some parallels with what happened to you in Denver, but it's not like somebody gave Brett a skull fracture with a can of tomatoes."

"So I'm off the hook because I didn't kill the first person I hit?" I stared out at the peach orchard. "Actually, that works for me. I'm just not sure Fowler will buy it."

Nate put his arm around my shoulders, pulling me close. "You'll be okay, Rox. There may be parallels with your story, but they won't find any evidence that you were involved. Whatever evidence there was at the scene won't implicate you. Have you ever been inside High Country?"

I shook my head. "Not lately. I ate there before Brett took over, but that's been a while ago."

"Like I said, no evidence. I watch a lot of TV these days, so I'm halfway to being a detective." He grinned at me. "Trust me, if they find DNA—and they probably will—it won't be yours."

That raised another vaguely depressing possibility: that Fowler would be asking me for a DNA sample. I'd probably give it to him since turning him down would look really bad. I took a healthy swallow of my wine.

Resting next to Nate's warm body was amazingly comforting. I felt like cuddling closer, letting him hold me for a while. Which was a very scary thing to consider. I hadn't really wanted to get close to anybody since Denver.

"What if they never find the person who did it? People might think I got away with it. There wouldn't be any way for me to prove I didn't kill him."

"You were born and raised here," Nate said slowly. "People know you. Nobody's going to assume you're a killer."

"You don't know how the town gossip works. And I wasn't born here, by the way. I was born in New Mexico."

"Yeah? How'd you wind up in Shavano?"

"My dad and I moved here when I was three. We lived in the main house with Uncle Mike and his wife. My dad invested all his money in the farm—he owned half when he died." Which meant I owned half now, although I didn't think about it much.

"What about your mom? Or is that a touchy subject?"

"Not especially. She left us when I was a toddler." Hence the move to Shavano. I always figured my dad wanted to put as much distance between himself and his ex-wife as he could.

"Have you had any contact with her since then? Do you know what happened to her?"

I shook my head. "Nope. Don't know. Don't care." That wasn't exactly true, of course, but I'd sucked up my anger and confusion over the years. And to be clear, she'd never tried to get in touch with me either.

"So you were raised by two guys?"

"Right, after Uncle Mike's wife died. They also had a long line of housekeepers and cooks. I learned the basics from a couple of them, Albonita and Carmen, who's still here but not cooking anymore."

"Did you work in the fields?"

"Sure. Nobody sits things out on a farm. If you live here, you work. How about you? Did you work in the family restaurant?"

"Same goes. Nobody sits things out with a restaurant to run. We started off busing tables and loading the dishwasher. Dad moved us up to being cooks when we were old enough to use a knife without losing a finger."

"You know, I didn't mind it much. I mean, the work was hard and sometimes I ended up with an aching back and a sunburned nose, but it made me understand what it takes to get food on the table. I think I had a lot more respect for the vegetables and fruits I worked with in culinary school than some of the other people there."

"Yeah, I know what you mean. In a small kitchen, you have to make do. You don't have a lot of people to rely on, and you sure as hell can't waste anything. Some of the people I worked with in Vegas had no freakin' idea what they were throwing out. Although the sous chef would usually tell them right before he kicked them out of the kitchen." Nate gave me a grim smile.

I bit my lip. I really wanted to know more about his time in Las Vegas, and I was tired enough that I'd lost all discretion. I dropped my head on his shoulder. "Why did you come home, Nate? Didn't you like it in Vegas?"

"Yeah, I did." He sipped his wine. Then he seemed to make a decision. "I had a heart attack, Rox. Well, it was more like A-fib, but it was close enough to an attack to make everybody nervous, particularly my mom. She packed up my stuff and collected me from the hospital. I didn't even get a chance to talk to the sous chef who hired me. Not that he wanted me to stick around."

"Why not?"

"I had the attack in the kitchen. After I'd been up for over twenty-four hours, covering other people's shifts and drinking tequila shots. The chef was probably afraid I'd have another one on his time, which I can understand. Still, when Mom whisked me off to Colorado, I ended up leaving my best knife behind. I would have liked to have picked that up."

"Ouch." Good chef's knives were expensive. I'd grabbed mine on the way out of Denver, and I still had it. "Do you think you'll ever go back?"

"It's an option. My mom would probably throw herself across the door bodily to prevent it. I haven't decided yet what I want to do long term." He wrapped his arms around me, pulling me closer, and I tucked my head beneath his chin.

"Shavano's a good town," I mumbled.

"Shavano's a great town. If I didn't have any problems at the café, I'd be happy to stay here long term." He pressed his lips against my forehead. "More than happy."

My heart did another of those odd thumps that seemed to happen a lot when he was around. "You mean the problems you have with Bobby?"

"Yeah. We're locked in this struggle over who's in

charge. I don't want to be in charge of the kitchen, but I do want to be able to make decisions about what goes on in my end of it. Bobby wants me to be a line cook, doing what I'm told and not making waves. Mom's trying to mediate, but I'm not sure there's a compromise that would work."

A timer dinged somewhere inside the kitchen, and Nate checked his watch. "That's the lasagna. Are you ready for some dinner?"

I nodded against his chest. The wine was making me a little sleepy, and I needed some food to get my blood sugar up again. "I can eat."

"Let's do this then." He let go of me to push himself to his feet, and I missed his warmth.

Watch it, Roxy. You don't want to get used to this.

I let him pull me up so that we stood knee to knee, staring into each other's eyes for a moment. Then he leaned forward and brought his lips to mine.

As kisses go, it was a definite winner. I put my hands on his shoulders in case my knees actually did turn to jelly, as I feared they might.

After a long moment, he raised his head. "Thanks for the conversation, Roxy. It's good having somebody to talk to."

"Yeah. It is."

And it helped that that *somebody* kissed like a champ.

Chapter 15

Nate's lasagna was transcendent, as I'd expected it to be. He wasn't one of those cooks who throws in a ton of cheese to cover up everything else. He had just the right proportions of cheese and sauce and spinach and the Italian sausage he'd found in the fridge. I ate three helpings with no apologies. I'm a big girl, and I hadn't had any food that day.

We had the strawberry shortcake for dessert. I didn't have any whipped cream, but I did have some crème fraiche. Nate put on a couple of dollops, then gave me a blissful smile. "This is first rate. Where does the crème fraiche come from?"

"Corona's dairy farm. They're just down the road. We barter some—I got the crème fraiche for a jar of raspberry jam."

"Win/win." He studied his dessert for a moment. "Do they do cheese?"

"Not so much. Just farmer cheese. But there's a goat cheese place over in Antero. It's really good."

Nate took another bite and sighed. "I can think of a half dozen things I'd like to do with this crème fraiche, but I'll never get the chance at the café. Damn it."

I didn't know what to say to that. He was right, and there didn't seem to be any remedy. Other than him leaving Shavano. That thought started a little pang somewhere in my gut. Clearly I wasn't following my own advice about keeping my distance.

"Have you ever thought about starting another restaurant here?" I threw the idea out before I'd really had time to think about it. But it made a certain amount of sense. Shavano was a great restaurant town, and there were lots of niches that hadn't been filled yet.

Nate raised an eyebrow. "Compete with the café? That wouldn't sit well with the family, trust me. I've got my differences with Bobby, but I don't want to cut into his business."

"Maybe not to compete with them. A different kind of restaurant, with a different set of customers." I shook my head. "I'm not being too clear right now. I'm tired from a day of jam making and worrying."

Nate took my hand in his. "The jam you did is terrific. Or it will be, once it's had time to set. And you shouldn't be worrying. They'll find who killed Holmes, and this will all blow over."

"Let's hope so." That would, of course, be the best outcome for everybody. But I wasn't sure it would happen.

Nate pushed his bowl to the middle of the table. "Need help with the dishes?"

I shook my head. "I've already washed all the jam making stuff, and the lasagna pan is soaking. Loading the dishwasher is low stress." Particularly since I'd installed a king-sized model once I realized just how many implements I was going to get dirty every time I made a batch of jam.

"I guess I'll head home, then. I've got the breakfast shift tomorrow." He paused, giving me a long look.

I thought about it. I really did. If I asked him to stay over, maybe he could keep me from panicking at two in the morning. And maybe he could also get me over my nervousness about having sex again.

But that seemed like a rotten reason to ask him to stay. And I decided I wanted our first time to be good. To be better than just reassurance sex.

"Okay," I said. "Thanks for coming out. It meant a lot to me to have you here."

He extended a hand to me, and I took it, letting him pull me to my feet. When I was up, we were standing close. I put a hand on his shoulder, and he bent down to meet me.

The kiss was almost enough to make me re-evaluate my decision. Maybe it wouldn't be so bad to have him stay. Maybe I could adapt. Maybe I really wanted to adapt.

After a moment, he raised his head. "I meant what I said, Rox. You choose the tempo. Fast or slow, it's up to you. But when you decide—*if* you decide—I'll be ready. Believe me."

I rested my head on his collarbone for a moment. "It's *when*, not *if*. Just give me a little more time."

"Whatever you want." He kissed the top of my head, gently. "But now I've got to go. Call me if anything happens."

Like Fowler arresting me? But it was a nice offer. "Thanks, I will. Drive safe."

I did, in fact, wake up at two in the morning and worry for an hour or so, but at least Nate probably got some sleep.

The next morning, I told Uncle Mike about my interview with Fowler. His reaction was predictable. "Wow, Rox, that was a really lousy idea."

"The idea was fine," I corrected through gritted

teeth. "The interview wouldn't have been a problem if Brett hadn't been killed that way. Even so, going to Fowler probably makes me look more innocent." Or anyway, I really hoped it did.

"If you say so."

Uncle Mike offered to let me pick strawberries to help me work off any anxiety. I told him I could work off my problems by making jam, which I did for the rest of the day.

The next day, I had a delivery to make at the Made In Colorado store in downtown Shavano. They did a good business in my jams, and I tried to keep them supplied, although it was a little tougher in the summer when I was trying to make sure I had enough to sell at the market. I packed up some pepper peach, along with some strawberry and some apricot. It made a case, and I figured I could spare that much.

I parked my truck on Second, ready to walk to the store on Main. The case wasn't that heavy and there was unmetered parking there. The streets were full of the usual summer tourists: families with small children, mountain bikers, rafters, and the occasional girls' weekend group. I balanced the case of jam in my arms and detoured around window shoppers, heading for the shop at the end of the block.

Just then, I saw someone I didn't particularly want to see—Evelyn Davidson. Our last encounter had left a bad taste in my mouth, and I didn't have much I wanted to say to her. Still, I didn't want to be rude. When she looked in my direction, I managed a smile, though it wasn't much of one.

Evelyn paused, staring, no smile in evidence. And then she turned on her heel, walking across to the far side of the street.

That was weird. It was almost as if she was giving me "the cut direct," although I had no idea why she'd want to do that. Our last conversation hadn't been *that* hostile.

I turned and kept walking toward the store. Whatever was bothering Evelyn had nothing to do with me, and I had other things to take care of. The shop was busy, with a lot of tourists turning over the merchandise. I headed for the office to find the manager, so I could drop off my jams and get a receipt.

The manager, Janet Leonhart, was new in town, but she seemed to be doing a good job finding artisans and others who wanted their stuff featured in the store. She glanced up as I walked in, and for a moment, I thought she looked a little shocked. Then her expression smoothed and she gave me a professional smile. "Hi, Roxy, how are you?"

"I'm fine, Janet. I've brought you some more jam, although I may have to cut back a bit during the rest of the summer while the farmers market is running. I'll be doing most of my selling there."

"Oh." Janet's professional smile wavered a bit. "Well, you don't have to consign your jam to us if you can't spare it. We don't want you to run low on supplies. If you don't want to leave anything for the time being…"

"That's okay. I can give you this much." I kept my pleasant expression in place, but it was a stretch. The situation was getting weird. Janet had never been anything but enthusiastic about my jam before this. Now she didn't seem to want it.

She blew out a breath. "Fine. You can just leave that case in the store room. We'll put it out when we have the space."

I paused. "You don't have space now?"

"Well, we've got a lot of products at the moment. Deirdre Michaelson just brought in a new bunch of her tie-dyed silk. And Carol Gottlieb has her stained glass." Janet smiled again, this time steely. "We'll put the jam out when we can. I'll give you a receipt." She turned to her laptop, bringing up a page on the screen. "Twelve jars, right?" She filled in the form quickly, then grabbed the receipt off the printer, handing it to me. "We'll let you know if we sell any."

For a brief moment, I considered grabbing the jam and heading to my truck. But that would basically cut off any future relationship with the store. Of course, at the moment, I wasn't sure we had much of a relationship. But I didn't want to close off the possibility that we might have one again sometime.

Maybe if Janet got a job somewhere else.

I placed the case in the store room, trying to make it as prominent as I could, then walked out to Main. I had nothing else I needed to do in town, but I decided to go to Bianca Jordan's bakery to get some bread for dinner. Even if I didn't buy anything, maybe I could hear some gossip about Brett's murder. I was curious about how much information Fowler had let slip.

Bianca's shop was at the end of Main nearest River Park, where the farmers market was held. I walked down the street, detouring around tourists and nodding at locals I knew.

At least I started out nodding. After a couple of minutes, I noticed a strange development. Some people smiled, but others glanced at me and looked away. If it had only happened once, I could have said it was just a mistake. But it happened three or four times, enough to make me pay attention.

Then, across the street, I saw a couple of women I knew by sight from the farmers market, where they bought my jam. They'd always seemed really friendly and really enthusiastic about my stuff. Now they stood together across the street, peering at me and whispering together, not smiling so much as smirking. It reminded me of high school when somebody had done something scandalous—or was rumored to have done something scandalous—and the gossip mill started going full bore.

And I was the scandalous person.

At that point everything fell into place: Evelyn, Janet, the people on the street. Either they thought I'd killed Brett Holmes, or they thought I was involved somehow.

My first impulse was to run across the street and tell those two women I was innocent and they were stupid to think otherwise. Fortunately for all concerned, my common sense kicked in and kept me standing where I was. I took a deep breath and resumed my trek to Bianca's place, but now I was sensitized. I started looking at the people on the street, trying to see if they were staring at me or if I was imagining it. And it seemed to me that I wasn't imagining it. That thing where someone I knew glanced at me and then looked away really fast happened two or three more times.

Was going to Bianca's place really such a great idea? What if she gave me the cold shoulder? I wasn't sure I could take that. Bianca was my friend, Uncle Mike's friend, my dad's friend. If she turned against me, I'd probably have a panic attack in the middle of Main.

By the time I got to the shop, I must have looked

wild. The sales clerk behind the main counter backed away slightly when I approached. "What?" she blurted.

"Is Bianca here? I need to talk to her."

The clerk gestured at the back, and I headed to Bianca's kitchen.

She was kneading some dough on her large wooden counter, her shoulders flexing. Bianca seems like a nice little old lady when you see her in the park, but she's actually really tough the way most cooks are really tough. She's around five seven or so, with gray hair she keeps pulled into a bun. Her arms and shoulders are roped with muscle. Bakers like her spend a lot of their time lifting heavy pans in and out of ovens. You don't want to mess with them, believe me.

Bianca heard me come in and glanced up, smiling. "Hey, kid. How's it going? Got any jam you want to unload?"

I was so relieved to see her smile that I almost collapsed on the floor. I'd been so afraid she'd tell me to get out. "I don't have any with me, but I could give you a good price on last year's peach preserves. The new crop is due to come in soon."

"Sounds good." Bianca paused in her pummeling of the dough, forehead furrowing. "Is something wrong? You look upset."

I sighed. "I am upset. I just figured out a lot of people in town must think I killed Brett Holmes. Or that I know who did?"

Bianca raised an eyebrow. "Do you?"

I shook my head. "No. Of course not. I hadn't seen Brett for a week before he died. You saw that altercation we had at the market two weeks ago. After that we avoided each other."

"Yeah, I can believe that. But the rumor is Brett shot down your bid to be on that ridiculous TV show. I can see how that might piss you off. Particularly when it was Evelyn Davidson who vetoed you."

"She did? Why?" That was one thing I was genuinely curious about since Evelyn's reasons had seemed a little thin.

"Because Holmes asked her to." Bianca shrugged. "Apparently they had something going on. Or she wanted them to. Don't ask me—I always thought Holmes was a slug, but apparently Evelyn didn't agree."

"Evelyn was having an affair with Brett?" My mind boggled.

"So I hear. Holmes was a hound, though, so Evelyn for sure wasn't his one and only. That's probably why he couldn't figure you out. All these other women fell for him. Maybe he thought you should have been a pushover." Bianca shrugged again. "No accounting for taste, I guess."

I sank into one of Bianca's chairs. "Do people in town think I killed him?"

Bianca paused, giving her dough a pat. "Some do, I'm sure. The story about the fight with you and Holmes and Nate Robicheaux went around town pretty quickly. So when Holmes was done in, a lot of people figured you were involved."

I closed my eyes for a moment. "Well, shit."

"Stupid people are always looking for something to gossip about. That's one of the things that makes them stupid. I wouldn't worry about it if I were you." Bianca grabbed her bench scraper and started dividing the dough into mounds, rolling them into balls.

"I might not," I said slowly. "Except it could affect

my business. Janet at Made In Colorado wasn't enthusiastic about putting my jam out with the other products, and a couple of my regular customers looked at me like I was Jack the Ripper."

"Could be your imagination." Bianca frowned as she said it, like she didn't entirely believe it. "Anyway, all of that will go away when they find the person who killed Holmes. Then people can go back to treating you like any other struggling artisan."

"What if they don't?" I said slowly.

"Who doesn't?" Bianca looked confused.

"Fowler and his minions. What if they don't find out who killed Brett? What if it stays a mystery? Will people go back to treating me the way they did before? Or is this my new normal?"

Bianca gave up rolling the dough into balls, leaning against the counter. "That could be a problem. People like to have things tied up and tucked away. Loose threads make them uneasy. They might decide you were a loose thread."

I bit my lip as I contemplated a future full of people avoiding me on the street and muttering about me behind my back. The tourists would buy my jam, but the locals might avoid it since it wasn't a good idea to reward a murderess. And I couldn't get by without the local business. I knew that for a fact.

Bianca gave me a quick smile. "Don't buy trouble, honey. Trust Fowler. He may seem sort of dour, but I think he knows his stuff. Leave it to him to find the murderer. And then everything will return to normal."

"Thanks, Bianca." I pushed myself to my feet, pretending I felt renewed and ready to go confront the world.

But inside, I felt wobbly. I'd let myself be chased out of Denver without a fight. I didn't want to lose Shavano, too. I was running out of places where I could hide.

But I wasn't entirely sure how I could prevent it. Maybe it was time to call in reinforcements.

Chapter 16

Susa usually worked from her house, a former miner's cabin turned bungalow near downtown. There was a discreet sign near the front door, *SS Systems* in a sans serif font that she argued looked both high tech and tough. Which described Susa, too.

I felt a little guilty about going there during the work day. She had a lot of clients and not a lot of time. But I really couldn't wait to explain the whole thing to her. Normally we were equally pragmatic, but right now my pragmatism was being overwhelmed by my panic.

I needed Susa to talk me down.

I rang her doorbell, telling myself I'd leave if it looked like she was crazy busy. When Susa answered, it was hard to tell how busy she was. Mainly she looked surprised to see me. She had on leggings and a sweatshirt that said *Unix* in rainbow letters, and she had a number two pencil stuck behind her ear.

"Hey, Roxy," she said, frowning slightly. "What's up?"

"Have you got a minute to talk? I mean, if you don't, I can call you later or maybe come back tomorrow," I babbled. "I don't want to interrupt you. Maybe I should come back later."

Susa grabbed my arm, pulling me into the house. "I'll make you some tea. And you can tell me what's going on. You look like Herman just ate a yellowjacket."

She paused. "Herman's okay, isn't he? I didn't mean to imply he wasn't."

"He's fine. He stayed with Uncle Mike last night, and he probably got pampered within an inch of his life. I'm the one who's falling apart."

"Good. I mean, not that you're falling apart. Good that Herman's doing fine." She ran a hand through her hair. "Sorry. I've been working on a bug report all morning, and it's got me cross-eyed."

I immediately felt like a jerk. "I'm sorry. I can come back some other time, when you're not struggling with something."

"Don't be ridiculous." Susa shoved me into the tiny kitchen at the rear of her house. "I'm taking a break so that my brain can recalibrate. Listening to you could be just what I need."

She pulled down a couple of mugs and a box of teabags. "I'll make tea while you talk. Tell me what's been going on, and why you look so weird."

I couldn't argue with that. I looked weird because I felt weird. I'd been accused of a lot of things in my life, but until now murder hadn't been one of them. I watched Susa fill her electric kettle and described yesterday's meeting with Fowler and today's experience downtown, ending with Bianca's matter-of-fact description of my possible future.

Susa leaned against the counter, her arms folded across her chest. "So I assume you're not buying the idea Fowler will find the killer and you should wait for him to do that."

"Not so much, no." I picked up the mug of tea she'd handed me. "I mean he may well be a great chief of police, but unless he comes up with something within the next week, I'm afraid people are going to permanently associate me with Brett's death. And even if they catch his murderer, that may not be enough to convince people I wasn't involved. Not if it takes too long."

"So what's your plan?"

"I don't have one. Except I feel like I should be doing something."

"Like what?"

"Like finding out what Brett was really like and telling the world. Bianca thought he was a hound, chasing women and treating them badly. If that's true, shouldn't that lead to a lot more suspects? Other women who resented what he did to them, or tried to do to them? Maybe even some men who were pissed at him for coming on to their girlfriends?"

"I don't know much about Brett Holmes. Was he any good as a chef? Did the people at High Country like him? Did he actually have a steady girlfriend, or did he have a string of women around town?"

"I never heard much about him. I avoided him as much as possible. Every time he saw me, he came on to me."

Susa grimaced. "He was a pig. That much is clear. But it might help to know more about his life. Who he hung out with, what he did in his spare time, that kind of stuff. He had to have friends or people he partied with. Who were they?"

"I feel honor bound to point out this is what Fowler is probably investigating. Assuming he hasn't decided charging me would save time and money." I took a sip of my tea, which had gone lukewarm.

"I'm sure Fowler will find out as much about Brett as he can, but you're in a better position to talk to the foodie community. Besides, it might be fun to do a little investigating. What can it hurt?"

I was sure Fowler would have a very specific and probably negative answer to that question. But I was beginning to think Susa had a point. If nothing else, it would make me feel like I was doing something to clear my name rather than sitting around and hoping Fowler would do it for me. Maybe it was a slightly crazy thing to do, but I was in the mood for crazy right then.

Being sane hadn't gotten me very far.

"Okay. Who should I start with? Evelyn Davidson probably won't talk to me, but I'd really like to know if she had an affair with Brett. Or if she wanted to."

"She won't talk to you, but she'll talk to me. I'm the one who keeps her computer virus free." Susa picked up her teacup. "Besides, I'm also dying to know if she hooked up with Holmes. She seems so buttoned up. I can't picture her falling for a sleaze. Of course, maybe that's why she fell for him."

"Okay, I'll leave Evelyn to you. I'll try talking to people at High Country. I know one of the waitresses over there, although I haven't seen her in a while. Maybe she can tell me about Brett and suggest other people to talk to."

"I'll start a file for us. We can do document sharing. You'll upload your notes and I'll upload mine."

Trust Susa to automate the whole thing. "You really think we should write things down?"

"Why not? That way we'll both have access to whatever we're finding, and we won't forget what we heard."

That sounded very reasonable, but I could think of one very good reason not to. "What if Fowler finds out what we're doing? Notes would be evidence we were intruding into his investigation."

"This file space is going to be so thoroughly protected Fowler would need his own pet nerd to crack in. And since I'm the pet nerd he'd have to come to, I can pretty much guarantee he won't succeed." She took a sip of her tea and grimaced. "Yuck. It's gone cold. Want to warm it up?"

"That's okay. I should get back to making jam." Although for the first time I wondered just how much I'd sell that weekend. I could count on the tourists, but anything beyond that was an open question.

"All right, I'll email you the details when I get our file sharing set up. This is going to be fun." She gave me a sunny smile, as if we weren't going to be meddling in a murder investigation.

I wondered just what Fowler would do if he found out what we were up to. Was there actually a law against involving yourself in an official investigation? I didn't know, and I didn't want to find out.

I went home then. I really did have some jam to make, although my marathon session the day before had left me with a good supply. Still, I needed something besides strawberry.

I thought about calling Nate, but then I didn't. What could I say to him? I didn't want to cry on his shoulder about people being mean to me. I was already spending too much time complaining to him. And besides, it wasn't his job to be my sounding board. I already had Susa doing that. I had a far more interesting role in mind for Nate, assuming I ever got my courage up to take that final step.

My contact at High Country was Bridget Sullivan.

We'd volunteered together at the library a couple of years ago. She was a single mom with a couple of kids, and she told me High Country was a great place to work for salary and tips. But that had been before Brett had taken over the kitchen. I wondered if she still felt that way.

I thought about finding her at High Country, but then I decided against it. Hanging around Brett's former workplace struck me as faintly creepy. In the end, I decided that straightforward was probably best, so I called her.

I was prepared for her to sound wary or maybe even hostile, but she just sounded like herself. "Hey, Roxy, good to hear from you. Everything okay?"

"Passable. Could I buy you a cup of coffee or something? I need to ask you some questions."

"Sure, I guess so. What kind of questions?"

I took a breath. I'd thought of several things I could pretend to be interested in, but I went with straightforward. "I need more information about Brett Holmes. Some people seem to think I had something to do with his death, and it's creeping me out."

"Yeah, I'd heard that. I said it was bullshit, but that's because I know you." Bridget sounded almost as matter of fact as Bianca. Was I the only one who found this whole situation horrifying?

"Thanks for standing up for me. But I'd like to get a handle on who Brett was. I didn't really know him at all."

Bridget sighed. "To know him was not necessarily to love him. But I'll tell you what I can. How about lunch somewhere?"

"Dirty Pete's?" I suggested. At least I wouldn't get any side-eye there. Harry would protect me. Unless

159

Harry was giving me side-eye himself, a possibility that made my stomach clench.

Bridget agreed to meet me around noon, and I took the first in a series of deep breaths. Harry was my friend. He'd be like Bridget and Bianca—he wouldn't turn on me. But I'd thought Janet Leonhart was my friend, too, and she'd thrown me under the bus without a qualm.

Fortunately, Harry grinned when I walked in the door. Less fortunately, he boomed, "How's the murder suspect today?"

After one look at my expression, his grin disappeared. "Geez, Roxy, it was a joke. Supposed to be one, anyway. Sorry, okay?"

"It's okay. I'm just not ready to laugh yet, I guess."

I sank into a chair at the same window table where I'd been sitting the time Brett had tried to pick me up. This might have been bad luck, but it gave me a view of the street. I was a little worried about Fowler walking by.

Bridget came in a few minutes later, waving a quick hand at Harry, who gave her a cautious smile. Apparently he didn't want to risk another greeting *faux pas*. She dropped down at the table opposite me. "You're buying, right? You're the jam queen."

"Right. Although I don't know how much of a queen I'll be if Fowler decides I'm a murderer."

"Fowler's not that dumb. He'll come around."

We ordered lunch and Caroline brought our iced teas. I let Bridget take a couple of sips and settle in before I broached the subject of Brett.

"What exactly do you want to know?" she asked, frowning.

"I'm not all that sure. I mean, he kept making passes at me, but I don't think we ever had a normal conversation. Did he do that at the restaurant, too?"

"Not to me, he didn't. At least not twice. He made an offer once, and I told him where to stick it. I don't think I was his type. He sure as hell wasn't mine." Bridget is a few years older than me, and she looks like a mom. She definitely doesn't look like somebody who'd like to have an evening of tequila shots and wild sex.

"Who was his type?"

"Hard to say—I mean he'd come on to anybody in a skirt. But I did notice he seemed to go after low mileage types."

I frowned. "And by 'low mileage' you mean…"

"Young," Bridget said flatly. "We have a few waitresses straight out of high school, although Denny doesn't like to hire too many of them because they can't serve booze, not even beer. Those were the ones Holmes really went after. I know one of them went out with him for a while. I think she was eighteen, so she wasn't a minor, even if it was just barely. Then he dropped her. She quit a couple of weeks later. Hard to think of anybody pining over a jerk like Holmes, but she was really young, like I said."

"Did anybody call him on it?"

"Like who? Outraged dad? Her parents are divorced, and her mom waits tables in Norcross, gets home around midnight. Carrie didn't have anybody to give her advice. Not that she wanted any. Believe me, I tried to give her some."

Caroline delivered our lunches, and we spent a few minutes eating, while I tried to think of other things to ask that might give me useful information. "How did Denny feel about Brett?"

Denny was the manager at High Country. The owner

lived in Aspen and dropped by maybe once a month.

"They didn't fight much. But I got the feeling Denny wasn't too impressed with him. Holmes kept trying to add stuff to the menu, expensive stuff usually. Denny's not what you'd call a big gourmet. He's more a bottom line type. He and Brett disagreed on food choices pretty regularly."

"Is there anybody in the kitchen I could talk to? Somebody who could tell me how he ran things?"

Bridget paused for a moment, thinking. "The best one would probably be Spencer Carroll. He's the one who's running the kitchen now. He stepped in the day the cops let us reopen. They'll probably bring in somebody else to be the head chef eventually, but Spence is in charge at the moment. And he's doing a good job. My guess is Denny would like to hold onto him, but the owner will probably bring in another hot shot from Denver."

I took a bite of my ham and cheese sandwich. Spencer Carroll would possibly be someone who could tell me the kind of kitchen manager Brett had been. That might not give me much insight into his possible enemies, but it would tell me a lot about what kind of person he was. When you work with somebody in stress conditions, you get a good idea of their character.

"How could I get in touch with him?" I had a feeling if I just showed up at High Country, he'd be too busy to see me.

Bridget gave me a slightly sneaky grin. "Why not ask your boyfriend? I've seen the two of them hanging around together. And it's a beautiful sight to behold, believe me."

I blinked at her. "My boyfriend?"

"The cook from Robicheaux's, the younger one." Bridget's grin faded. "Aren't the two of you together? I thought I heard you were."

My cheeks flushed pink. *What are you, fifteen?* "We've gone out together, yeah."

"So ask him to get you an introduction to Spence. Maybe even have him come along. The restaurant scene is pretty clubby around here. Everybody knows everybody else."

Except Nate didn't know Brett. Or he said he didn't. *Don't go there.*

"Okay, thanks. I'll call him. Anything else you remember about Brett?"

Bridget picked up her last potato chip. "He was really full of himself, but you probably know that already. He wanted us all to understand he'd been sous chef at this big restaurant in Denver, Solo. Every other thing he said started with 'When I was at Solo.' I mean, who cares, right? The chef at Stumptown had a place in Napa before he came here, and the guy at South Fork was a head chef in Chicago. It's not like we're the back of beyond in Shavano."

"He *was* pretty impressed with himself."

"But he wouldn't have stayed here much longer. That's the irony of it. If somebody killed him to get him out of the way, they wasted the effort. But my guess is whoever killed him did it because he was such a dick."

I found myself nodding slowly. "That makes sense."

Professional rivalries were real, but I didn't know anybody who'd kill over a job. And Brett had other problems, most of them arising from his winning personality. Whoever killed him probably had a very good reason.

Chapter 17

After I went back to the farm, I took a few minutes to do what Susa had suggested and wrote up my notes. I hadn't wanted to write anything while Bridget was talking, but I did want to remember what she'd said. Unfortunately, my notes looked pretty thin.

Young girls, anybody in a skirt, heartbroken waitress, Carrie, run-ins with Denny over costs, worked at Solo, Spencer Carroll, impressed with himself.

If somebody knocked me off before Susa and I solved the case, no one would be able to make sense of this except me.

It did give me some leads, though. For one thing, I knew people who worked at Solo, the place where Brett claimed to have been head chef. I doubted that was true, but I knew someone I could ask.

And then there was Spencer Carroll, the new head chef. I could ask Nate for help if they were friends. That had its good and bad points, however.

I couldn't decide how to approach Nate. If I asked him to dinner again, he might think I was ready for more than dinner. I wasn't sure I was, but I wasn't sure I wasn't. Plus asking him to set me up with another man while we were on a date seemed a little crass.

I needed to talk to him in a neutral setting where I could lay out the whole project and explain how Spencer Carroll fit in. The farmers market would be a good bet.

I decided to try texting him.

—Are you doing a demo at the market this weekend? Want to do lunch?—

He texted a few minutes later:

—Yeah, and yeah.—

So at least we had a date. Now I needed a plan. I needed to give Nate the entire story so he could see why I wanted to talk to Spencer Carroll.

Only I wasn't sure what that entire story was. I was pretty much going on instinct, talking to people in hopes that I'd hear a piece of information and something would go *ping* in my mind. In my ideal scenario, everything would suddenly be clear in an instant. That happened to me sometimes when I was cooking—I'd think of a combination of flavors and suddenly I'd know just what I needed to do.

But that was cooking, and this was murder. I knew how very unlikely it was that I'd figure everything out in a flash. Nonetheless, it was the best idea I had at the moment.

Spencer Carroll might be part of that *ping* moment. It wouldn't hurt to hear someone else's story about Brett as part of my information gathering.

On Saturday, I loaded several cases of jam into the truck. It didn't hurt to be optimistic, even though I was more and more convinced that my sales were going to be lackluster. *Nothing like starting with a positive attitude.* On the other hand, I'd rather be pleasantly surprised than bitterly disappointed.

The market was even more packed than the previous weekend. The local farmers had more produce to sell since their crops were beginning to come in, and tourist season was in full swing. Some itinerant musicians had set up in the park, playing jug band music over a modified amp. A few craft booths had been set up along the paths, with people selling wooden toys and stained glass window ornaments and jewelry. It was busy and hectic and crowded. Dolce and I sold a lot of jam.

I tried to convince myself that I'd sold as much as I usually did, but that wasn't true. During the summer, each weekend's sales normally exceeded the one before it until we hit Labor Day and the tourists headed home.

While my sales that Saturday were healthy, they weren't much over last Saturday's sales. I'd obviously had the advantage of a lot of tourists buying my stuff to take to their rented condos. But I'd had fewer locals than usual.

Of course, I'd still had some. Bianca had stopped by to pick up the case of peach preserves she'd ordered from me. Harry grabbed a couple of jars of apricot, proclaiming loudly to anyone listening that my stuff was the best in the state. And there were those who dropped by to get a glimpse of the woman who might have murdered the chef last week. They didn't stay long and they didn't buy much of anything, but they stood just beyond the edge of the crowd, watching me with avid eyes.

I decided I never wanted to be famous again. Or infamous, for that matter.

Nate swung by around eleven with a paper plate. "Here you go—mac and cheese."

It looked heavenly, all thick sauce and buttery crumbs on top. I took a quick bite and tasted cheddar and cream, along with a little kick of chili. "Very nice. Thanks."

"You're welcome. Will you be through by two?"

"Oh, yeah," I said. I might even be through before that depending on when the tourists flocked off to grab lunch.

"Maybe we can do a picnic. I've got a couple of things I want to go over with you."

That sounded serious, but given that I had a couple of things to go over with him, too, it worked for me. "A picnic sounds fine."

The rest of the market passed quickly. I paid Dolce and then packed up the case and a half I had left. That was a bit more than last week, but I'd brought more so it probably evened out. Probably. I wouldn't know for sure until I looked at my spread sheets and checked the sales figures. I had no reason to be concerned about it.

Except I sort of did. I knew I hadn't had the customers I usually had, and I knew the ones I was missing were my locals. Some of them might have stayed home rather than buck the crowds, but some of them were avoiding me. I needed to get them back, and the best way to do that was to find out who killed Brett.

Good luck with that, Roxy.

Nate showed up at two with a cooler over his arm. "Give me a ride to my place? I figure we can eat in the backyard again.

"That works," I said, trying to tamp down my worries. Nate didn't need to hear me whining again. At least not until he'd had a chance to eat some lunch. "I really like your yard."

"I do, too." He grinned at me. He seemed a little more excited than usual although I wasn't sure why. Surely a picnic wasn't that big a deal.

The grass in Nate's yard was long and lush, waving slightly in the afternoon breeze. I could smell pine and a hint of the roses just beginning to bloom in Madge's front yard.

He brought out a classic red-checked tablecloth and spread it on the picnic table. Then he dragged up a couple of Adirondack chairs and I sank into one, stretching my legs out in front of me.

"I've got chicken sandwiches and potato salad, courtesy of Coco. Also a bottle of wine, courtesy of me." He pulled a chilled bottle of white out of the cooler and placed it in the middle of the table, along with a couple of plastic wine glasses. "And there's chocolate cake for dessert."

"Also from Coco?" I asked.

He shook his head. "I did that one. I'm trying to brush up some of my skills so I don't get rusty. I don't get many chances to experiment around the café."

He handed me a sandwich wrapped in parchment paper, and I sank into my Adirondack. I'd spent the last several hours worrying about my sales and trying to keep up with the tourists, who tended to scrape the sample bowls dry at a great rate. It felt wonderful to be sitting in the shade, dining on something civilized. The chicken was thick and juicy, piled on Bianca's four-grain with some kind of special spread, maybe a flavored aioli.

It was terrific. The potato salad was terrific. The wine was terrific. I could feel my tense muscles relaxing, feel at least some of my stress slipping away.

I thought about bringing up Spencer Carroll and decided to let that slide for a while. I was enjoying myself too much to bother at the moment.

"So I had an idea," Nate said, a little hesitantly.

I glanced up from my plate. I'd forgotten he'd said he had some things to discuss. "What idea is that?"

"I entered the café in the Taste the Market contest. For Best in Shavano."

Taste the Market was a big competition the farmers market held on Fourth of July weekend. It featured a lot of the vendors from the market, all vying to get to the top of whatever category they were entered in: best pie, best cheese, best salsa, best jerky, and so on. There was a best jam category and I'd won it pretty consistently, but I was a little nervous about entering this year.

The judges were locals, and I was afraid they'd drop me to the bottom of the rankings.

"That's great," I said. "What are you going to fix? Do you have to do a whole meal?"

"Main, sides, and dessert."

"Good for you. It's great publicity." Best In Shavano was the most competitive part of the contest. Even if the café didn't take home the prize, they'd get a lot of good exposure.

Nate took a quick sip of his wine, like he was fortifying himself. "I was hoping you'd give me a hand."

I frowned. "I don't do many main dishes. Unless they involve jam." Other than the cooking I'd done for Uncle Mike over the past couple of years, I hadn't really done much in the kitchen beyond my business.

"Mine might involve jam, but that's not when I need your help with. I wanted to include as many local products as I could in whatever I fix. I know some of the producers around here, the ones at the market, but I don't know them all. I figure you do."

I took another bite of my sandwich. "I probably do. I can certainly help you find anything you need if it's produced around here. Using locals is a really smart strategy, particularly if you can use other market vendors."

"Great." Nate's grin had that flush of excitement again. He was really into this. "And maybe you can give me a character reference if anybody needs one."

My own smile faded a bit. "I'm not sure a character reference from me would be helpful right now. In fact, you might want to limit any references to me when you talk to people."

Nate shook his head. "Come on, Rox. These people know you. You grew up around here. They're not going to suspect you of murder. Not seriously."

"Some of them won't. Some will. But of course I'll help you regardless. What kind of menu are you thinking of?" It was a clumsy redirect, but I didn't want to waste time complaining about the gossip.

Nate ran through a list of possible main dishes, with me kibitzing and making suggestions for suppliers. He actually had some ideas for main dishes that involved jam, usually pork or chicken with jam-based sauce. I had more ideas for things I tried out myself: duck breast with blackberry jam, lamb with sour cherries, even a killer baked bean recipe with apple jelly instead of maple syrup. Uncle Mike ate well.

By the time we'd finished lunch we were both grinning with excitement, jazzed with recipes and food joy. And white wine.

Nate grabbed my hand to pull me out of my Adirondack, then held me close in a warm hug. "This is great. Thanks, Roxy, I knew you'd be the one to talk to about this."

I was caught between really liking the feel of his arms and having a mild panic reaction to being held. I decided to go with the liking rather than the panic. "You haven't told Bobby?"

He pulled back slightly to look at me. "I haven't told anybody but you. And the people at the contest when I turned in our entry."

That struck me as a bad idea, given Bobby's probable reaction to being out of the loop. "You should maybe discuss it with him. Or at least with your mom. I mean, you'd be representing her restaurant."

"I know." He rested his forehead on mine for a moment. "I will. But I wanted to go in with a main dish in mind so it won't seem quite so crazy."

"You've got a lot of good ideas. It's not crazy at all."

Another moment, and he raised his head again, smiling down at me. "Want some cake?"

"Love some." I followed him to the picnic table where he lifted out what looked like a chocolate torte, with a dense, luscious chocolate frosting.

"I haven't done much baking since I was in school," he said. "It was never my big thing, but Spence was talking about flourless chocolate cake the other day. Made me want to try it again."

As an opening to talking about Spencer Carroll, that seemed almost too perfect, like the gods were smiling. Given that they hadn't smiled at me much during the past week, I decided to grab my chance. "Is that Spencer Carroll from High Country?"

"Yeah. We ran into each other at City Market last week."

"I need to talk to him. Could you introduce me?"

Nate frowned. "Spence? Sure, I guess so. Why do you want to talk to him?"

"He worked with Brett Holmes before…well, before. I'm trying to get as much information about Brett as I can, so that I can maybe figure out what happened to him and why."

Nate's brows arched up. "Isn't that what Fowler's supposed to be doing?"

"And he is. I mean, I guess he is. But I want to know for myself. I'm losing business over this, losing customers. And I'm losing sleep. I'm worried about my future. I need to know what happened to Brett, or at least I need to find out as much as I can."

Nate looked like a whole squadron of objections were floating through his mind, but in the end he shrugged. "Okay, I can introduce you to Spence. But I want to go with you. Otherwise he might think you're like all the other budding tabloid reporters he's been fending off. A lot of them have come out of the woodwork since Holmes died."

The staff at High Country had probably been getting a version of the same gawkers I'd been dealing with. A lot of people had probably gone to the restaurant to see the scene of the crime.

"I'd be glad to have you come with me. Maybe you'll think of things I don't."

"Have you talked to other people about Holmes?" Nate looked like he was a little afraid of the answer.

"I talked to a friend of mine who's a waitress at High Country. That's about as far as I've gone. But she mentioned Spencer Carroll." I decided not to tell him Susa was part of my investigation since that would probably make me sound even nuttier than I already did.

Nate cut us both wedges of the torte, which looked dark and chocolate-rich. "Have you found out anything yet?"

I sighed. What had I found out anyway? "I found out

he was a sleaze at work, so it wasn't just me. He came on to a lot of different women, and he didn't necessarily like taking *no* for an answer. And he worked at Solo in Denver, which is a place I know so I can ask other people about his time there. That's about it so far."

"Are you looking for something in particular?"

"A confession would be nice."

Nate narrowed his eyes.

"I guess I'm looking for something that would give me some insight into the kind of man Brett was. What made him someone who got killed. I mean, there are a lot of sleazy people in the restaurant business, and nobody kills them. What pushed someone over the edge with Brett?"

Nate speared a bit of cake with his fork. "What got him killed may have less to do with Brett's character and more to do with the person who killed him. Maybe he just pushed somebody's buttons."

"That's true, but it still might help to know more about what kind of man he was. At least it would tell me who he was most likely to offend."

"When do you want to talk to Spence? He works dinners, although I think High Country does Sunday brunch, too."

Given that brunch was the best way for a restaurant to burn off last week's leftovers, it made sense that High Country did one. "Maybe we could get together for a beer sometime."

"Let me see if he's free tomorrow after his brunch service. Mid-afternoon work for you?"

"Sure. I'll even buy you dinner." It was the least I could do after I talked him into this.

"Or I could cook for you. I do a great dinner. And

I'm not bad on breakfast."

My heart thumped hard. Was I ready for this? "Dinner would be fine."

Nate gave me a quick grin. "Dinner it is. Would you like to take some cake home for Mike?"

"Sure." I watched him divide the cake as my heart rate returned to normal. At least I wouldn't have to make any decisions.

Not until tomorrow night.

Chapter 18

I was going to check Susa's file sharing folder when I got home to see if she'd had a chance to talk to Evelyn yet, but Susa beat me to it. She was playing with Herman in my front yard when I got back.

"There you are," she called when she saw me drive up. "I was about to go up to the main house to get Mike to let me in."

"If I'd known you were waiting, I'd have gotten here sooner," I said, although that wasn't entirely true. I wouldn't necessarily have rushed home from Nate's place.

"I was out here checking a glitch in the farm's billing system, and I figured I'd stop by to tell you what lousy notes you leave." She bent down to scratch Herman's ears, and he gave her a blissful grin.

"When did I leave you a note?"

Susa gave me an impatient look. "Online. Your notes from talking to Bridget. Those were probably the most opaque notes ever."

I sighed. "Right. Come on in. I'll give you a blow-by-blow."

"And tea. I need tea if we're going to talk about murder. It's a requirement."

Fortunately, I had some tea. Also some thumbprint cookies from a couple of days ago. No way was I sharing Nate's torte. We sat at my kitchen table with Herman sprawled at our feet, angling shamelessly for more scratches from Susa.

She dropped a printed copy of my notes on the table. "*Young girls, anybody in a skirt, heartbroken waitress, Carrie, run-ins with Denny over costs, worked at Solo, Spencer Carroll, impressed with himself.*" She raised an eyebrow at me.

"Okay, it's not that opaque. Or anyway, it's not if you're me. That's what Bridget told me about Brett. Not that it's anything we didn't already know. He was a womanizer, went after 'anybody in a skirt.' He particularly went after the young and naïve, like this Carrie who was a waitress there and dated him for a while. He also didn't get along with Denny, the manager at High Country, but I'm not sure that's relevant because why kill him when he could just fire him?"

"They could have fought. Maybe it wasn't premeditated."

"I'm guessing it wasn't. But Denny Rohrbacher has never struck me as the type to hit somebody over the head in a rage."

"There's a type who does that?"

"You know what I mean. He's really buttoned up and professional. I can't even imagine him losing his temper, let alone killing somebody in a rage."

"Buttoned up people can have meltdowns. What's this about Solo?"

"Solo is the restaurant where Brett worked in Denver. I know people there. Maybe I can find out why he left his job."

"I thought he left because High Country offered him more money."

"Unlikely. A Denver restaurant's always going to

176

pay better than one in Shavano. But the job at High Country was probably a promotion. My guess is he worked on the line at Solo. Getting the head chef job at High Country would be a definite move up."

"And *impressed with himself* is pretty clear." Susa glanced up at me. "Next time I recommend complete sentences."

"I'll see what I can do." I grabbed a cookie. "Did you talk to Evelyn?"

Susa gave me a slightly smug smile. "I did indeed. I even bought her a latte at Beans On the Rocks."

"What did you find out? Was she going out with Brett? Did they have a 'thing'?"

Susa's smile lost some of its smugness. "Yep and yep. She's broken up over Holmes, which I don't understand. She says they weren't dating any more. Or not exactly dating, anyway. But she still seems to be hung up on him."

"What does 'not exactly dating' mean?"

"In my opinion, it means he was going out with other women while occasionally sleeping with Evelyn, but she's not ready to admit it. She says they were 'on a break' and seeing other people. But I got the feeling he was the only one doing that. She was waiting around for him to come back full time."

"Oh. That's sort of sad."

"Sad but also annoying. I mean I think she tossed you out of the running for *Sweet Thing* just to make him happy. And he still cheated on her."

"Did she know who else he was dating?"

"She didn't mention it. And based on what the waitress at High Country told you, it could well have been more than one woman. I don't think Evelyn's much of a possibility as a murderess, though. She's passive, if you know what I mean. More likely to sit around and mope than take a club to him."

"No, not a probable suspect," I agreed. "Plus she doesn't seem strong enough to bash him over the head. Of course, we don't know how much force that took. I mean, maybe whoever did it just happened to hit a weak spot."

"I could see if I could access the autopsy report. It might be on the city computers." Susa gave me a bright smile.

I shook my head quickly. "No. Don't do that. We don't need it, and it could get us both into big trouble if they found out you were doing it."

"You're no fun." Susa pouted. "So who's Spencer Carroll?"

"The chef at High Country. The guy who took over for Brett. I figure he'd be a good source of information about what Brett was like professionally. I want to find out if he was as annoying in the kitchen as people said he was."

"You're going to try to talk to Carroll?"

"Yeah. Nate knows him. He said he'd introduce me."

Susa gave me a long look. "You told your boyfriend you want him to introduce you to another man? And he agreed? That sounds a little sketchy."

I started to say that Nate wasn't my boyfriend, but then I paused. He *was* my boyfriend. Sort of, anyway. He was closer to being my boyfriend than anyone had been in a while. "I explained why I needed to talk to Carroll. And Nate's going to come along to vouch for me."

Susa grinned. "To vouch for you and maybe to keep

an eye on this Spencer so he doesn't make a play for you."

"Oh, come on. I'm not some femme fatale. I'm a six-foot Greek with crazy hair."

Susa raised her eyebrows almost to her hairline, a really good trick I wished I could imitate. "How many times do I have to tell you this? You are gorgeous. Men look at you and their jaws drop. You are like one of those models from the eighties, like Cindy Crawford or, hell, Verushka."

"Verushka was the sixties," I mumbled, blushing.

"So you're a throwback. Anyway, stop running yourself down. The guy in Denver doesn't represent all men."

"It's not about him, not really."

"Yeah, it is. And believe me, I'm not telling you to get over it. I know it's not something you get over. I am telling you to stop blaming yourself. And to stop thinking what happened in Denver means there's something wrong with you. There's something wrong with men like that guy."

Susa gave me a fierce hug, as I fought tears. She was right, and I knew it on some level. I just hadn't been able to convince myself entirely.

But I was working on it.

"Okay." Susa folded her arms. "What's next? Where do we go from here?"

"I need to talk to the people I knew at Solo and to Spencer Carroll. But I thought of something you could check out. You're friends with the principal at Shavano High, right?"

"Dolores Cantu? Yeah, I have a contract for the high school administration Web site. They wanted me to do the student site, too, but I said no way. I'd be spending all my time stopping those little jerks from hacking each other."

"Okay, Brett did some kind of program over there. Cooking demos or something. He bragged about it at the Merchants Association, but I don't remember the details. Could you find out what he did and what they thought of him?"

"Sure. Should be easy enough. He's still the number one topic around town."

Brett and the possibility I'd killed him. We were both trending. "Great. I'll call you when I've talked to Spencer Carroll."

"Yeah, I want to hear about that. I'm guessing there'll be some definite male displays going on. Maybe even a little antler clashing." Susa swallowed the last of her tea. "Gotta go. Complete sentences, Rox. Remember."

"I will. I promise."

Nate and I met Spencer Carroll in a tavern off Second. He'd picked the place, and it was about as far from High Country as you could get, at least culturally—old school Shavano grunge with a juke box and a couple of pool tables. But since it was Colorado, they also had an extensive craft beer list.

Carroll was playing pool when we walked in. He wasn't quite as tall as Nate, but he was stockier, with a butcher's build—well-developed chest and arm muscles, like he'd been wrestling beef carcasses for a while. His curly black hair stood out in a corona around his head, and he had a short beard and moustache with a few silver threads. He looked up and grinned as we walked in.

"Hey, Robicheaux, gone any further with that short

rib recipe?"

Nate grinned back. "Haven't worked on it much since the last time I talked to you." He put a hand on my elbow. "This is Roxy."

Carroll put down his pool cue and stepped forward. He had that same slightly glazed look I was used to by now. *Yes, I'm six feet, and I've got a lot of hair. Get over it.*

"A pleasure." He sounded a little choked.

"Can we sit down somewhere?" Nate asked. "Roxy's got a couple of questions for you."

Carroll nodded toward a table at the side. "Take the booth. You want a beer?"

Nate shook his head. "Seltzer for me. I've got prep waiting."

"Me, too," I said quickly. "I mean, not prep but jam stuff." Off duty chefs are known to knock back a few, and I wasn't ready for that in the middle of the afternoon.

Carroll shrugged, then headed for the bar as I sat down on one side of the booth. Nate sat beside me, a little closer than he needed to. *Male displays,* Susa had said. Maybe she had a point.

Carroll came to the booth, sliding in opposite me. He pushed a glass of seltzer my way, smiling. "Here you go. Now what can I do for you?"

"I wanted to ask you about Brett Holmes," I began.

Carroll's smile faded. "Oh, man, not Holmes. I'm so sick of that son of a bitch. Hard to believe he's more of a pain in the ass dead than he was alive, but that's what's happened."

I couldn't argue with him. "Believe me, I wouldn't be asking you about him normally, but the cops seem to think I'm a suspect, and I feel like I need to know as much about him as I can."

"A suspect? Why the hell would you be a suspect?"

"I had a couple of arguments with him. Public ones. And I don't have an alibi because I was home alone when he was killed."

Carroll raised his eyebrows in Nate's direction. "You weren't around?"

"Unfortunately, no. They've looked at me, too. But since I only met Holmes once, they didn't seem to think I was much of a suspect. Even if we did have a run-in the one time we met."

Carroll turned to me again. "This is getting interesting. But let me tell you, you weren't alone. A lot of people got into fights with Holmes. Regularly. The guy couldn't keep his mouth shut, and a lot of people wanted to shut it for him."

Nate frowned. "Including you?"

"I wasn't his biggest fan. But I didn't get into it with him much. He pretty much left me alone—if I ever walked out, he'd have been up the creek. He'd have actually had to do some serious cooking."

"What kind of cook was he?" I asked. "He talked a lot about what a kitchen stud he was, but I never ate at High Country, so I don't know what you guys turned out."

"He talked a lot," Carroll agreed. "Most of it was crap. I don't know why he left Denver, but I doubt he was as big a kitchen stud as he said he was. He had decent skills, but so do most of us in the kitchen. I wouldn't say he was much ahead of the rest of us."

"But the owner brought him in to be head chef, right?"

"Theoretically. My guess is Holmes talked his way

into that job. He didn't have head chef skills. He made menu suggestions, but they were mostly crap that he heard other restaurants were doing. I mean he heard some restaurant on the Front Range started using CBD oil in their drinks, and he was ready to start adding CBD to everything on the menu. Denny told him to get a grip."

"Okay." Brett had always struck me as the type who was more interested in talking than actually doing anything innovative. "How'd he get along with the rest of the kitchen?"

Carroll gave me a dry grin. "Shitty, thanks for asking. Most of the guys ignored him as much as they could. But he could be a real jerk. We had a woman on the line for a while. Really great on stuff like steak frites. But Holmes kept hitting on her until she got fed up and quit. She moved on to Breckenridge. The guys were so pissed at him one of them dropped a steel skillet on his foot, accidentally he claimed."

"Ouch." That struck me as a bad thing to do to a good piece of carbon steel.

Carroll smiled. "It was full of mushrooms and hot butter. Lucky for Holmes he was wearing steel-toed boots and jeans."

"Okay, so he was unpopular with the other cooks, and he was a hound around women. I knew that already, but it's good to know I'm not the only one who had trouble with him."

"He was a jerk, like I said. Everywhere he went he caused trouble. He had some kind of deal at the high school in town, and he even got into trouble over there."

I'd heard about Brett doing something at the high school, but I hadn't heard he'd had problems over it. "What did he do that got him in trouble?"

"Don't know exactly. I just heard he was kicked out of the program for high school mentors. Although I gotta say I'm amazed anybody thought that asshole would be a good mentor in the first place."

I was, too. But Brett struck me as someone who'd be good at talking his way into things, even if he had no intention of following through. "Thanks for telling me. I'll check it out and see what information I can find." I'd let Susa know what Carroll had told me. Maybe she could get the high school principal to share a few details. "You remember anything else about him?"

Carroll shook his head. "He wasn't all that interesting, to tell you the truth. Just another kitchen blowhard."

"If you do remember anything else you think would help, would you let me know?"

Carroll's grin turned sultry. "Absolutely. Just give me your phone number, and I'll call you if I think of anything helpful."

"Why don't you call me," Nate said flatly. "You've already got my number, and I can let Roxy know what you've got to say."

Carroll chuckled. "Can't blame a man for trying, Robicheaux. But okay, I'll call you if I think of anything."

"Good enough. Any more questions for Spence, Rox?"

I shook my head. "Not that I can think of."

I'd had more than enough antler clashing for one afternoon. Spencer Carroll was cute, but Nate was cuter. And I was still shaky about dating one guy, let alone two. "Thanks for your help." I slid out of the booth, following Nate.

"Any time." Carroll grinned up at me again. "Nice meeting you."

I followed Nate to the street, pondering what I'd learned, if anything. Brett was a jerk. I already knew that. He thought he was God's gift to women. I knew that, too. He talked a good game, but he wasn't much of a cook. I hadn't known that, but I could have guessed it. He was more talk than action.

"Sorry about that," Nate said. "You know how cooks are."

I paused in my ruminations. "What about them?"

"Spencer. He was hitting on you."

"Right. No problem. I'm fine." I'd been more interested in what Carroll was telling me than the flirting. But the flirting was low key. Nothing like being attacked in a pantry.

"Are we still on for dinner Saturday night?"

I was abruptly pulled from considering Spencer Carroll to considering Nate and dinner and…everything else. "Sure," I said brightly. Or as brightly as I could manage. "What time?"

"Why don't I come to your place? You've got a better kitchen than mine."

That was undoubtedly true. And if we were at my place, I could suggest it was time for him to go home at the end of the evening.

Or not.

"That sounds good." I cleared my suddenly dry throat. "Maybe I can suggest something for dessert."

"I'll look forward to it." He leaned down before I could anticipate it and gave me a quick, very hot kiss. "See you at the market."

185

"See you." I touched my fingers to my lips, then began wandering to my truck. I suddenly had a lot to think about.

Chapter 19

Rainstorms usually come in the afternoon in the mountains, but that Saturday it looked like we might get a downpour in the morning. All the merchants were installing roofs on their booths, some improvised with the nearest piece of plastic. Fortunately, when he designed our booths Uncle Mike had foreseen the probability that changeable mountain weather would occasionally dump rain or snow on our retail efforts, and mine came with a roof attached.

The rain fell intermittently throughout the morning, and the tourists scrambled from booth to booth between downpours. I sold a fair amount of jam, but people who took shelter under my roof tended to fill up on samples, too, so I gave away a lot more than I usually did.

A fair number of the locals who passed by still regarded me with suspicion, and Evelyn did her "cut direct" thing again. But now I knew she and Brett had once had a thing, or at least Evelyn thought they did, and I felt a little sorrier for her. Not much, mind you, but a little.

Still, I was determined to go on asking questions about Brett, to see if I could find out who might have killed him. I wanted those suspicious glances to stop, and I didn't want to worry about declining jam sales.

I was making a mental list of people I needed to talk to—my friends who worked at Solo, the high school principal, maybe Carrie, the waitress who was dating Brett before he died—when someone cleared his throat pointedly behind my right shoulder.

I turned to see Chief Fowler watching me with narrowed ice-blue eyes.

"Morning," I said. "Would you like to sample some strawberry preserves?"

He raised his eyebrows while maintaining his narrowed eyes, a very neat trick. "I need to talk to you."

We didn't have many customers at the moment because of the rain, so I nodded to Dolce. "Keep an eye on things for a few minutes, okay?"

"Sure."

I followed Fowler to a bench on the opposite side of the path. "What's up?"

"You've been talking to people about the Holmes case." There wasn't a hint of a question about it.

How the hell had he found out what I was doing? Had somebody complained? I shrugged. "Yeah. I talked to some people I knew. Did somebody tell you?"

Fowler gave me one of those inscrutable looks of his. I hate inscrutable looks. "Well, stop it. This investigation is none of your concern. Amateurs mess things up for the professionals."

He gave me another inscrutable look. That probably intimidated some people. "There's nothing illegal about me talking to people I know. Are you tracking down everybody who's been gossiping about Brett Holmes?"

"You're not gossiping. You're investigating Holmes. That's my job."

It *was* his job, but I wasn't happy leaving him to it. "I've got good reasons to want to know more about Brett Holmes and his activities around town. I'm under suspicion. People are whispering about me. I'm losing sales because local people think I might be a murderer. That won't stop until Brett's killer is found."

One corner of his mouth edged up in a smirk. It wasn't much better than his inscrutable look, and it was even more annoying. "They'll get over it. As soon as they have somebody else to gossip about."

"They may gossip about other people, but they won't stop gossiping about me. Or suspecting me. I can't sit around and let my reputation get trashed. I've got a business to run." I reined in my anger, which, after all, wasn't getting me anywhere. "Look, what if I pass on whatever I learn about Holmes? Would that satisfy you?"

He shook his head. "Nope."

"Sorry, then. That's the best I can do."

We stared at each other. I can glower with the best of them when I have the motivation.

After a long moment, he sighed. "All right, what have you learned?"

I took a breath trying to put what I knew into some kind of order. "Brett was a pickup artist who went after any woman he came across, including fellow employees. He had a relationship with Evelyn Davidson, but they broke up, probably over his cheating. He had another relationship for a while with a young waitress named Carrie at High Country. They broke up, and she quit. The other cooks at High Country thought he was a phony, and they didn't want to put up with his crap. He was involved in a mentoring program at the high school, but he got bounced for some reason. He worked for a restaurant called Solo in Denver, and I'm going to try to find out why he left because I know people who work there."

I paused to catch my breath.

Fowler smirked again. "You've been busy."

I gritted my teeth. "Did you know all of that?"

"Some of it."

"So I've added to your investigation?"

He gave me another long look. "Are you telling people you're working for the police?"

"No. I'm just talking to people. I told them I needed to know more about Brett because some people thought I'd killed him."

"Make sure you don't misrepresent yourself." He pushed himself to his feet. "For what it's worth, I don't consider you a suspect."

"Could you publish that in the *Shavano County Sun?*"

"Nope." He touched two fingers to the brim of his Stetson. "See you around."

"Right." I went back to the booth to relieve Dolce.

Nate showed up around noon with a paper cup and a spoon. "I did chili again today. I've been working on dishes for the Best in Shavano competition, so I didn't have time to do anything more adventurous."

"I love your chili," I said, quite truthfully.

"What if I come over around six this evening and fix dinner? I want to try out a couple of recipes for the contest. Will that work?"

My heart promptly did a little flip. "Sure."

"Great. See you then."

I took a breath to calm my nerves. "See you."

I wasn't sure why I was so nervous. I wanted Nate to come over, to explore whatever was happening between us. But I hadn't quite moved beyond that to knowing what else I wanted. What if we didn't work? What if I blew it? What if I couldn't remember how to

190

have a normal relationship with anybody, even a great guy like Nate?

If you don't try, you'll never know.

Which was the sensible way to look at it. Why was it so hard to do?

By two, all the customers had given up for the day, and most of the vendors had already packed it in. The rain was still falling off and on, and there were some spectacular rainbows down the valley. I packed the booth away, ready to spread it out to dry once we got home. As I loaded the last set of poles into the truck, I saw Annabelle and Dorothy Dorsey pulling a wagon loaded with the poles from their booth and cases of their pickles. "How was business?" I asked.

Annabelle shrugged. "It's been better. I think I gave away more samples than I sold."

"Same here. How's your summer going, Dorothy?"

Dorothy stopped, half-turning to look at me over her shoulder. It was the most hate-filled glance I think I'd ever gotten from anyone.

What the hell?

"Dorothy," Annabelle snapped. "Roxy asked you a question."

Dorothy gave her mother a different searing glance, then turned toward the parking lot and took off at a run. Annabelle glared after her. "God save me from teenagers," she muttered, then turned to me. "Sorry about that. She's in a phase."

I thought she was in more than that, but what did I know about teenage girls? It had been a while since I'd been one myself. "No problem."

"See you next week." Annabelle turned toward the parking lot herself, dragging the wagon behind her.

I went on loading the truck so I could head toward home and my dinner with Nate. At least the experience with Dorothy had given me something else to think about. Was she another person who believed I'd killed Brett Holmes? Why should she care? Was she some kind of disinterested seeker of justice, outraged at my escape? Somehow I didn't think so. Far more likely she was upset about something else I'd done.

Maybe she had a crush on Nate. He was certainly the type to inspire crushes among the young and impressionable. Hell, he was the type to inspire crushes among the not so young and much less impressionable, judging from the way my own heart sped up whenever he walked up to the booth. And she'd probably seen us together around the market.

Or maybe it had nothing to do with Nate. Maybe she wanted to work at my booth again and make some money, and she was upset that I hadn't asked her. Of course after the way she'd snarled at me, I wasn't likely to ask her to work for me again.

I pulled the cover over the truck bed and climbed into the driver's seat. I had more important things to worry about than Dorothy and her grudges.

I made a little more jam that afternoon. The first crop of apricots had come in, and I'd bought a couple of flats from Peterson's Orchards down the road. I figured I'd start with straight apricot jam and then do the exotic stuff like apricot tarragon preserves later in the summer when I had more fruit to play with.

Besides, doing straight apricot jam didn't require a lot of thought, and my brain was decidedly elsewhere that afternoon. I kept telling myself that Nate might just be coming over to try out some possible Best In Shavano dishes without considering anything else, but even I didn't believe that. We were approaching a point where I'd need to make a decision, but I wasn't ready yet.

How much longer would Nate put up with me dithering around? I probably needed to take the plunge and either go to the next level with him or let him go off to find someone else. Someone who didn't come complete with a set of hang-ups.

Unfortunately, I wasn't ready to commit to either option. At least not entirely ready. Sort of ready, though.

Geez, you really are *a wimp.*

I was, and I hated that I was. But I was also waiting for something, a special kind of *ping* in my head that would mean I was absolutely ready to move forward. It made no sense to be thinking that way, and it marked me as an idiot, but there it was. I needed some kind of sign from above before I was ready to go all the way.

Sue me.

At six, Nate knocked on my front door before he let himself in. I was cleaning up the kitchen, making sure there was no lingering stickiness anywhere that would get in his way. "Hi," I called. "I'm in here."

"Where's Herman?" He set a couple of tote bags onto my counter, then began lifting out jars and packages.

"He's up at the main house with Uncle Mike." Where he would be out from under our feet and unlikely to be overwhelmed with protective feelings.

Nate went on unloading. "I've got the ingredients for dinner, but I was hoping you could help me out with the dessert."

"Sure. What are you making?"

"We'll get to that later." He grinned at me, that same

golden grin that made my knees slightly weak. *Wimp.*

"I decided to go with the pork chops in apricot sauce because it was something we could actually serve at the café, assuming Bobby would ever agree to it. I mean, we do pork chops regularly, so I wouldn't have to fight as hard as I would for duck or lamb." He glanced around the kitchen. "Sauté pan?"

"On the rack," I pointed to the pan rack near the stove. "Did you go ahead with the farmers market specials at the café?"

"Yeah, for what it's worth. I've been keeping it small, and they sell out regularly. But Bobby always looks at them like they contain plutonium."

"He'll come around. People like the market. And we've got more adventurous eaters around here than we used to." Although they still shied away from my pepper peach. But I was gaining on them.

Nate pulled a jar of my apricot preserves out of his sack. "It's a simple sauce, but it's got a little kick." He lifted out some greens and a couple of ripe tomatoes, amazingly ripe for June.

"Where did those come from?"

"Aram Pergosian's greenhouse. I don't know how he does it, but his tomatoes taste ripe way earlier than anybody else's."

"You're getting to know all the right people at the market. Aram is a wizard with vegetables. I'm just glad he hasn't gone into fruit or we'd be in real trouble."

Nate washed his hands in my sink, then turned toward the stove. "Okay, let's do this."

Dinner was sensational, but I'd figured it would be. The apricot sauce had just a hint of chili, along with a splash of white wine and a touch of tarragon. It made the pork chops taste simultaneously rich and faintly exotic. The tomatoes and salad greens were dressed with a champagne vinaigrette, and we drank the rest of the wine he'd used with the sauce. All in all, I was a very happy diner.

I slid back in my chair, dabbing my lips with my napkin. "That was terrific. I can't imagine anybody doing anything better at Best in Shavano."

"Thanks. I'm pretty happy with it, but Spence is entering, too. And he's doing lamb since High Country has lamb on the menu. Here's hoping he doesn't outclass us."

"Pork chops can be classy," I said loyally. "These certainly qualify."

He rested his elbows on the table, giving me a searching look. "About dessert."

"Okay." I leaned forward to match his posture. "What about it?"

"I need some jam, but maybe something more than regular jam. In the end, the jam's going to count for a lot in the recipe. I'm making crepes using whole wheat flour from a mill in Saguache. I want to do a filling with your jam. What do you suggest?"

I bit my lip, running through my inventory in my mind. I had a little of the strawberry basil around, and it was more than ordinary. In a couple of weeks, I'd have apricot with sherry, but he probably wouldn't want to use apricot jam with his dessert when he was already using it in his main dish.

And then, just like that, I knew just what he needed. "Hang on." I pushed to my feet. "I've got to make sure I have enough of this left."

I usually make a few jars of rose petal jam in late

summer when the mountain roses are blooming. I use roses from the bushes that grow around the fence at the main house. I don't know who planted them, since neither Uncle Mike nor my dad were the type to plant flowers. Maybe they came with the place. Anyway, these bushes have small, open flowers, sort of like wild roses. The petals come off easily, and I can usually collect enough for about a dozen jars of jam without totally denuding the plants. But there's never enough to sell. I give a few of them away at Christmas. Then I hoard them through the winter because they taste like summer. It's lovely on a snowy day to spread a few rose petals on your toast.

I went to the pantry, crossing my fingers that I had a couple of jars left. And I did. Exactly two jars, in fact.

I brought them to the table, setting them in front of Nate. "These aren't for sale, but maybe that's not a problem. They're definitely mine."

He picked up one of the jars, holding it to the light almost reverently. "Rose petal jam. I've never heard of it. Rose hip jelly, sure. But rose petals?"

"Yep. Rose hips have seeds, which makes them a pain in the ass to work with. You have to strain the liquid after you boil down the hips and mash them, and that means using many layers of cheesecloth and letting the stuff sit for an hour or so. With the petals, you just boil them. No straining allowed. And I think they taste like flowers, although not everyone agrees."

Nate pushed himself up from the table. "Let's try it. I really want to see how this comes out. This is great." He flashed me a quick grin that sent a shiver down my spine.

Oh, my. Oh, my, my, my.

Nate whipped up the crepe batter, then found a small omelet pan on the rack that would work. He melted butter, added it to the batter, then poured a ladleful into the pan, rotating it slightly to make sure the bottom was evenly covered. A few moments later he used a fork to turn the crepe. "Once upon a time, I flipped my crepes, but I'm older and wiser now. Plus I don't want to waste the flour."

"Okay, I'll take it on faith that you could flip them if you wanted to."

He slid the first crepe out on a plate. "This is where Herman would come in handy. First crepe usually goes to the dog."

"That crepe looks way too good for Herman. Besides, I'm trying to keep him from developing a taste for fine cooking."

Nate poured another ladle of batter into the pan, rotating it again. "I'll make four or five of these. That should be enough for the two of us."

"Absolutely."

When he'd made five crepes, Nate took the pan off the heat and reached for the jam. I took a quick sniff as he screwed off the top. Flowers. Just like always. He spread a couple of teaspoons of jam around the crepe, then started to flip the side across.

"Wait," I said and turned to the refrigerator. I had a small carton of Corona's crème fraiche left, also a demitasse spoon. I dipped a quick squiggle of crème fraiche across the top of the rose petal jam.

"Terrific." Nate extended the folded crepe toward me. "Here. Have a bite. Tell me what you think."

I took a quick bite and closed my eyes. It was…amazing. Sweet and tart and warm and cool and everything you want in a light dessert. And there was the added bonus of Nate's hand holding the crepe, brushing my lips as I bit. "Oh, gosh," I murmured.

Nate took a bite of the same crepe, then closed his eyes, too. "Yes. Oh, yes."

And just like that, it happened. I heard the *ping* in my mind that I'd been waiting for, almost like a chime being played. The combination of sublime taste and Nate had pushed me over the edge. And I knew. Being with Nate was absolutely, positively what I needed to do.

I blew out a long breath and looked up at him.

He was watching me, too. After a moment, he extended his hand to me.

I took it.

He leaned in. So did I. And then things got interesting.

Chapter 20

Breakfast was great. Better than great, actually. Of course Nate had stayed over. I'd thought he might choose to return to his place, but I was really glad he hadn't.

We had the rest of the crepes, this time with honey and yogurt because we didn't want to use up the rose petal jam before the contest. Nate said he'd take it with him and keep it well hidden where Coco wouldn't find it.

I suppose I should say something about the night before. Without going into details, I can say I had definitely turned a corner. Among other things.

Nate kept touching me while we cooked and ate. Little touches, like brushing my hair away from my face or running his hand down my arm when I passed him the honey. It was like he couldn't get enough of touching. And neither could I.

We'd gotten up early because Nate had to go to work eventually. But the café did a midday brunch rather than breakfast on Sunday, so he didn't have to get there until nine or so. That was just as well since I didn't think I could bear to let him go too early.

We were both still at the *I'm pretty sure this has never happened to me before* stage.

Uncle Mike showed up at my door around eight, bringing Herman for his breakfast. That could have been awkward except Uncle Mike had always been really eager for me to get back into the social scene. Clearly I was heading there with a vengeance.

His eyes widened slightly when he saw Nate at the breakfast table in his unbuttoned shirt and bare feet. Herman padded over to sniff at him, then turned to me, questioning. He wasn't used to seeing strange men first thing in the morning, but then neither was I.

"I'll get your breakfast in a minute," I said, trying to sound perfectly normal. It wasn't a normal situation, and we all knew it. But I didn't see any point in making it more abnormal than we had to. "Have you had any breakfast, Uncle Mike?"

Uncle Mike shrugged. "Cereal and toast." He looked longingly at the crepes we were eating. "Got any more of those?"

"Sure. By the stove. Help yourself. Nate made them."

"Oh." He gave Nate a neutral look. Nate gave him a smile, and Uncle Mike smiled back. *Okay, first crisis averted.*

After that we all ate crepes in companionable silence. Apparently Nate had passed some kind of test with Uncle Mike, although I wasn't sure what it had consisted of.

Nate left a few minutes later, after we'd made a date for that night after the café got done serving brunch. They were closed Monday, which opened up a lot of interesting possibilities.

Uncle Mike sat at my kitchen table, chewing crepes as Nate closed the door behind him. "Umm…" he began a moment later.

"You don't have to say anything. I know you're concerned, but everything is okay. You don't need to worry."

"I wasn't going to." He gave me a small smile. "Did he make you dinner?"

"It was terrific. He made the crepes for dessert. We used the rose petal jam, and I gave him the last two jars."

"Well, that's okay then." Uncle Mike got up and carried his plate to the sink where he washed it carefully. "Thanks for breakfast."

"You're welcome."

"Come on, Herman." He patted his leg, and Herman lumbered to his feet.

"You're taking him to the main house?"

"You won't want him around tonight." He gave me a quick nod and ambled out the door, followed by our mutual dog.

I took a while to finish my coffee, ruminating about life and sex and families. Having Uncle Mike's approval wasn't a necessary requirement for my boyfriends, but it didn't hurt.

I decided I should probably make dinner for Nate tonight, which might mean going into town to hit City Market. At the moment, though, I enjoyed the fact that I was feeling a lot closer to "normal" again than I had for a couple of years. I'd never wanted my Denver experience to define my life, and maybe this was the final step to making sure it didn't.

Susa called me while I was cutting up apricots. "Well?"

I considered saying *Well, what?* But that would just be annoying. "It was fine. Very nice."

That was putting it mildly, but I didn't feel like getting into specifics right then.

"*Fine?*" Susa exploded. "It was *fine? Nice?* Good

grief!"

"It was good, Sus. Really good. I'm happy."

There was a pause on Susa's end. Then she sighed. "Hallelujah, then. Remind me to give Nate Robicheaux a big hug the next time I see him."

"Nope. I won't be doing that. But you can pat him on the shoulder."

Susa chuckled. "Good enough. I don't blame you. What else is new?"

"What else?" I paused, guiltily. I hadn't bothered to write up my conversation with Spencer or the one with Fowler, which probably needed to be added to our records.

"You didn't write stuff up, did you?" Susa sounded more resigned than annoyed.

"No, but I will. I had a conversation with Spencer Carroll. He mostly talked about what Brett was like in the kitchen. No good, according to Spence. The other cooks all hated him."

"What a surprise."

"Oh, he also had a little more to say about the thing at the high school. Apparently Brett got bounced from the mentorship program." I settled into my chair with another cup of coffee.

"How the hell can you get bounced from the mentorship program? I've been trying to get out of it for a year, but Dolores won't let me go."

"Who's Dolores?"

"Dolores Cantu. The principal. She's the one who recruited me as a mentor. Believe me, once you're in, you never get out. Or anyway, that's what I thought."

I took another sip of my coffee. "I didn't know you were in that program. Did you run into Brett?"

"That isn't the way the program works. You meet with the kid you're mentoring a couple of times a month at the school. You have a project you work on together. I met my student in the school computer lab because that's where we were working. I have no idea where Holmes was."

"Probably in the school kitchen. Or the home ec room. Do they still teach home ec?"

"No idea. It wasn't one of my interests."

It actually hadn't been one of mine either, but I seemed to remember there was a room with several stoves and sinks. "Could I go with you to talk to the principal?"

"I guess so. You realize she'll probably ask you to join the program."

Somehow I doubted that, given my current reputation. "I doubt there'd be any student interested in jam-making as a profession."

"It would probably be someone interested in professional cooking or small business management, but who knows? I guess this means I'll have to call Dolores, which means I'll have to have a mentor meeting sometime this week. I'll let you know when she can talk to us. Meanwhile, write up your notes."

"I will. I promise."

It was only after we'd hung up that I realized I hadn't told Susa about Fowler. Just as well. There was nothing she could have done about it. Except maybe avoid him in case he'd heard she was asking questions, too.

I got the apricots on to boil, then I grabbed my phone to check my contacts. One of my roommates in Denver, Lauren, had worked at Solo for a while until she'd quit to take a better job at another restaurant. I hadn't talked to her much since I'd left, but we'd been friendly. I figured if I wanted the lowdown on Brett, Lauren would be a good place to start, assuming the two of them had overlapped at Solo.

She picked up after a couple of rings. "Yeah. Who's this?"

I checked the time a little guiltily. If Lauren had worked the Saturday night dinner shift, she might have wanted to sleep late on Sunday. "Hey, Lauren. It's Roxy Constantine."

There was a brief pause on the other end. "Wow, Roxy. Long time. How ya doin'?"

Fortunately, she sounded more friendly than annoyed. "I'm fine. Got a jam and jelly business going here in Shavano called Luscious Delights."

"No shit? That's great. You selling anywhere in Denver?"

I had a momentary pinch of guilt—I really needed to expand my distribution, just like I'd discussed with Uncle Mike when I thought I might be on *Sweet Thing*. "Not yet. Right now I'm just selling here in town and in a couple of shops in Salida."

"I'll keep an eye out for it. What else is new?"

We spent a few minutes talking about mutual friends and the food business before I got down to my real reason for calling. "I wanted to ask you—when you worked at Solo, did you know a guy named Brett Holmes?"

"Oh, the asshole? Yeah, I knew him. They hired him on just before I left."

"Was he head chef?" Not that it made any difference as to why Brett had been killed, but I was curious to know if he'd been telling the truth about that.

"No way—he was on the line. Just like the rest of us. Of course he ended up at Shorty's Italian, and they might have been dumb enough to put him in charge some of the time. Why? Is he up there where you are now?"

I paused, trying to figure out the right way to say it. But there wasn't any *right* way. "He was head chef at a restaurant up here, High Country, but he was killed last week. Someone murdered him at the restaurant where he was working."

"Holy crap," Lauren murmured. "He was an asshole, but I didn't want anything like that to happen to him."

"No," I agreed. "Even assholes deserve to live. But there are some people up here who seem to think I was involved in his death. Not the cops, but other people. There's some gossip around town. And I'm worried it may affect my business."

"Yeah, I can see how that might put a crimp in your sales. So you're trying to find any other people who might have wanted to kill him?"

"Something like that."

"Well, there's always the guy who owns Solo, Harry Moritz."

"His former boss? Why would he want to kill Brett?" I settled a little deeper into my chair.

"A couple of reasons. We can both agree, Brett wasn't the brightest bulb on the tree, right?"

"Right."

"He also had a pretty inflated idea of his own attractiveness. He was always coming on to all the women in the kitchen, including me, believe it or not. I told him I was a lesbian, but that didn't stop him. He kept saying I just needed to be with a 'real man.' "

I could almost hear the quotation marks in Lauren's voice. "That's genuinely creepy."

"Agreed. But that was the kind of guy he was." She blew out a long breath. "Anyway, he was convinced he was God's gift to women—all women, regardless of age."

"Uh oh," I murmured.

"*Uh oh* is right. He made a play for Moritz's seventeen-year-old daughter who worked in the front of the house. I never heard how far the whole thing actually went, but it was far enough that Moritz fired him. One of the guys I knew in the kitchen told me the daughter said she'd been raped, but I don't know that for a fact. I did hear Moritz actually beat Brett up pretty good and told him to get out of Denver. After he left Solo, Brett apparently talked some trash about Moritz's daughter, about how she'd come on to him and then lied to make him look bad. That pretty much finished him as far as Denver's concerned—Harry Moritz is a popular guy. I guess Shorty's got rid of him, too. My guess is that's when he started looking for something out of town. But that all happened after I left. So maybe he actually got a genuine offer based on his skills. Such as they were."

"Hah." I considered the implications of all this. Another person who absolutely hated Brett Holmes, with very good reason. Actually, more than one, assuming the daughter wasn't too traumatized to fight. Of course Moritz was in Denver, but Denver was only a couple of hours away. "What happened to the seventeen-year-old?"

"No idea. Like I said, that all happened after I left. But she wouldn't have had an easy time, what with rumors flying around about her character."

Something I knew only too well myself. "And Solo is still going?"

"Still going strong last I heard. Losing Brett didn't leave a dent."

That didn't necessarily mean that Harry Moritz didn't have time to come up to Shavano and clobber Brett, but maybe it was less likely. "Okay, thanks, Lauren."

"Keep in touch, okay? Denver always needs good women chefs."

"I'll do that. Come up to Shavano and have some mountain food sometime."

"I might. I just might."

I could hear the smile in her voice, and I was smiling myself when I hung up. I should have done a better job of keeping in contact with my Denver friends. Maybe it was time I did a little fence mending.

I sat down at my computer then and typed up all my notes for Susa. And, of course, as I did, I started to see connections. Which was probably why Susa wanted us both to do it in the first place. So much of Brett's life seemed to revolve around his relationships with women, which were uniformly lousy.

Did that mean a woman had killed him? Maybe. Women certainly had lots of reasons to resent him. But the fact that he'd been killed in his kitchen might indicate a professional connection.

His fellow cooks disliked him enough to dump a skillet full of mushrooms on his foot, which risked injuring him seriously at the very least. I didn't think Brett's obnoxious nature was enough to murder him for. But kitchens were high stress environments. Who knew what Brett could have done to piss someone off? Maybe that someone had stuck around after work to call him on it, and Brett had said or done something even worse. I could easily see one of the cooks being so furious that he'd hit him with whatever was handy, most likely a pan or a heavy implement.

If that's what had happened, it was an accident with lethal consequences. And whoever had done it would be horrorstricken but also eager to cover it up. Spencer Carroll hadn't seemed that temperamental, but I didn't know the other people in the kitchen. And even Spence might have his temperamental moments. Brett tended to bring out the worst in people.

I wondered if Nate knew any of the other people in the High Country kitchen. I couldn't think of any way I could meet them myself without diving into the off-duty cook scene, which I didn't want to do. I was happier staying out of bars like the one where we'd met Spence.

On the other hand, I could try to find Carrie, the waitress who'd had a relationship with Brett. Maybe Spence knew her last name, and if he did, I could check around and see if she was still working in Shavano. Good servers were always needed around Shavano, and she might well have found a job with another restaurant in the area. Preferably one where the head chef wasn't a jerk.

Now, however, I needed to think about dinner. I checked the freezer and found some stew. I had a bottle of red wine that would work. I wished I had some of the exquisite greens and tomatoes Nate had gotten from Aram Pergosian, but I didn't have time to go to his farm stand. Instead I found a half bag of Uncle Mike's arugula and some sliced strawberries I could sprinkle over it with a vinaigrette. None of it would be particularly gourmet, but it would mean Nate didn't have to cook. And for someone who'd spent two or three hours frying eggs, that had to be a major relief.

Nate arrived around five, carrying a paper sack. "I should have asked you what you wanted for dinner. We had some leftover pie, so I brought that. And I can do eggs. Trust me, when it comes to eggs, I'm in the groove." He paused to inhale. "Something smells delicious."

"It's stew I had in the freezer. And I made an exceedingly minor salad."

He grinned at me. "Exceedingly minor is fine. Stew and salad with pie for dessert. Works for me."

I grinned back. "Me, too." I pulled the wine out of the rack and handed it to him. "You open this, and I'll get the stew out of the oven."

"Deal." He grinned again, a lot more sultry this time.

And right then and there I decided to forget about Brett Holmes for the rest of the evening. There were more interesting things to think about.

Chapter 21

I succeeded in pushing Brett out of my mind for the rest of the evening, but I couldn't keep him away much longer than that. Susa called me the next morning while Nate was in the shower and I was getting eggs and ham for breakfast. I didn't know if we'd have Uncle Mike and Herman to feed, too, but there was enough for everybody.

"I talked to Dolores," Susa said. "She can meet us this afternoon after school, around four. And of course she wants to talk to you about joining the mentorship program."

Apparently Principal Cantu hadn't heard about my scandalous reputation. "That might be fun. At least it would get me out of the house and show everybody I'm an upright citizen."

"I doubt that anybody thinks that about me, but whatever. Now what the hell is this with Fowler?"

I heard Nate come into the room behind me. "Just what I wrote. He tracked me down at the market and told me to keep out of his investigation."

"He can't do that." Susa sounded outraged. "We have a right to ask questions, and people have a right to answer them if they want to. He can't limit our access to information any more than he could limit a reporter's."

Actually, I wasn't sure about the real legal limits we faced. There were probably laws against interfering with an investigation. "We reached a compromise. I told him everything we'd found out so far. But he didn't seem impressed."

"Well, impressed or not, he's got no right to stop us. He's probably used to having people back down when he gives them one of those intimidating looks of his. We won't back down, right?"

"Right." Although if Fowler leaned hard enough, we might have to. Susa's professional skills were essential to the town of Shavano—nobody would put up with Fowler bullying her. But my jam production fell into the luxury category. People might sympathize with me, but I doubted they'd go to the mat for my right to talk to Principal Cantu.

After promising to meet Susa at the high school at four, I hung up and turned around to find Nate watching me, eyes troubled. "You didn't tell me Fowler was after you."

"It wasn't a big thing. He tried to browbeat me into not talking to people, but I didn't want to be browbeaten. We compromised."

"Compromised how?"

"I'm telling him what I find out. He's telling me zilch."

Nate settled into a kitchen chair. "Did you ever consider this quest might be dangerous? Whoever killed Holmes is out there somewhere. If they think you're getting close, they might decide to do something about it."

My shoulders suddenly felt tight. "How would they find out?"

"The same way Fowler found out, I guess. If I was a murderer, I'd have my ear to the ground to keep track of any investigation."

"I don't know how Fowler found out. I guess somebody might have complained, but I don't think Bridget would have done that. Or Spence. I suppose Evelyn Davidson might, but I didn't talk to her. That was Susa. And I got the impression Evelyn was glad to talk. She wanted to vent to someone."

"Maybe Evelyn or Bridget or Spence told somebody in passing that they'd talked to you or Susa, and maybe that somebody told somebody else who told Fowler without knowing what they were telling him. I mean, there are lots of ways Fowler could have found out without it being a complaint." Nate poured himself a cup of coffee.

"Yeah, that's true. And I'm pretty much done with my investigating now. Susa and I are going to talk to the high school principal to see what Brett did to get kicked out of the mentorship program. But that's pretty much everything I had in mind, unless I can find that waitress who had a relationship with Brett and quit after they broke up."

"What's her name?"

"The waitress? Carrie."

Nate frowned. "That's all, just Carrie?"

"That's all Bridget remembered. I guess they don't do much with last names at High Country."

"I worked for a guy once who called all the waitresses Rose because that was the name of the last waitress he remembered. It's not always a great job."

"I guess I could check at some of the restaurants around town to see if they have a waitress named Carrie."

"Hell, just ask my mom." Nate took another

swallow of his coffee. "I swear she knows every waitress in town, where they're working and if they're likely to move on. Whenever somebody quits at the café, Mom's got a replacement lined up within a day."

"Okay, that would save me some time." Of course, talking to Madge after starting a relationship with her son might be a little charged, but maybe she was as eager for Nate to get into dating as Uncle Mike was for me. "What would you like for breakfast? I've got ham. And I could scramble some eggs."

Nate pushed himself to his feet. "No way. You made dinner. I make breakfast. Besides, eggs are my life. At least most mornings they are."

Uncle Mike and Herman wandered in a few minutes later as Nate was working on his first omelet. He made a couple more and slipped some ham to Herman when he thought I wasn't looking. That, of course, ensured Herman's lifelong devotion.

After we'd finished eating, Uncle Mike strolled off, leaving Herman with me. Just as well—Herm needed to get used to new people entering his life, particularly if Nate stuck around.

And I was beginning to think he might.

Nate stretched in his chair, luxuriating in the sunshine. "I could snooze in the sun today. What have you got on your plate?"

"Jam. As usual. I need to check the seals on the apricot preserves I put up yesterday. And I've got to make some more of my staples before the weekend."

"Can I help?"

I paused. I'd never had anyone help me make jam before. It was pretty much my deal. On the other hand, I still might hire an assistant, particularly if I could get my local business in shape. And Nate was the best cook I knew. "Sure. You can chop."

And he did. We were almost at the end of the strawberries by then, but I had a couple of flats. And I had some rhubarb, although we don't get much of it in Shavano. I figured I'd do some strawberry rhubarb jam since it always sold well.

Nate chopped up the rhubarb after I'd told him what I wanted. He was very precise, but that wasn't a surprise. If you tell a good chef you want one-inch chunks, one-inch chunks is what you'll get.

I got everything into jam kettles, then filled the canner with water and jars and set it on the other side of the stove. "How long?" Nate asked.

"Around fifteen minutes to cook, with stirring every few minutes. Another ten or twenty minutes in the canner to process."

"Ten or twenty minutes?" He gave me a slow smile.

"I have to be vigilant," I said quickly. "I can't get to it too late."

"You won't be too late."

"Ten minutes?" I raised an eyebrow. "Really?"

"Oh, lady, you have no idea how efficient I can be when motivated."

I didn't then, but I certainly did twenty minutes later.

After I'd gotten all the jam jars out on the cooling racks, we decided to head to Nate's place since Madge would probably be at her house on her day off. I'd follow him in my truck so that I could go on to the high school after I asked Madge if she knew anything about a woman named Carrie who'd worked at High Country.

I was a little nervous about talking to Madge since I figured she probably knew what was going on with Nate and me. After all, he lived above her garage. She probably had a pretty good idea of when he left and when he came home.

I didn't know if she'd approve or not. I just hoped we could still be friendly.

As it turned out, I shouldn't have worried. Madge was standing on her front porch as we walked up, with a grin almost as wide as Uncle Mike's had been. "Nathan, Roxy, come in, both of you. Would you like some coffee? And I've got some of Bianca's cinnamon rolls."

"I'd love some coffee. We had a big breakfast." I felt my cheeks flush. I hadn't meant to bring up the fact that Nate and I had eaten breakfast after spending the night together, but I'd done it straight out of the gate.

Madge didn't seem to notice. Or she didn't care. "Come on into the kitchen. You, too, Nathan."

I followed her through the house, a cozy Craftsman bungalow with lots of dark wood and a red brick fireplace in the living room. Her kitchen stretched the width of the house and had the kind of appliances I'd expect to see in a chef's house. I wondered if Nate's dad had done all the cooking when he was alive. Madge was clearly at home there now.

"Come on, sit down." She gestured toward a large golden oak table in a breakfast nook. I grabbed a captain's chair and sat opposite her with my coffee mug, while Nate dropped into a chair nearer the windows. "Now," Madge said, "tell me what's up."

"I'm trying to find some information about Brett Holmes, the chef who was killed last week." I'd decided on the way there to be direct. I couldn't have thought of a way to tiptoe into the subject anyway.

Madge's forehead furrowed. "Why would you want

to do that?"

"Because some people in town think that I killed him. I didn't," I added hastily.

"Of course you didn't." Madge sounded as outraged as Susa had. "What kind of people would think something like that?"

"Some of them are women who had relationships with him, like Evelyn Davidson."

"Oh, like that woman at the Colorado crafters store, Janet or Janice, something like that?"

"Janet Leonhart?" I managed to keep my jaw from dropping. Brett had certainly gotten around.

"That's the one. I don't know that they had what you'd call a relationship, but I certainly saw them together a few times."

"She's one of the ones who thinks I killed Brett. She wasn't interested in putting my jam out for sale at the store." And now I understood why.

"Well, it's her loss. I don't imagine that's cut into your sales that much."

"Not yet. But I've lost some local customers. Enough that I'm a little worried."

"Roxy's just talking to people she knows," Nate explained. "And she's passing her information on to Chief Fowler." He gave me a looked that reminded me he really wanted that statement to be true.

I'd pass anything on to Fowler I thought would be of use in his investigation, but I wasn't promising to give him everything I found out.

"So how can I help?" Madge asked. "I don't think I ever talked to Brett Holmes, but I knew who he was. Most people in the restaurant business around here know each other."

"I'm interested in a waitress who used to work at High Country. She and Brett dated, but then he broke up with her, and she quit. I'd like to talk to her."

"I know some of the waitresses who work over there. What was her name?"

"I've only got a first name. Carrie."

"Oh." Madge paused for a long moment, then sighed. "Carrie Bremer, probably. I don't know how Denny could justify hiring that child. She was much too inexperienced to work in a fine dining joint like High Country. But I think he was scrambling to fill some openings, and she showed up at his door."

"You knew her?"

"I knew her mama, Stacy Bremer. She waited tables, too. At that Italian place near the highway. I think Carrie was her only chick. Stacy was holding down a couple of jobs to pay for Carrie's school expenses."

I felt a little shiver work its way down my backbone. The way Madge used past tense when she talked about Carrie didn't sound good.

"Is she still here in town?"

"Carrie?" Madge shook her head. "She took a job in one of the ski towns, I'm not sure which. Maybe Winter Park. Or Breckenridge. She left after Brett Holmes broke her heart. Or anyway, that's what Stacy said."

"Broke her heart?" Nate raised an eyebrow.

I had to agree with him. I had a hard time believing anybody could get a broken heart over Brett. Most of us would be more likely to sigh in relief.

"She was just a child when she worked there, Nathan. Just a little over seventeen."

"Seventeen?" Nate frowned. "Why the hell would they hire a seventeen-year-old at High Country? She wouldn't even be able to bring drinks to the table."

"Well, like I said, Denny was scrambling. And Carrie really was a conscientious little thing. A very hard worker. Still, she would probably have been better off working for us than for Denny."

"Her mom and dad didn't care?"

"Stacy's divorced, and I never heard anything about her husband. I assume he's long gone. And from Stacy's point of view, Carrie was making more money than she was. The tips are a lot better at High Country. She probably thought the job was good for her."

"So Brett was dating someone under age?" This was the second seventeen-year-old Brett had taken up with, counting the one in Denver. I only hoped the relationship had been better than the one he'd had with Harry Moritz's daughter.

"Yes, he was. Stacy worked long hours. She couldn't really ride herd on Carrie. And besides, the child would probably have resented her mother trying to tell her who to date. But a seventeen-year-old probably wouldn't have been able to see through Brett Holmes as easily as some of the other women around town." Madge took a sip of her coffee. "From what I heard, I don't think Denny liked it much. He may have told Brett to knock it off."

"And Brett did?" Brett had never struck me as the type to obey orders.

"Perhaps he was already tired of her." Madge looked like her coffee tasted bitter all of a sudden. "Maybe it fit his own inclinations."

"That sounds like Brett. He could blame Denny and duck out of a relationship he wanted to duck out of." And Denny hadn't beaten him up the way Harry Moritz had.

At least I didn't think he had.

Unless Denny had given him that skull fracture.

"Brett and Denny had a lot of run-ins over things like the menu at High Country," Madge mused. "We talked about it at the Merchants' Association meeting one time, Denny and I."

"Talked about what?" Nate asked. "Brett's love life?"

Madge shook her head. "Denny wanted some advice about managing a chef. I didn't really have any to offer him because our kitchen has always been family-run. And of course you boys do exactly as I ask whenever I ask it." She gave him an angelic smile, and Nate snickered.

"Was he thinking of firing Brett?"

Madge turned to me. "I don't know that he could fire Brett, unless he cleared it with Ethan O'Reilly first."

Nate frowned. "Who's that?"

"Ethan O'Reilly owns High Country, along with a couple of restaurants in Breckinridge. He hired Brett. Denny's the manager, and he hired everyone else. In my opinion, that shows Denny knows a lot more about managing a restaurant than Ethan does. But Ethan's the one with the money."

"So Denny didn't like him but couldn't get rid of him," I said slowly.

Madge shook her head. "Don't make more out of it than it was. A lot of managers are in that position. But Ethan listens to Denny, and if Brett had become a real problem, my guess is Ethan would have fired him without a second thought."

"So dating kids wasn't a problem?" Nate still looked a little annoyed.

"Nathan, you know as well as I do it's not our business to manage our employees' personal lives," Madge said flatly. "As long as those personal lives don't impact the work. From what I heard, Denny did tell Brett to leave Carrie alone. On the other hand, I'd guess Brett wouldn't have stopped dating Carrie if he hadn't wanted to. So maybe it was just a fling for him, and poor Carrie got in over her head."

I gritted my teeth. Brett seemed to have had a lot of "flings" around town and left a lot of women unhappy. I still considered him a creep, but maybe if he'd appealed to me, I'd have been more sympathetic.

Of course if he'd appealed to me, I might not have had a relationship with Nate. And that really would have broken my heart.

"Thanks, Madge," I said.

"Did I help at all? I could ask around at the next Merchants' Association meeting, but I don't know how Denny would feel about that. He's trying hard to make people forget about Brett being murdered in his kitchen. That's the kind of thing that makes customers decide to eat elsewhere."

I could see their point. "You confirmed what I already knew. He was a womanizer, and his ethics weren't sterling."

"No, they definitely weren't. Still, that's true of a lot of chefs. And nobody fires them, more's the pity. I'm just glad I'm related to two wonderful chefs who have the café running better than it has for a long while." She beamed at Nate, and he gave her a slightly half-hearted smile in return.

I figured he was thinking about Bobby, who was a lot more *my way or the highway* than you'd expect from a family member.

Still, that was better than working with a sleaze who treated women as if they were disposable. On reflection, I wasn't surprised that someone had lost it with Brett. I was only surprised that they'd apparently gotten away with it.

Chapter 22

I drove to the high school at four, parking in one of the side lots where the faculty parked. I was surprised at how many cars were still around. Apparently, summer school was in full swing. I didn't envy the teachers trying to hold students' attention when the sun was warm and the mountains were shining blue against the horizon.

Susa climbed out of her truck as soon as I parked, her lips curving into a Cheshire Cat smile. "You have a nice Sunday?"

"I had a lovely Sunday. And a very nice Monday, too." *And no, Sus, I'm not going to fill in any details.*

Susa gave me a mock pout. "Fine. Don't tell me. I'll probably imagine something a lot hotter."

Doubtful. Definitely doubtful.

She turned toward the main high school building, a granite pile constructed in the sixties that we'd actually attended ourselves back in the day. They'd added on a new wing five years ago that looked a little more contemporary, but the overall style was institutional bleak.

Susa glanced up, shaking her head. "You'd think they'd try to make schools look like places kids might want to go."

We pushed the main door open and walked down the hall toward the central office. Nothing much had changed about the interior either, but at least somebody had posted some cheery wall decorations that covered up the institutional beige.

We stepped through the door to the principal's office. "Hey, Susa," someone called. "Right on time."

The woman who came forward to greet us wasn't as tall as I am, not surprisingly, but she was taller than Susa by a few inches. Her dark hair was cut in a swinging chin-length bob, and she wore a blue dress shirt and jeans. And sneakers.

She was about as far from the high school principal of our school days as I was from Betty Crocker. "You must be Roxy Constantine." She extended her hand. "I'm Dolores Cantu."

"Hi, Dolores," I said, shaking her hand, "nice to meet you."

"I'm so glad you're interested in our mentorship program. I'm sure you'll love it."

Susa rolled her eyes behind Dolores's back, but I was willing to start with a pitch for the program before we worked our way into just what Brett Holmes had done to get kicked out of it. "Well, I'm not sure most high school students would be interested in making jam, but I'll be glad to work with anyone who's willing."

"Your jam is wonderful," Dolores enthused. "I always buy the apricot tarragon. You'll be making more of that this summer won't you?"

"Assuming we get a good apricot crop in this year."

"Love it, just love it. Come on into my office, and I'll give you some information on the program. We can probably get you started this fall—we don't really do much with mentors in the summer."

"Except for a lucky few like me," Susa murmured.

Delores marched purposefully toward her office

door as Susa and I fell in line behind her. The woman had a great command voice.

We had a little more conversation about the program once we were sitting in her office, how to list my interests (emphasizing cooking in general rather than jam in particular) and other topics I might talk to students about. Apparently, a lot of students were interested in how to start a small business, everything from homemade wind chimes to fruit leather. I could expect loads of questions about what Dolores generously referred to as my "area of expertise."

I began to relax as I talked to her. It actually sounded like fun—passing on what I'd learned to people who might be really interested. Maybe getting a chance to help someone realize her dreams. Or maybe help someone avoid a few nightmares.

Which brought us to our original mission. I glanced at Susa, who was staring out the window at a soccer game in progress.

"Maybe Susa can fill you in on her experiences," Dolores said dryly.

Susa gave her a flat smile. "My experiences aren't likely to make her want to sign up, considering the number of potential hackers I've had to warn away from a life of crime. But maybe cooks are more law-abiding than nerds."

"Not necessarily," I muttered.

"Right." Susa rested her hands on the edge of the desk. "We had other reasons for coming today, Dolores, along with getting Roxy signed up. We're trying to get some information on Brett Holmes. I've heard he had trouble here, in the mentorship program. I don't know if you'd be comfortable talking about it, but we'd be grateful for anything you could tell us."

Dolores frowned, glancing back and forth between us. "Well, first of all I need to know why you're asking. Why should you be looking for information about Brett Holmes?"

I blew out a breath. Every time I explained our project it sounded a little more farfetched. But it was what it was. "Brett and I had a couple of run-ins before he was killed. There's a lot of gossip flying around that I had something to do with his death. It's not true, but I've noticed local people avoiding me. I'm afraid it'll affect my sales if I don't do something about it."

Dolores was still frowning. "But the police are investigating, aren't they? Why not just wait for them to find the murderer? They're more experienced in this kind of thing than you are, surely."

"They are—both more experienced and carrying out an investigation. But I can't just do nothing. I mean, I know that's the logical thing to do. But I'm tired of having people cross the street when they see me coming. And I know the people in this town—Chief Fowler may not."

Dolores sighed, leaning back in her chair. "I suppose if I were in your place I'd feel similar. It's always hard when you feel like nothing's happening and it's something that affects you directly. Even harder when you're a 'take charge' type." Dolores struck me as the "take charge" type herself.

"So can you talk to us about Holmes?" Susa asked. "Or is it protected by mentor-principal privilege or something?"

Dolores shrugged. "Weirdly enough, I think the fact that Holmes is dead makes it easier for me to talk about him. If he was alive, I'd worry about violating his rights, and maybe getting sued for talking. But I don't think that's a concern anymore."

"Probably not. Has Chief Fowler been here to talk to you about him?"

She shook her head. "I don't really expect him to. Not many people knew that Brett Holmes was part of the mentorship program, and he wasn't part of it for long. By the way, how did you hear about that?"

"He talked about being a mentor in the kitchen at High Country, bragged about it. One of the cooks told me. But I don't think they ever heard why he got kicked out. Assuming that's what happened."

Dolores grimaced. "Yeah, that's what happened. A first for the program. I usually have more trouble keeping mentors from semester to semester than getting rid of them."

Susa looked faintly guilty, but Dolores ignored her. "He came in originally to do some of the things we've been talking about—mentoring students who wanted to be professional cooks. There's a lot of interest now that so many chefs are on television. As a career choice, it's a lot more glamorous than it used to be."

I snorted. Lots of people believe being a professional chef is a prestigious job, but I'd been in enough professional kitchens to know that was a crock. "Did he get a lot of students who wanted to work with him?"

"Yes, at first." Dolores stared up at the ceiling. "We had around ten students who applied, but that's far too many for one person. I advised him to look at the applications and choose a couple he thought he could work with. Then the others could reapply later."

"And did he?"

"Oh, yes. He even interviewed a few of the students himself. And he ended up choosing two. Both girls."

Uh oh. It wasn't like I hadn't had a feeling this would be where we ended up, but it was still unsettling. "How did that go?"

"At first it seemed fine. The two girls both worked with him. We have a classroom with cooking facilities for our family and consumer sciences classes, and they used that. They both seemed to be having a good time. And then one of them dropped out of the mentorship."

"Is that common?" I asked. "Students giving up?"

Dolores shook her head. "The students who are in the program all want to be there. They're very motivated. We've had a few dropouts, usually because of something outside the program, like family or health problems. But most students stick it out."

"Did the student who dropped give you a reason?"

Dolores stared down at her hands. "Yes and no. She said she didn't have time to be in the program and her parents wanted her to drop it."

"And you didn't believe her?"

"I wanted to. I really wanted to. Because at some level I wasn't sure I wanted to discover what the real reason was. I had some suspicions, and some fears. But in the end I did try to find out. That's my job, and I can't sidestep it."

"Did she tell you?" I was almost as afraid to hear as Dolores had been.

"Not exactly. She danced around the reason. She didn't have time. She wasn't getting as much out of it as she thought she would. And then finally she said she felt uncomfortable."

Oh, crap. "Brett made her feel uncomfortable?"

"That's what it amounted to, but she didn't explain it. Just said that she felt uncomfortable and didn't think she was getting much out of the experience."

"Did you talk to the other girl? Did she give you any more information?" Susa asked.

"Oh yeah, right away. I had a heavy load of suspicions by then and nothing concrete, so I needed to make sure she was okay."

"Was she?" I really hoped so.

"Apparently. She wouldn't say anything against Brett Holmes. She argued Dolce had just been too uptight. That she didn't understand what Holmes was trying to teach them."

My shoulders went rigid. "Dolce? Dolce McCray?"

Dolores stared at me for a long moment. "I shouldn't have let that slip. Believe me, I didn't mean to. The students' identity is absolutely confidential, particularly in a case like this. You understand?"

I nodded slowly. I understood. But maybe I could find a way to ask Carmen and Donnie about Brett. Or Dolce, when she worked at the market with me next week.

Dolores rubbed her eyes, and I got the feeling she was regretting ever having agreed to talk to us.

"What happened to the other girl?" Susa was gripping the arms of her chair so tightly her knuckles were white.

"I'm not entirely sure," Dolores said slowly. "After…the first girl…dropped out, I kept a much closer watch on Holmes and his mentee than I had with any of the other groups. But I couldn't always be there. I had other duties I had to attend to. I tried to get the consumer science teacher to stick around, and she was there at least part of the time, but Holmes turned out to be very good at slipping away from observation. Then the student's mother complained."

"About what?"

"Holmes took the student to his restaurant without any prior notice. He told her he wanted to show her what a real professional kitchen was like. The mother wasn't sure anything had happened, but she didn't trust Holmes, and she didn't like the fact that he'd left the school grounds. So she told me she was pulling her daughter out of the program. That effectively ended Holmes's mentorship since both of his students had dropped out. Of course I would have terminated him anyway since he broke a major rule when he left the school without permission."

"How did he take it?" Knowing Brett, I was guessing not well.

"He offered to go to the applications and choose another student or two. I told him that wouldn't happen. Honestly, it was too late in the semester for him to start working with someone else, but even if it hadn't been, I wouldn't have allowed it."

"And he wasn't happy."

She shook her head. "He definitely wasn't happy. He wanted me to promise him he could be part of the program next year. I said he couldn't. I told him it was because he'd taken a student off campus without authorization."

I could imagine how little he liked that idea. Brett wouldn't have accepted that he needed authorization to do anything he wanted to do. Particularly not if it involved women.

Or girls in this case.

"Let's be clear here," Susa said. "Do you suspect that Brett Holmes sexually harassed these girls? Or perhaps went further than that?"

Dolores sighed. "I was afraid that he had, but I couldn't prove it. When the first girl said she felt uncomfortable that rang all kinds of alarm bells with me. That's standard code people use for inappropriate behavior. It could mean anything from suggestive language to unwanted touching."

"But she—the girl—wouldn't tell you what made her uncomfortable?"

"No. I think she was embarrassed. And she may have been afraid of what would happen if she told. I think she realized I was on her side, but if there was a stink about Holmes, she'd be the one who'd get the blame. Teenagers being what they are, a lot of them would probably assume she did something to make Holmes come on to her."

"Like breathing in his presence," I muttered.

Dolores raised her eyebrows. "You said you had problems with him?"

"Yeah. He was one of those men who was absolutely convinced he was irresistible. So if you resisted his charms, he took it personally."

"That fits with what I saw." Dolores gave me a dry smile. "He never tried anything with me, but I'm a lot older than you two. Plus I've got a husband and three kids."

"What about the other girl, the one he took to High Country? Did she give you any idea of what he did while he was mentoring?"

Dolores shook her head. "She wouldn't talk to me

about anything. She was really angry with me because she thought I was responsible for Holmes leaving the program. Which I was, of course. But her mother was the one who'd pulled her out. I don't know if she realized that. Actually she was furious with us both. And the world. She's at that stage."

"If she thought she'd had a relationship with Brett…" I began.

Dolores squared her shoulders. "He was an adult. She was a child. There can be no 'relationship' there. If I'd had any concrete evidence of something like that, I would have gone to the police without thinking twice. There are times when I still think I should have done that anyway. Even if they couldn't have proven anything, they might have put the fear of God into that man. Enough so that he'd avoid doing anything like that again."

I couldn't argue with her. We'd heard enough about Brett's preference for young girls for me to think it was quite possible he'd said or done something inappropriate with his mentees. But, of course, there was no proof as long as the second girl refused to support Dolce's uncomfortable feelings.

Susa sighed. "Thanks for talking to us, Dolores. I know it wasn't easy. We'll probably have to pass this on to Fowler, just because it could be a motive. Brett was an asshole, but even assholes…"

"…deserve to live," I finished. "For what it's worth, this seems to fit into a pattern with Brett. He pursued other underage girls, and in at least one case it got him into some serious trouble."

Dolores's eyebrows went up. "Legal trouble?"

I shook my head. "No. The girl's father beat him up

and ran him out of Denver."

"Too bad. If he'd had a record, I could have weeded him out when we did the background check." Dolores pushed herself to her feet, and we followed suit. She handed me a folder. "I hope you'll still consider joining the program. Holmes was an aberration. Most of the people who take part have a good experience. And the students are really grateful."

"I'll fill out the paperwork. If you want me, I'll be happy to join you."

Dolores's expression cleared a bit. "Good. I'm glad you're still interested. If you get me the application by August, we can get it cleared and get you into the program by September."

"I'll do that." And I would. Along with sounding like an interesting thing to do, I figured I owed it to Dolores as thanks for passing on the information about Brett. Of course by September I might be the outcast of Shavano if Fowler hadn't arrested Brett's killer. I'd need all the contacts I could get.

Susa followed me to the parking lot, her steps slower than usual. "You think that girl was your Dolce, Carmen's daughter?"

I sighed. "I don't know for sure. It's possible. She never mentioned anything about working for Brett, but I don't know why she would. I don't think he ever came around the booth when she was there."

"Are you going to ask her?"

"Maybe." I paused next to my truck. A tension headache was gathering at the back of my neck. "I'm not sure how to approach this. I don't want to get Dolores in trouble for leaking her name. I don't think she meant to do it, and it was just by chance I knew who Dolce was."

Susa shook her head. "No, I'm pretty certain Dolores didn't mean to tell you her name. She looked like she really regretted it as soon as she let it slip."

"I guess I'll talk to Dolce Saturday. Maybe just ask her about working with Brett and what it was like, let her think I found out some other way. Like maybe Carmen or Donnie told me." I took a breath. "You don't think he actually got physical with her, do you?"

"I think if he had, she'd have told someone, like maybe her parents. And then Donnie would have torn him apart." Susa paused. "Crap. You don't think that's what happened, do you? You don't think Donnie killed him?"

I thought about Donnie—late forties, balding, slightly overweight, perennially sunny. But with a lot of hard muscle. "I can't picture him doing that. Unless it was an accident, or he was really provoked. And I can't picture Brett letting him do it. I mean Brett had a couple of inches on Donnie and he wasn't puny."

"He wasn't puny, but he was a sleaze." Susa sighed. "It sounds horrible to say it, but I'm not all that sorry he's dead."

I wasn't either, but it wasn't something I felt good about. "Even assholes…"

"…deserve to live. Let's go have a margarita or something."

That sounded like a very good idea.

Chapter 23

As it turned out I didn't have a margarita. I had some of Harry's lemonade at Dirty Pete's because I still had to drive home. I thought about telling Harry what we'd found. He was a bartender, after all. That was right next to being a psychiatrist in my book.

But in the end, I decided Harry wasn't the right one to tell. I phoned Nate.

He was finishing his prep for breakfast at the café and doing a little more fiddling around with his Best in Shavano entries. I told him I'd had a lousy day and I needed to unload on someone. "Come to my place. I'll meet you there. And I'll cook for you."

That was the best offer I'd had since the last time he'd cooked for me.

I was still upset about Dolce. Brett Holmes was a sleaze who preyed upon teenagers, but that fact hadn't really hit me hard until I'd understood that I knew one of the teenagers he was preying on. I wanted to do something, but there wasn't much I could do. Brett Holmes was dead, and letting everybody know what a creep he was might hurt Dolce and the other girl, whoever she was.

Nate was waiting for me. I followed him up the stairs to his apartment, a sunny room that spanned the width of the garage. His kitchen was very small, not much more than a galley, but he'd fitted it out with racks and cubbies so that his tools were stowed near at hand.

He started to pull a bottle of wine from his rack, then paused. "So how shitty was your day?"

"Pretty damn shitty."

He pushed the wine back and took a bottle of tequila down from the cupboard. "Time for some ranch water."

Ranch water is like a margarita without the agave syrup and with a slug of Topo Chico. It's also really potent. "I don't know if I should have a lot of alcohol."

"Stay here tonight. I have to get up early to fix breakfast, but you can sleep in if you want."

I paused. "Yeah, okay. I can text Uncle Mike to look after Herman."

"Good, that's settled." He picked up a bottle of triple sec and a couple of limes. I sent a quick text to the ranch, hoping Uncle Mike wouldn't mind.

"You can start your rant while I finish the drinks." Nate pulled a couple of bottles of Topo Chico from a carton beneath his sink.

I settled onto the couch in the living room and started to tell him what Dolores had said. Nate frowned as he listened, then stopped slicing the limes. "That son of a bitch was going after high school students?"

"Apparently."

"Holy shit. I'm only surprised it took him this long to get clobbered. And I'm trying not to feel like he deserved it." He tossed ice cubes into the glasses with a little more force than he needed to.

"You and Susa both," I said. And me, too, if I was being honest.

I worked through the rest of what Dolores had told us while Nate handed me a glass and sat down beside me. I felt like cuddling up to his warmth, but I restrained myself. I had a story to tell, after all.

"So I'm pretty sure the one who quit was Dolce, the girl who helps out with my booth on Saturdays."

Nate took a sip of his drink. "Are you going to ask her about it?"

"Yeah, if I can figure out a way to approach her without getting Dolores in trouble. She didn't mean to let her name slip."

Nate stared out his window at the setting sun. "What if Dolce knows something about Holmes's death? Do you think she'd tell you?"

"Dolce?" I shook my head. "Not possible. She wouldn't be involved. She's just a kid."

"Kids do kill people. If Holmes did something to make her angry, could she have done it without meaning to?"

"Maybe, but I don't think so. For one thing, she's not that big." Of course, standing next to me any girl would seem not that big, but Dolce really wasn't. "I don't think she's more than five feet four or so."

"She lives on a farm. She's probably stronger than she looks."

I shook my head. "I can't see her being strong enough or angry enough to hit Brett over the head with something. After all, she wanted Dolores to get her out of the mentorship because she felt 'uncomfortable.' That doesn't sound like someone with a hair trigger. She was going through channels to get an adult to help her."

"Okay, maybe not Dolce. What about her parents, her father? Could he have gone after Brett?"

I flexed my shoulders, trying to ease the tension. "Donnie? You know Donnie. Do you honestly think he could take Brett out even if he was angry?"

"He's the guy who works your uncle's booth at the market, right?"

"Donnie and Carmen have both worked for Uncle Mike for close to twenty years. They lease the acreage next to the orchard."

"He doesn't strike me as the type, but like I say, people can change under pressure." He paused. "What about Carmen?"

I considered it, reluctantly. "Carmen's actually tougher than Donnie, who's a sweetheart. When I was a teenager, Carmen used to ride herd on me. I was a lot more worried about pissing her off than Uncle Mike."

"So? If she found out Brett had been creeping around Dolce, would she go after him?"

"Maybe. Maybe not." I closed my eyes, rubbing a hand across the sudden ache in my chest.

"Take a break." Nate put his arm around my shoulders. "It's not your job to figure this out."

"Maybe I will." It felt so good to have his arm around me, and I felt so unsettled by everything we'd heard from Dolores. Suddenly, all I really wanted to do was drowse.

Unfortunately, my brain wouldn't let me. "There's the other girl," I murmured.

"The other girl?"

"The other girl in the mentorship. The one Brett took to High Country. She's got parents, too. Or at least she's got a mother who pulled her out of the program. If we're putting Donnie and Carmen in the running as suspects, we need to consider her, too."

"I guess she's as likely as they are." Nate pulled me against him. "Can you find out who she is?"

"Yeah, I'm guessing Dolce will be a lot more

willing to tell me that than to tell me what Brett did that upset her so much."

"So you'll decide how likely a suspect she is?"

"I could." I turned to face him. "You know what, I'm kind of sick of doing this. This thing with Dolce is really freaking me out. These are people who are close to me. I don't like thinking of them as suspects. I *can't* think of them as suspects."

"Then don't do it," Nate said, logically enough. "You were doing this to reassure yourself. If that isn't happening, stop." He rubbed his hand along my arm. "There are easier ways to reassure yourself, believe me."

"I think you're right." I took another sip of my drink. "I think I'm at an end here. There's really no reason to go on doing this, and there are lots of reasons not to."

"You're not still curious about who murdered Brett?"

"I'm plenty curious, but I'm not willing to push on with what we've got. I didn't know this would get close to home, and it makes me anxious." I rested my head on his shoulder. "I'm done. Can I be done?"

"Sure you can be done. You want some supper?"

"Yes, I do." I glanced down at my ranch water and was a little shocked to see it was mostly gone. "Can I help?"

"Sure. It's just spaghetti and marinara. You can do the salad."

"I can definitely do the salad."

We worked side-by-side, although given the size of his kitchen we didn't have much choice. If more than one person tried to cook, they'd be side by side. Finally, as Nate put the spaghetti on a platter, he turned to look at me. "Even if you're done with investigating, you need to promise me something."

That sounded ominous. "Promise you what?"

"Promise me you'll take all of this to Fowler. Drop it in his lap and let him deal with it. The murderer is still out there, watching. If you've found something that gives away his identity, even by accident, you don't want it to be something only you and Susa know about."

He looked so serious that I couldn't laugh it off the way I wanted to. Besides, he had a point. "I'll tell Fowler most of what we found out. I won't tell him that Dolce was one of the girls because I don't want to get Dolores in trouble. But I'll tell him about Brett getting bounced from the program and that it may have been over inappropriate behavior with teenage girls. He can ask Dolores for more, and she can tell him to get a court order or something."

"Or something." Nate poured me another glass of ranch water. "Okay, that's the end of our discussion of Brett Holmes for the evening. From now on, we talk about something less emotional. Like politics or religion."

"Or Best in Shavano," I suggested.

"Best in Shavano is very emotional where I'm concerned. Why don't we just talk about sex? That way we can work our way into the more fun part of the evening."

"That already sounds like fun," I said.

And it was.

The next morning we had breakfast at the café before service started. It was early for me, but normal for Nate. Madge came in as we were finishing up and gave me a broad smile. Bobby was there too and sort of acknowledged my existence—at least I think that's what the nod in my direction was supposed to do. I left at six thirty as they were getting ready to open and drove to the farm.

I figured there was no point trying to talk to Fowler until later in the day—afternoon seemed best. I wasn't looking forward to the conversation, particularly since I was pretty sure he'd tell me I shouldn't have gone on asking questions. But Nate was right. The information about Brett and his predatory ways was relevant. And according to Dolores, Fowler hadn't come to the high school to question her. Either he didn't know about Brett's time in the program, or he didn't realize it was significant.

I was less worried about the hidden murderer's interest in me. Obviously some people knew I was asking questions. That was how Fowler had found out in the first place. But the murderer would probably be a lot more nervous about Fowler and his investigation than about Susa and me.

Uncle Mike brought Herman down midmorning, and they both seemed fairly happy to see me. "Why don't you just let Herman stay with me at night?" Uncle Mike said. "I like having him around in the evening. We have some good discussions."

"He's an excellent conversationalist," I agreed. But he was also my dog, at least in part, and I kind of liked having him around in the evening. Not that I was nervous about being alone, but, yeah, maybe I sort of was. Maybe Nate's concerns had made a bigger impression than I realized. "I'll think about it."

I considered telling Uncle Mike about Dolce and Brett, but I decided not to. He'd known Dolce since she was a baby, and he was likely to lose his temper if he thought Brett had harassed her. I didn't want him heading over to Donnie and Carmen's place until I'd had a chance to talk to Dolce privately. I really wanted to know who the other girl was and maybe talk to her, too.

Yes, I'd told Nate I was through investigating, but maybe I wasn't as through as I'd thought.

So I spent a few hours doing what I always do when I want to think: making jam. This time it was peach because the early crop was in. The market always sells out on peaches during the first couple of weeks they're available because people are desperate for them. I don't take much from Uncle Mike's pick during the first rush, but I do stir up a little peach jam, usually with some added flavoring because the sugar content isn't as high as it will be later in the year. This time around I was doing whiskey to give it a real bump.

By noon I had a dozen jars done, which might be all I'd do for this week's market. I had a few more peaches left, but I might just wait until next week to work with them. I made a quick sandwich to have with a glass of milk, then got ready for my trip into town.

Herman was waiting hopefully next to the door, tail thumping, and I was hit with a quick attack of guilt. I hadn't been around him as much as usual over the past week or so. Maybe Uncle Mike had a point. Maybe he needed more human contact than I could provide.

I sighed. "You want to go for a ride, Herm?"

He pushed himself to his feet, his tail beating a wild tattoo on the door, and that guilt attack got a lot stronger. If I was going to have a dog, I needed to spend more time with him. "Okay, come on. Let's go to town."

Herman was pretty well behaved around people, so I figured he wouldn't be a problem in Fowler's office.

Besides, this was Colorado—everybody had a dog, and they went everywhere their owners went. After I finished with the chief, I'd take Herman to the dog park and let him run around with some other dogs for a change. That should take care of possible guilt attacks for at least a few days.

I parked my truck in the municipal lot next to courthouse. Herm allowed me to put him on a leash, then followed me cheerily up the street to the main door.

He padded down the hall beside me, his toenails clicking on the concrete floor. We got a couple of dubious looks, but nobody told me to take him outside. The chief's office was in a slightly obscure spur off the main hall, but we finally found it again. The receptionist glanced up at me. "Yes?"

"I'd like to see Chief Fowler. Is he available?" I tried to sound as official as possible. Of course, Herman's presence undercut that a bit.

"He's not in," the receptionist said neutrally. "Do you have an appointment?"

I shook my head. "Do you know when he'll be back?"

The receptionist shrugged. "He's at lunch. Maybe a half hour or so."

I thanked her and paced down the hall, Herman clicking happily at my heels. I could wait a half hour, but that didn't give me enough time to take Herman to the dog park, not if I wanted to be there in time to catch Fowler.

I headed for River Park instead. We could walk the trails for thirty minutes or so, and maybe I could let Herm off his leash for a few minutes if nobody was around.

There were a lot of people in the park, taking

advantage of a balmy summer day in the mountains. Kids waded in the shallows while their parents watched. Kayaks and tubers jockeyed for position for shooting the rapids. Dogs dashed after Frisbees, immersing themselves in the river.

Herman looked longingly after them.

"Not a chance." Taking a soggy dog to the chief's office struck me as a very bad idea.

I turned off the path that ran alongside the river, heading toward the general area where the market was usually set up. Nobody was there today, of course, except for a few joggers and one or two moms pushing strollers. The farther we went from the river, the fewer people we ran into. I trotted toward the meadow area where band concerts were held later in the summer, hoping I could let Herman do some running.

But as we got closer to the band gazebo, I heard voices. Loud voices.

"I've told you, you need to shut up," a woman said. "Just shut up about it. He's dead now. Let him alone."

"It is so true," another voice answered. "You just don't want to know. You don't want to know the truth about me and him."

It sounded like a girl's voice. A familiar girl's voice. At my side, Herm made a concerned noise. "It's okay," I murmured, moving closer. "No problem."

The woman was shouting now. "Stop saying that. You don't know what you're talking about."

"I do so know. He told me I was special. He said he liked me. He said we'd be great together."

"Liar," the woman shouted again, and I heard what sounded like a slap, followed by a cry of pain.

"Okay, Herm. Time to see what's happening here."

I trotted toward the voices, rounding a curve next to the band gazebo. "What's going on?" I called, peering at the two figures standing in the shade of the gazebo roof. Evelyn Davidson and Dorothy Dorsey stared back.

Chapter 24

Dorothy was standing a little in front of Evelyn, rubbing a hand across her reddened cheek. It was pretty clear who the slapper and the slappee had been.

I stopped at the foot of the gazebo stairs, trying for a smile. "Hey, Dorothy, are you okay?"

Dorothy gave me another one of those furious looks, like I was the last person she wanted to see right then. "Go away. I'm not talking to you. He said you were a bitch."

Right. So they really were talking about Brett. "Evelyn? What's going on?"

"It's none of your affair. Just go on about your business." Evelyn sounded like she had a clenched jaw.

"I don't think I can do that. I think Dorothy should go home. And you should go to…wherever it is you need to go." I had no idea what Evelyn was doing in the park in the middle of a working day, but I figured there were a lot of things she could be doing instead. Although their conversation about Brett had been interesting. I turned to Dorothy. "Why don't you go home now? It's lunch time."

Dorothy looked like she wanted to go, but she didn't want me to be the one who told her. "Maybe I will, maybe I won't."

"It's up to you," I said.

Dorothy glanced at Evelyn. "I guess we're done

here. I'm going home."

"No you're not. We're not finished talking yet. There are still some things you need to understand." Evelyn stepped closer behind her, resting one hand on the girl's shoulder. "We're staying. You're leaving, Ms. Constantine. The two of us have things to discuss that have nothing to do with you."

Dorothy seemed to have suddenly gone paler than usual behind her Goth makeup. Her black smudged eyes looked wide with something like fear.

Beside me, Herm strained against his leash, whimpering, but I held him in place. "Do you want me to leave you with Evelyn, Dorothy?"

Dorothy licked her lips, staring straight ahead.

Evelyn gave her a quick shake, her hand tightening on her shoulder. "Tell her."

Dorothy looked miserable. And very frightened. "Maybe…just go away?"

I took a deep breath. "Let her go, Evelyn. She's just a kid. Whatever she did that's got you so upset, she's still just a kid."

Evelyn gave me a smile that was basically a lip flex. "She's the one who threw mud on your truck and wrote 'slut' on your windshield, did you know that?"

Dorothy closed her eyes for a moment. Her lower lip trembled.

"Brett thought that was hilarious. He took a picture on his phone and showed me later." Evelyn darted a glance at Dorothy.

Now that I thought about it, that made perfect sense. The thing with the mud had been more like something a kid would do than an adult. Even an adult like Brett Holmes. "She's fifteen years old, Evelyn. That's a child

246

in anybody's book. Well, almost anybody. I guess Brett had different standards."

Evelyn's jaw looked rigid. "Whatever Brett did, it doesn't matter now. He's dead. Everybody needs to just move on, including you."

A nasty suspicion nudged the back of my mind. "You want me to stop asking questions?"

"I want you to mind your own business. It's all over now. You need to shut up. Both of you need to shut up." She gave Dorothy's shoulder another shake.

"He loved me," Dorothy cried out. "He did. He said I was special." She jerked away from Evelyn's hand, and I saw something flash behind her.

"What the hell, Evelyn…" I started, but Herm had had enough. He jerked loose from my hand, bounding up the steps and barking all the way. I ran after him, but he was too fast for me.

Dorothy ran across the gazebo, leaping down the steps on the other side. Herm hit Evelyn at full force, knocking her backward so that she stumbled against the gazebo railing. I saw her hand go up and I saw the hunting knife she was holding flash in the sun.

"No," I screamed and jumped the last step, grabbing for her arm. I missed and grabbed the knife blade instead. It hurt like blazes, but it made Evelyn lose her grip. The knife fell to the floor where I managed to kick it away.

Herm was barking desperately, and something moved at the corner of my vision.

"All right," a masculine voice said. "That's enough."

I had never been so glad to see anyone in my life as I was to see Chief Fowler in that moment. Evelyn, on the other hand, didn't look like she shared my opinion. "She attacked me," she said in a trembling voice. "Her dog attacked me." She pointed in Herman's general direction. "That's her knife on the floor. She tried to kill me."

"Nope," the chief said. "That's not what happened. I saw what you did, and so did these folks." He gestured to a small group of joggers, stroller pushing moms, and wide-eyed teenagers, all of them staring at Evelyn. The chief nodded at the knife, now several feet away. "That's yours."

"I never saw it before," Evelyn said stiffly.

"Interesting, since it was in your hand and will no doubt have your fingerprints all over it. Did she threaten you with the knife?" He turned toward Dorothy, who was now kneeling next to Herman, stroking his head.

"She was mad at me." Dorothy's chin went up at a mutinous angle. "Because Brett liked me better."

Oh, honey. "Evelyn and Dorothy were arguing about Brett. I don't know what the knife was about."

"I heard that," Fowler said mildly. "Did you decide to rescue Dorothy then?"

"I didn't know she needed rescuing. I didn't see the knife."

Evelyn gave me another of those killing looks. Clearly, I'd interfered with her plans. Whatever those plans might have been.

A uniformed cop stepped onto the gazebo beside Fowler, glancing a little apprehensively at Evelyn. "Ms. Davidson, you're under arrest," Fowler said pleasantly, pulling a pair of handcuffs from his belt. "For assault. We'll figure out other charges later. You have the right to remain silent. Anything you say can be used against you in court. You have the right to have a lawyer with you during questioning. If you can't afford a lawyer, one will be appointed for you if you wish."

Evelyn looked stunned, so stunned she let him handcuff her wrists behind her back without complaint.

Fowler nodded to the cop. "Take Ms. Davidson to the station. I'll be along in a bit. After I've taken care of Ms. Constantine."

I stared at him. "I don't need to be taken care of."

"I disagree." Fowler took hold of my wrist, gently raising my hand, and I noticed the blood dripping down my fingers for the first time.

"Oh, shit." I collapsed onto the bench that ran around the inside of the gazebo. My hand suddenly hurt like a bitch. I guess the adrenaline had finally worn off.

Fowler handed me his handkerchief, which I wrapped around the cut. "We need to get you to Urgent Care so they can fix you up," he said easily.

"I grabbed the knife because she was going to hurt my dog. Oh, God, my dog. Herman?"

Herman padded across the floor, grinning happily. Dorothy picked up his leash.

"I can't take him to Urgent Care, can I? I need to call my uncle so he can come and get him. I need to wait until he's here."

Fowler sighed. "I don't think that's a good idea." He lifted my hand so I could see the blood soaking through the handkerchief. "Waiting, I mean."

"I can stay with him," Dorothy said. "I mean, I can come along with you to the clinic and stay with him outside until your uncle comes." She glanced between us, suddenly looking like a fifteen-year-old with a lot of eye makeup. "If that's okay."

"That's good," I said quickly. "That'll work."

Fowler shrugged, resigned to having an entourage. "All right then. Let's get this show on the road."

The Urgent Care people got me into the exam room quickly, leaving Fowler in the waiting room and Dorothy in the parking lot with Herm. I had a deep cut across my palm, but the doctor decided it didn't need stitches, much to my relief. She was wrapping my palm in gauze when Uncle Mike walked in.

He looked almost as pale as Dorothy had when Evelyn had held a knife to her back. I didn't know what Fowler had told him when he'd called, but apparently it was dire.

"I'm okay," I said quickly. "It's just a cut. I'm getting a bandage. Did you see Herman outside?"

Uncle Mike nodded, then sat down rather heavily in the exam room chair.

"She's going to be fine," the doctor said briskly. "Although she'll have to keep her hand elevated until the swelling goes down."

"Elevated?" I said, as the level of my catastrophe began to sink in. "I can't do that. I have jam to make."

"She'll keep it elevated," Uncle Mike said. "Don't worry. She'll keep it elevated and bandaged and whatever the hell else she needs to do." He gave me a fierce look, and I promptly shut up.

The doctor gave me antiseptic and printed instructions for taking care of my hand. She also gave me a couple of painkillers and sent me on my way. We found Herman and Dorothy sitting on a bench outside, looking like they'd bonded.

I picked up his leash. "Thanks for taking care of him."

Dorothy stared down at her flip-flops, then looked

up at me. "Thank you for, like, saving me and all."

"Glad to do it." I thought about saying something about Brett, but I decided to let it go. Annabelle could lecture her daughter.

"And I'm sorry about your truck. The mud. Sorry." At least I think that's what she said. Her head was down and she was mumbling.

"Okay. Do you need a ride home?"

Dorothy shook her head. "It's not far."

"Thanks, then," Uncle Mike said. "Come on, Roxanne, time to get you home."

That sounded ominous. When Uncle Mike calls me *Roxanne*, it's serious. But he didn't say much on the drive. He pulled my truck into its parking space in front of the cabin, but he made no move to get out. He also didn't look at me.

When he finally raised his gaze, his eyes were as dark as mine, Constantine genes all the way. "Roxanne, you're all I have left. Your dad and I lost our folks a long time ago, and then I lost Rhoda and then your dad. You're it. I can't spare you."

I took a deep breath, trying to stave off tears. I knew they'd be coming, but I didn't want to break down just yet. "I know. I'm sorry."

"Why should you be sorry? This wasn't your fault. None of it." His jaw tightened. "Two people were at fault here—that bastard Holmes and his idiot girlfriend. And don't you try to tell me she wasn't an idiot." He gave me a fierce look, although I had no intention of defending Evelyn.

"Is that what Fowler told you?" I had my own theories about Evelyn's motivations, but I hadn't really discussed them with anyone.

251

He shook his head. "Fowler told me squat. He did say you'd gotten hurt taking a knife away from Evelyn Davidson. I figured the rest out for myself. Now let's go inside and you can tell me what happened."

Chapter 25

So I did. I wasn't sure where to start, but I decided I'd go with today's adventure and then add details as needed. Uncle Mike had questions, a lot of them rhetorical.

"Why did you go to that gazebo? Why didn't you call the cops?"

"I didn't know what was going on there. I heard a woman and a girl arguing, and then I heard someone get slapped. Sounded like they needed an intervention. I had Herman with me, and I thought I'd be safe." Which gave Herman a lot more credit than I usually did.

Uncle Mike sighed and motioned for me to keep talking.

The description of seeing Evelyn's knife made him sit up straight, eyes blazing. "She had a knife, and you charged up there? What the everlasting hell, Roxy?"

"It wasn't me," I said quickly. "It was Herman. He pulled away from me. I think he wanted to help Dorothy." Or maybe bite Evelyn, which amounted to the same thing.

Herman wandered across the room to rest his head on Uncle Mike's knee. Apparently, he was a little concerned about the loud voices coming from people he loved. Uncle Mike reached out to scratch his ears, a little absently.

I felt a new jolt of guilt as I watched him. Uncle

Mike wouldn't have let Herman charge into danger like I had. Maybe Herman would be better off with him full time. I'd have to think about that. Maybe later.

As I went on with my story, his eyes widened but he kept his peace.

I explained about Fowler appearing in the gazebo after I'd grabbed Evelyn's knife, and Uncle Mike blew out an angry breath. "Did he bring in a SWAT team?"

"No. I think he constitutes a SWAT team on his own." I hadn't had time to think about Fowler much, but now I took a moment to consider what he'd done. Walking into a crazy situation with a knife-wielding psycho and a bleeding woman. And he'd calmed everything down.

I stumbled through telling the rest, summarizing Evelyn's arrest and our trip to the Urgent Care clinic, along with Dorothy and Herman. "I still have Fowler's handkerchief," I finished. "I'll see if I can wash it and get it back to him." Although if I were him, I might not want it.

Uncle Mike sat in silence, staring down at his boots. "Well," he said.

I bit my lip, waiting for him to go on. If he wanted to yell at me again, I'd take it.

Uncle Mike pushed himself to his feet, then walked over and put his arms around me, giving me a fierce hug. "You okay now? You need anything for that hand?"

I shook my head. "I'm okay. My hand hurts, but I took some ibuprofen. I'm coping."

He gave me a concerned look. "Why don't you come up to the house with me? Watch some TV. Pop some corn."

"I'd like that, but I'm really tired. Maybe after I take

a nap."

"Okay. Take your nap. Don't worry about supper." He turned toward the door, motioning Herman to follow him. "I'll order pizza or something."

That sounded like a good idea, but I still needed to take that nap. After I called Nate and Susa. The news must have gotten around town by now, and I didn't want anyone worrying about me.

I had picked up my phone and stared at it for a moment, trying to decide who to call first, when someone rapped on my door.

Maybe it's Susa. Or Nate. Either or both would be welcome, as long as I didn't have to go through the whole story again. Just thinking about it made my throat ache.

I pulled the door open and saw Chief Fowler standing on my porch.

It's safe to say he was among the last people I'd expected to come around the place. If nothing else, I thought he probably had more than enough to do at the station, what with booking Evelyn for assault and all. I hadn't seen him since he'd dropped me at the clinic and bullied the staff into treating me immediately.

"Can I come in?" he asked, and I realized I'd been staring at him blankly.

"Of course, sure." I stepped aside to let him into the living room.

He glanced around the place as he removed his Stetson, taking in the cases of jam I had stacked against the wall, the slightly worn furniture, and my *It must be jelly, cause jam don't shake like that* poster. Okay, so I wasn't a whiz at interior décor. Nate hadn't seemed to mind.

"If you've come to tell me I was an idiot with Evelyn Davidson, you can save yourself some time," I said. "I've already concluded that for myself, believe me."

"I don't know that it was all that idiotic," he said mildly. "You were trying to help a kid who was being threatened. And you had your dog." He glanced around the room, probably looking for said dog.

"Herman's with my uncle at the main house."

"According to Dorothy Dorsey, the dog deserves a medal." Fowler gave me a dry smile. "I'm here because I need to take your statement, Ms. Constantine."

"Roxy. After all this you might as well call me Roxy."

"Right. I need your statement, Roxy."

"Okay. Have a seat. Would you like some something to drink? Coffee or iced tea?" I figured I wouldn't bother offering him a beer. I'd seen enough cop shows to know he wouldn't drink on duty. Probably.

He shook his head as he dropped into the easy chair, placing his hat on the floor near his boot. "No, thanks. How did you end up in between Ms. Davidson and Dorothy?"

I sat down on the couch opposite him. "Herman and I were on a walk. I was waiting for you to get back to your office."

"Me?" He frowned. "Why did you want to see me?"

"Because I'd found some stuff about Brett I thought you should know."

"What information is that?" He pulled out a notebook and rested it on his knee.

"About Brett and the high school mentorship program. I talked to the principal, Dolores Cantu, and she told me she suspected Brett of inappropriate behavior with female students. I didn't know Dorothy was one of the girls, though. I mean, I guess she was, judging from what she said."

Fowler nodded slowly. "Actually, I already found out about that. Ms. Cantu called me yesterday. She said she'd been talking to you."

I steeled myself for another lecture on staying out of his investigation. "I was going to tell you about it."

"Ms. Cantu said she'd decided to talk to me because of her conversation with you. Until then, she hadn't realized her problems with Brett Holmes might be relevant to the investigation." Fowler gave me a level look.

"Were you going to talk to her before that?"

He shook his head. "You'd mentioned the mentorship thing, but I didn't think it was important. It was on my list, but not high on my list."

"So I helped you." I let myself smile. Cautiously.

One corner of his mouth edged up. "I wouldn't go that far. But I'm less inclined to yell at you than I was before."

"I'll take that as a yes." I leaned back in my chair, feeling better than I had since I'd seen Uncle Mike at the clinic.

"I still need your statement."

I described my encounter with Evelyn and Dorothy a lot more succinctly than I had when I'd told Uncle Mike, but Fowler didn't interrupt, which made it go a lot faster.

"You didn't know she had a knife?"

I shook my head. "Not at first. She had one hand on Dorothy's shoulder, and I guess she had the knife pressed against her with the other hand. I only saw the knife when Dorothy moved. How much did you see?"

He frowned slightly, as if this was some kind of academic exercise. "I need your version of it first. Then I can fill in the blanks."

I told him about Herman rushing Evelyn, and that I'd been afraid she'd stab him. "I tried to grab her arm and I grabbed the knife instead."

Fowler winced. "Painful."

"Very. But I got the knife away from her and kicked it across the floor. Dorothy helped."

"Yeah, I saw most of that. So did a lot of witnesses in the park."

"Did you hear what she said?"

"Some of it. You want to give me your version?"

I tried to remember all the stuff Evelyn had been yelling at Dorothy. At that moment, it seemed important. "She told Dorothy to shut up about Brett. She said nothing Dorothy said would make any difference since he was dead, and she ought to let him be."

"What did Dorothy say."

"She thought Brett was in love with her. He'd said she was special."

Fowler sighed. "I was afraid of that. Is that when Ms. Davidson hit her?""

"I didn't see it, but I heard it. And I got there right afterward."

"So then what did they say?"

"They both told me to leave, but I thought Dorothy might need help, so I suggested Dorothy leave, too. Dorothy started to go—that's when Evelyn grabbed hold of her. I guess she had the knife then, but I didn't know that."

"What else?"

I made a quick decision not to tell him about Dorothy mudding my truck. I'd let Dorothy tell him herself if she felt like it. "I told Evelyn to let her go, that she was just a kid. So then we argued about that, and I made some crack about Brett liking young girls. That's when she said we both needed to shut up about it and move on. Dorothy tried to get away and Herm went charging in."

"Right. I was there for that."

"How did you happen to be in the park anyway?"

He shrugged. "It's where I eat my lunch usually. I heard the shouting and figured I might need to check it out."

"What was Evelyn doing in the park with Dorothy anyway? Did she say?"

"She didn't, but Dorothy did. Apparently, Ms. Davidson had been telling people she and Holmes were in a, quote, committed relationship, unquote." Fowler's smile was more like a grimace. "That didn't sit right with Dorothy, so she went to Davidson's office to confront her. Davidson suggested they go to the park to discuss it."

I figured Evelyn probably wasn't excited about people in her office hearing Dorothy claim she had a relationship with Brett, too. "Did she take the knife to threaten Dorothy? To make her keep quiet?"

"Possibly." Fowler shrugged. "That may be what she'll claim."

I took a deep breath. "Do you think Evelyn killed Brett?"

Fowler gave me an owlish look, but then he shrugged again. "Probably. There's evidence that she was there that night. My guess is she found out Holmes was trying to seduce teenage girls. That would be enough for any woman to decide a guy was a scumbag. They may have fought. And then she hit him with a cast iron skillet."

"Why would she bother about Dorothy? Why not just let it go?"

"She was playing the bereaved lover, grieving for her man. How would it look if a fifteen-year-old claims she was Holmes's great love? And maybe she was even a little jealous. Who knows?"

I bit my lip. There were some things I was probably better off not knowing, but I felt like I needed to ask anyway. "Did Brett molest Dorothy?"

Fowler stared down at his notebook for a moment. "She says he didn't. I choose to believe her."

I chose to believe her, too, since the alternative was awful. But I hoped Annabelle would make sure Dorothy got some help.

Fowler closed his notebook and put it back in his pocket. "You may be called as a witness, depending on what Ms. Davidson's lawyer decides to do."

"She attacked me in front of a crowd of witnesses, including the chief of police. What can her lawyer do about that?"

"Lawyers can do all kinds of things. But I don't think getting Ms. Davidson off is in the cards. At least not on the assault. And we'll do our damnedest to add a murder charge to it." He pushed himself to his feet. "Do you need any help out here, with your injury and all?"

I shook my head. "My uncle's here, and I have friends I can call." Of course, I didn't trust any of those friends to make jam for me. Somehow I'd have to figure out a way to get to work, even if I had to do it one-handed.

"Fair enough." Fowler turned toward the door, then paused, looking at me. "Do you drink beer, Roxy?"

"I'm a Colorado girl. What do you think?"

He gave me another of those half smiles. "Maybe I can buy you a beer sometime."

I blinked at him. *What the hell?* "Maybe you can."

He replaced his Stetson on his head. "See you around, Roxy."

"See you." I watched him go, then dropped onto the couch. I wasn't at all sure whether he'd just made a tentative pass or not. But it wasn't something I wanted to think about.

Which led me to a subject I'd been avoiding. Nate. I really needed to call him and fill him in. But I was dreading it. I figured his reaction would be like Uncle Mike's, only maybe louder. He'd asked me to go tell Fowler what I knew, and I'd tried. But the result hadn't been what either of us expected. I knew he'd be upset, but I also knew I needed to talk to him anyway.

Big girl panties, Roxy. Nate deserved to hear the story from me and not from some town gossip.

I dialed his number and then listened to it ring, wondering if I could leave a message without being a total coward.

"Yeah," Nate answered, finally.

"I've got some stuff to tell you, stuff that happened to me today. Do you have some time?"

"I've got lots of time. I'm also at the turnoff to your place."

I stepped to the doorway and saw his car rolling down the road toward me. Which meant he'd already heard about Evelyn and Dorothy. Or a version of it, anyway. This should be loads of fun.

"Okay. I'm here. Waiting."

A couple of minutes later, Nate walked into my living room and straight to me. He put his arms around me and held me close for a few moments. "Good lord, Roxy," he muttered. "Christ almighty."

I moved against him, letting myself feel his warmth and the protection of his arms. It was just what I needed, and it made me feel guiltier than ever because I should have called him before I did anything else. "How did you hear?"

"It's all over town that Evelyn attacked you and tried to attack a teenager. Coco told me. Before she told Mom, which is saying something." He leaned back to look at me. "Is there more to it than that?"

I really wanted to say no, but *big girl panties* and all. "There's a lot more. I'll tell you, but Uncle Mike's doing dinner. And I want you to stay after that. Can you?"

"Sure. I'll tell Bobby to start breakfast without me. Is it that bad?"

I blew out a long breath. "Evelyn held a knife on Dorothy Dorsey. Herman went after her, and she went to stab him. I tried to grab her arm, but I grabbed the knife instead. But Fowler was there, and he stopped her." Short, but fundamentally correct.

"Good for Fowler. Did Evelyn kill Holmes?"

"Probably. When Fowler took my statement, he said there was evidence against her, but I don't know how solid it is. I'll probably have to testify if she goes to trial for attacking me and Dorothy."

"You don't want to?"

"I'd rather forget the whole thing."

Nate sat down on the couch, pulling me down next

to him. "That's a lot more dramatic than the story I heard. You sure you're okay?"

I started to say I was fine, but I wasn't. And I was tired of pretending I was, particularly since tears were beginning to leak down my cheeks. "I'm not, but I will be."

Nate put his arm around me again, leaning over to kiss my forehead. "You're okay, Rox. You got through it."

I had. But I wasn't sure that was enough. On the other hand, I was sure I wanted to stop thinking about it. I put my arms around Nate, resting my head on his shoulder. "I'm glad you're here."

"I'm glad I'm here, too. Do you want to go up to the main house?"

"Eventually," I murmured, leaning in a little closer. "Just now I want to cuddle. If you've got the time."

"I've got the time." Nate pulled me deeper into his arms. "I absolutely have the time."

So for an hour or so, I didn't think about Evelyn or Dorothy. Or the fact that I had a cut hand that might make it impossible for me to make enough jam for the next market.

Chapter 26

As it turned out, my jam production wasn't a problem after all. I had more volunteers than I could use. Carmen spent several hours chopping fruit and then helping me pour the jam into the jars. Susa, pretty much a non-cook, did things like lifting the jars out of the canner. Nate helped when he came over in the evening. One night Coco showed up, claiming that she needed a refresher course in jam making. She was, of course, terrific. By the end of the week, I had enough jam for that weekend's market and the one after that.

All of which reinforced my earlier decision to start looking for an assistant as soon as I got a chance. Being a one-woman jam factory had some definite drawbacks.

The Best in Shavano competition was a week or so later, which distracted everyone from the Evelyn Davidson adventure. I'd entered this year's version of my pepper peach jam, using the full-strength Pueblo chilies, without much optimism. After all, at the time I'd entered, a lot of people in town had thought I was a murderer who'd gotten away with it. I figured since I was unlikely to win anyway, I might as well go with a jam I was proud of instead of a safe choice. Hence pepper peach instead of peach preserves.

At least that particular misconception about my guilt had been largely taken care of, although some people still seemed to be regarding me with a mixture of suspicion and confusion. They thought I'd done something, but they weren't quite sure what. Still, it seemed a lot more likely that Evelyn had killed Brett, given her attack on me and Dorothy. She'd been charged with assault, and she was still in jail. I only hoped the case against her was solid, and that they'd eventually charge her with Brett's murder, too.

The contest happened on the weekend after the Fourth of July so the organizers could take advantage of the extra people in town for the holiday. That meant the regular farmers market took place in the morning, and the competition got started in the afternoon in the same general area. There were always a lot of tourists hanging around the weekend after the Fourth, and I figured we'd probably sell out of whatever I brought to town.

Dolce was still supposed to work as my assistant in the booth. I hadn't told her I knew about Brett being her mentor, and I wasn't sure I would. There was an argument to be made for keeping quiet and hoping the whole thing would just go away. But as it happened, Dolce was more mature than I was.

"Mom told me what happened to you," she said, "with Evelyn and Dorothy and all. Mr. Holmes was my mentor for a while at school. He was a creep."

"Yeah, I heard he created some problems in the mentorship program," I said with what little tact I could muster. "I'm glad he got kicked out."

"So was I," Dolce said. "Ms. Cantu said you were going to be a mentor next year. Is that right?"

"I am." I'd turned the paperwork in to Dolores's office a few days after my afternoon with Evelyn. It was my payback to destiny for having saved Herman and me.

"Could we work together? I mean, I work with you

here, but that's the business side of things. I don't know anything about jam making, not really."

Dolce looked so hopeful I was a little dumbfounded. I'd wanted an assistant jam-maker. Maybe this was the answer. She could find out if she liked cooking, and I could find out if we worked well together. Although I was already pretty sure we would. "I'll talk to Mrs. Cantu about it. It would mean leaving campus so you could work at my place. But since we know each other already, and since you live nearby, that might not be a problem."

"Great." Dolce gave me a lovely smile and got to work charming the customers.

Nate wasn't doing a demo that day because he needed the time to get ready for his Best in Shavano competition. The final version of his pork chops used some of this year's apricot preserves. He served it with roasted potatoes and a zucchini gratin. Dessert was, of course, the crepes with my rose petal jam.

I was a little nervous for him, although I thought his food was delectable. I knew he'd been taking some flak from Bobby about the time he'd spent developing a recipe they'd probably never serve at Robicheaux's. Their clientele liked their pork chops with applesauce and their potatoes fried.

I plunged into selling jam for the rest of the morning, keeping the sample bowls filled and smiling to beat the band. We had more peaches available now and I was trying a new exotic jam every week. This week it was peach with bourbon and vanilla. There was a hint of almond extract in there, too.

And of course we had the usual: raspberry, strawberry, apricot, and the tail end of last week's exotic, raspberry peach.

Lines of customers jostled one another at the samples counter. I kept track of the little kids who tried to raid the cracker supply, while Dolce threatened the wrath of God toward one nine-year-old who'd almost upended the bowl of apricot preserves. I was ringing up a customer who'd bought one of everything when a guy in a man bun and a vintage T-shirt leaned over the counter in my direction.

"So where do you get your fruit?" he asked.

I was tempted to point to the sign that said *We use Colorado produce,* but that seemed rude. "We buy our produce from local farmers. A lot of it comes from my uncle's place, Constantine Farms. Their booth is just down the line here."

The guy's eyes widened as he looked at me, and his face flushed a bit. He cleared his throat. "Are you the owner?"

I nodded, smiling as I handed the bag of jam to the customer who'd bought it. "This is my place. I'm Roxy Constantine."

"Oh." He picked up a cracker and dipped it into the pepper peach. Then his lips spread in a smile. "Oh, wow. This is great."

"Thanks." Another customer handed me a couple of jars of raspberry peach. Normally I'm delighted to talk about my stuff, and compliments are always welcome. But we were crazy busy right then, and I really wished the guy would just move on.

However, he seemed to have settled in. "So how long have you been in business?"

"A couple of years."

"Where else do you sell?"

"Just here in town for now. Although I sell a limited

number of jars at a place in Salida. Most of our business is here at the farmers market."

"Oh." He looked around the booth and seemed to notice the crowd for the first time. "Looks like you're being swamped."

"It's busy," I agreed. *To state the obvious.*

"Maybe I'll come back and talk later."

"You do that," I muttered as he walked away.

After noon, business began to slack off a little. People were moving over to the craft fair next door with its array of food trucks. I heard a band tuning up in the gazebo, which meant another draw for the crowds. I took a moment to check the stock. We'd sold out of the bourbon peach and the raspberry peach. We had a few more jars of pepper peach, apricot, strawberry, and peach preserves. The raspberry was running dangerously low.

"Do you need to go to the truck to get more jam?" Dolce asked.

I shook my head. "It's all out here and in the cases under the counter."

Dolce's eyes widened. "Wow, we've really been selling."

"We have at that." I glanced around the booth as I added jars to the stock we had out for sale. "I wonder how everybody else has been doing?"

"We've been doing okay. Not record breaking but good."

I turned to see Annabelle Dorsey examining a jar of strawberry preserves. "Is this from this year?"

"I put up a lot when the fruit came in." That had been the weekend I'd been accused of murder. I'd been a jam-making machine that day.

"I'll take it." She put the jar on the counter where I

could ring it up, then handed me her money. "I need to thank you for what you did for Dorothy. And I need to apologize for her." She raised her gaze to mine, looking flinty.

"You mean when she ran off to the parking lot that time?"

Annabelle shook her head. "When she threw mud at your truck and wrote a foul word. I didn't know she'd done it until Fowler came to talk to us both."

I blew out a breath. "Oh, that. I didn't know it was Dorothy at the time. I thought it was Brett Holmes. Dorothy already apologized."

Annabelle stared down at her strawberry preserves. "She's been having a hard time. Apparently, she thought she was in love with that jerk. It's been a nasty awakening. But learning about men is a life skill we all need."

I didn't know much about Annabelle's history with men, just that she'd divorced Dorothy's father. Something about her expression made me think she hadn't had a great experience. "She's a teenager. All of us were dumb when we were teenagers. I hope there's someone she can talk to." Which was as close as I could get to saying Dorothy needed a counselor.

"There is." Annabelle picked up the jar. "At least he didn't get away with it."

"No, he didn't get away with it." In fact, he'd made the fatal mistake of underestimating one of the women he'd jerked around. That didn't mean I thought Evelyn was justified, but it did mean Brett's sins had caught up with him. Poetic justice if you will.

Annabelle turned and walked up the path toward her booth. I wondered if Dorothy was helping out today, but

I wasn't going down there to find out.

At two I broke down the booth and put everything away, even though there were still a few potential customers hanging around. I wanted to get to the exhibit hall in plenty of time for the end of the Best in Shavano competition, the part with the live judging. I was also a little curious about where my jam had placed in that competition, although I still wasn't optimistic.

The entries in the various competitions were placed on tables ranged around the edge of the room. Jams had been placed next to pies, which made a certain amount of sense. They hadn't yet posted the winners of the side competitions—they'd get around to that after they'd finished judging the restaurant contest that constituted the main event.

I found a seat near the front, and Susa slipped into the chair next to mine. "How's Nate doing?"

"Too early to say. They haven't started judging yet."

"Well, anyway, he looks yummy."

He definitely did, but all the chefs had cleaned up for their audience. They stood at the front, dressed in their chef's jackets and toques or beanies. For a moment I felt a touch of nostalgia. Back in the day I'd worn that outfit, and worn it proudly. Of course now I cooked in jeans and T-shirts, and I wore those proudly, too.

I found Nate easily, standing near the front in a black chef's coat and beanie. I wondered if they'd been his uniform in Las Vegas since I was sure he didn't wear anything like that to cook at Robicheaux's. Spencer Carroll was nearby, dressed in crisp whites and a toque. I recognized a couple of the other chefs, too, one from the Jade Garden and one from Moretti's. The other two were strangers.

The contest entries were on trays in front of the chefs: three complete, plated entrées, with sides and desserts. They'd be taken up to the judges table, with each chef coming up to explain his plate. According to some texts from Nate that morning, they'd done their cooking in the commercial kitchen behind the event center, trying to share the stoves and ovens. Keeping your cool was probably part of the competition.

I figured Nate's stuff was better than the entries from Jade Garden and Moretti's, but I wasn't certain about Spence. High Country was a more haute cuisine kind of place than Robicheaux's, and of course Spence had something to prove. A win might mean they'd keep him on as head chef instead of hiring somebody from Denver.

An announcer came out to introduce the chefs and the judges, a newspaper critic from the Front Range, a rep from the Shavano tourist board, and a celebrity chef from Aspen. Nate looked calm as the entries were taken to the judges' tables. I felt nervous enough for both of us.

The tasting took around thirty minutes. I noticed the Aspen chef kept clearing his palate with water, but the other two judges dug in enthusiastically. I hoped they'd hit Nate's entry early in the process since they'd probably be too full to judge the last ones fairly.

Nate stepped forward after a few minutes. For some reason they hadn't chosen to let the crowd hear the questions and answers from the contestants and judges, so I found myself watching the judges' faces, trying to see if they were happy or not, if maybe they were licking their lips. Nate kept his bland smile in place as he answered the questions. One of the judges pointed to something on the plate, and Nate gave him a genuine grin as he answered. That had to be a good sign, I decided. Finally, he stepped aside to let Tal Nguyen from Jade Garden take his place.

"That went okay, didn't it?" Susa asked.

"Maybe. I don't know for sure."

The other chefs took their places as the judges went through the entries. Spencer's entrée looked like lamb with some kind of potato side. He wore the same noncommittal smile that Nate had had when he stepped back in line, both of them trying hard not to give anything away.

Finally, the judges stood up and left the room, going somewhere to confer and maybe swallow a few antacids. Nate walked toward us. He looked more tired than he had before, his smile fading when he got to the chair I'd saved for him. Before he could sit down, he was intercepted by Madge and Coco who both hugged him with broad smiles. Nate pushed his lips into something like a smile again, but I had the feeling his heart wasn't really in it.

Oh, hell. Maybe the questions hadn't gone well. Maybe he'd already heard the results or had reason to think he knew what the judges were going to do. He gave his mom another hug, then sat down beside me and Susa.

"How'd it go?" Susa asked. "You look great, by the way."

I gave him a quick hug, pressing my lips to his cheek. "What she said."

Nate sighed, running a hand across the back of his neck. "They asked me about the sauce on the chops, and they were intrigued by the rose petal jam. But Spence did rack of lamb with a rosemary crust and duchess potatoes. I can't compete with that. We don't have the resources at Robicheaux's."

"Of course you can compete with that," I said loyally. "It's not about how expensive the food is, it's about how well prepared it is. And yours is super."

Nate gave me a very faint smile. We both knew that wasn't entirely true. "Thanks, babe, but I'm okay. I think we'll place, but I don't think we'll win."

And who knew how Bobby would react to that.

The door at the back of the room opened, and the judges filed in again. "Gotta go," Nate murmured, hastening to his place at the front.

I took a breath, squaring my shoulders. Nate could always be wrong. His pork chops could have blown Spence out of the water, which would be great for Nate and not so great for Spence. *Focus, dammit.* I was supposed to be sending positive vibes to Nate, not worrying about Spence's future at High Country.

The announcer stepped to the microphone, and my shoulders tensed. "First of all, we want to thank you all for attending our fifth annual Best in Shavano."

"Yeah, yeah," I muttered. "Get on with it."

"The judges have made their choices in all the other competitions. You'll find ribbons at each booth and lists of all the winners are posted outside."

"Hey," Susa said. "Want to go see if you won?"

I shook my head. "I didn't. Not this year. I want to stay here and see how Nate did."

The announcer turned to the assembled chefs. They were all still in their chef's coats, but some of them had pulled off their hats. Nate and Spence, though, were still wearing their full uniforms.

"The judges have awarded prizes in three areas: entrées, sides, and desserts. We'll only announce the first place winners here, but the others will be posted outside. So let's get underway." He opened an envelope, pulling out a sheet of paper. "And the winner for entrees is…" The announcer did a *British Baking Show* pause, grinning. I felt like strangling him.

"Spencer Carroll and High Country Restaurant," he said.

Nate kept smiling. So did everybody else. I guessed all of them had probably figured rack of lamb would cancel out whatever they'd chosen to do. Spence stepped forward with a big grin, and the judges shook his hand, murmuring what looked like compliments as they did.

"Okay. So rack of lamb wins. No biggie. Nate can take the sides."

Susa glanced at me, then kept her focus on the announcer.

"Best sides. The winner is…"

I decided the announcer deserved to die. Or at least have his tie stuffed down his throat.

"Spencer Carroll and High Country Restaurant."

I sighed. Spence had done duchess potatoes and haricots verts. Again, high ticket items. Maybe the competition should introduce categories so the expensive restaurants would compete against each other and the places like Robicheaux's would have a better shot.

Nate's smile seemed fixed now, and my heart ached for him. He'd put in so much time, worked so hard developing those recipes. And he'd gotten nothing.

"Now the all-important dessert category. You know what they say—life is uncertain, eat dessert first." The announcer looked around as if he'd come up with that quip on his own. I gritted my teeth.

Nate raised his head, not really trying for a smile this time, but managing to look pleasant.

"And the winner for desserts is…"

Death. The man deserved death.

"Nathan Robicheaux and Robicheaux's Café."

Nate stared at him for a moment, as if he wasn't sure he'd heard what he'd heard. Tal Nguyen from Jade Garden pounded him on the shoulder and even Spence managed a smile. The announcer I'd been consigning to perdition just a couple of minutes ago handed Nate a trophy, and Nate finally let himself grin.

It wasn't the entrée, but it was still important. Maybe even more important, given that a lot of people went to Robicheaux's for dessert and coffee. And my jam had been part of it. I'd helped. I grinned at Nate as we applauded, and he gave me a particular kind of grin in return.

That was when I remembered: his dessert had also convinced me to go to bed with him the first time.

A winner all around. Maybe our mojo had helped to put it over the line. It was worth a repeat performance. Maybe tonight.

Chapter 27

We headed to Dirty Pete's for a celebratory beer after the competition was finished. The three of us were joined first by Madge and Coco, and then by Harry, who divided his time between the table and the bar where he was working. Uncle Mike slid into a seat beside Madge, whom he watched with hopeful eyes.

I wasn't sure how I felt about that. I liked Madge, but I loved Uncle Mike. If she broke his heart, I might get cross with her. Still, I thought Madge had a gleam in her eye when she glanced in Uncle Mike's direction. It might work out after all. We'd have to wait and see.

Spencer Carroll came in a few minutes later with his two awards. I tried to feel annoyed with him, but he was so happy it was hard to keep any resentment going. He had indeed nailed down his place at High Country, at least for the time being. And Nate seemed genuinely happy for him. If Nate could be magnanimous, so could the rest of us.

Spence couldn't stay long because he had to get dinner started at High Country. He high fived Nate over their awards, then ambled off across the street. After he'd left, I saw a vaguely familiar guy at the bar, taking a martini from Harry. The guy glanced at our table, then paused, frowning before he grabbed his martini and walked toward us.

I was a little nervous about that frown, but so far as

I knew I hadn't done anything to piss anybody off recently. Not counting Evelyn Davidson, of course.

"You're Nate Robicheaux, aren't you?" he asked when he reached tableside.

Nate turned to him, then put down his beer. Apparently, he recognized the guy. "That's right."

The guy placed his martini carefully on the table, then extended his hand. "I wanted to let you know those were superlative pork chops." I finally placed him: the chef from Aspen who'd been one of the judges.

"Thanks. I appreciate that." Nate smiled a little tentatively. Harry bent forward on the bar so he could hear better.

"I voted for you on all three dishes," the chef continued. "You almost won on the entrée. But I couldn't convince the others in the end." He shrugged, his mouth twisting in a sour grin. "Some people will always go with what's expensive instead of what's tasty."

"This is Roxy Constantine." Nate nodded at me quickly. "I used her apricot jam on the chops."

The chef glanced at me without much interest, then returned to Nate, pulling his card from his wallet. "If you're ever interested in moving to a bigger market, let me know. I can always use a talented chef."

Madge's smile faded as she regarded the chef with something like loathing. If she'd been Medusa, the Aspen chef would have been stone.

"Thanks again. I'll keep it in mind." Nate tucked the card into his pocket as the chef took his martini toward the back of the room.

Madge took a swallow of her beer, very deliberately not looking at her son.

"Don't worry, Ma. I'm not going anywhere."

"At the moment," Coco muttered.

I decided to ignore both of them. Maybe they had a right to be worried, but this was Nate's day, and I wanted him to enjoy it. I picked up my beer. "Here's to you, Nate. You nailed it, just like we knew you would. Congrats."

Everybody else raised their bottles, too. "To Nate." Susa grinned. "I can't wait to taste those pork chops myself."

Nate gave her a slightly rueful grin back. "I may have to come by your house to fix you one. They aren't on the menu at the café."

"Yes, they are. They will be. They'll be a special sometime this month." Madge gave Nate a fierce look.

"With Roxy's apricot jam? The apricot jam made the dish."

"Of course. If you've got any apricot jam for us to buy, Roxy?"

"Sure. As much as you want."

"Good. That's settled. Come on, Coco, I'll give you a ride home."

Coco looked as if she might have preferred to stay, but she shrugged. "Okay." She moved over to Nate, kissing his cheek. "You did good, bro. Congrats and thanks."

I frowned as I watched them go. "Thanks for what?"

"For taking on Bobby and winning. Although I may not have won all the way yet. The market specials we've been doing have sold well, but Bobby's still not convinced anything at the café needs to change. Still, we get to tweak the menu a little more, and that's a definite plus."

"Good for you, then. And good for the café—it's

going to appeal to a new bunch of customers, without losing the old ones."

"And we're buying your jam." He grinned at me. "Did I tell you what the judges said about the crepes?"

"What?"

"They said the combination of flavors was like nothing they'd ever tasted before. The guy from Denver said it was like eating a bouquet. In a good way."

Uncle Mike swallowed the last of his beer. "Better be getting home myself." He looked out the window where Madge and Coco were climbing into Madge's car. "Got stuff to do."

I tried to read his expression but I couldn't entirely. Longing was involved, though. "Okay. I'll be home later."

"Take your time." He smiled at Nate. "Celebrate."

"We will. I'll make sure she gets home okay."

I noticed he didn't specify which home he was referring to.

"Well, I'm not leaving," Susa said. "I want another beer."

Harry set up more beers for all of us, then sat down at our table again as the door behind us swung open.

Chief Fowler walked in.

It might have been my imagination, but the room seemed to go quiet for a moment. Harry stiffened, and I wondered if he was worried about possible liquor law violations.

"I'm off duty." Fowler gave us one of his half smiles. "You all can relax."

"Good to know," Susa said. "Join us."

I gave her a wide-eyed stare, but she ignored me. Fowler dropped into the chair beside her, removing his

Stetson. "Competition over?"

I nodded toward the trophy. "Yep. Nate won for dessert."

"Congratulations. You serving the winning dessert at the café?"

Nate shook his head. "One of a kind. I used Roxy's rose petal jam, and there's none left. I'll buy up all she makes next fall, though. Exclusive production." He gave Fowler an intense look.

I had a weird feeling there was some kind of silent dialogue going on between them. Then I decided it was probably my imagination. "How's the police business?"

He shrugged. "Same old. Normal."

Normal meaning no murders, which struck me as desirable. "That's good, isn't it?"

He gave me another half-smile. "That's good."

One of the customers at the bar leaned over Susa's shoulder. "Roxy Constantine, right?"

"Right." It took me a minute to recognize him. Man bun. Vintage T-shirt. Oh, yeah, the guy who'd wanted to have a conversation. "You were at the booth earlier."

"Yeah. When I came back, you weren't there."

"We closed down a little early today. Because of the competition."

"Oh, right. The competition. Congratulations."

I narrowed my eyes. He hadn't said anything to Nate so far or even looked at him. "Congratulations?"

"On winning. The pepper peach. I actually wanted to buy a couple more jars of that if I could."

"She won?" Susa stared up at him. "Roxy won the jam contest?"

"Yeah." He gave me an incredulous look. "You didn't know?"

"I forgot to check." My cheeks flushed because what kind of idiot forgets that she's entered in a big contest?

"Rox, that's great!" Nate put his arm around my shoulders, giving me a quick hug. "Is it too late to pick up your ribbon?"

"Probably. I'll do it tomorrow." I turned to the man bun guy. "You want some pepper peach? I can go get you a couple of jars." I figured he deserved something for giving me the news. I might never have found out otherwise.

"Actually, I needed to talk to you." The guy pulled out one of the empty chairs and slid up to our table.

Both Nate and Fowler stiffened slightly, but I figured he had a right to join us. "What's up?"

"I'm Toby Hartshorne. From Gold Plate productions." He reached into his pocket and pulled out a card. Nate gave it a narrow-eyed glance as I dropped it into my purse. "We do a show on Food Network called *Sweet Thing,* and we're going to be filming here next month."

My pulse promptly began to thunder in my ears. "Yeah, I'd heard that."

"Usually we do restaurants and ice cream parlors, but I'd like to include your jam. Maybe shoot at the farmers market. Assuming the market's okay with it."

"I think I can guarantee the market would be fine with it."

"Well, good. Would you be interested?"

"Definitely. I'm definitely interested. I'll talk to the market management and set it up." I dug around in my purse until I found one of the business cards I give out once in a blue moon. "That's my cell. Just give me a call next week."

"Great. I'll get the wheels in motion and then we can discuss how to go about this." He gave me another smile. "About that pepper peach."

"I've got a couple of jars in my truck. I'll get them for you." I pushed to my feet.

Hartshorne stood up, too. "I'll walk there with you. Maybe you can suggest a good place for dinner. With a dessert, of course."

"I'll help," Nate said quickly. "I'm good with restaurant recommendations." He moved beside me, taking my hand.

Hartshorne shrugged. "Fine."

I glanced at Susa, a little concerned about stranding her with Fowler. She gave me a small, curving grin. If anyone could handle the chief, it was Susa. Assuming, of course, he wanted to be handled.

We hiked to my truck where I got Hartshorne his pepper peach. Nate directed him to Moretti's, which really did have a good tiramisu and decent cannoli. Then he put his arm around my shoulders again. "You want to go out for dinner? Or I can make cacio e pepe at my place."

"Your place. We've got a lot to celebrate."

"We do at that." He grinned. "You're going to be on TV."

I grinned back. "A famous chef offered you a job. Sort of."

Nate shook his head. "I wouldn't take it. I'm not ready to enter the rat race again."

That left open the question of what he'd do when he was ready, but I ignored it for now. "Still, it's good to know the one pro on the panel thought your stuff was the best."

"It is. And it's great to know that your pepper peach ruled. We should have checked it before we left."

"I didn't want to. I figured I lost. Good to know I didn't." I glanced up as we rounded a corner. "Where are we going?"

"To the café. I need to pick up some pecorino romano. I've got everything else I need to fix dinner."

I followed him into the kitchen, then paused. Bobby stood near the prep table, putting some containers into the refrigerator. Probably prep for tomorrow's brunch. Nate stepped up beside him, reaching for a large container of cheese.

"What do you need?" Bobby asked.

"Romano. Just a cup or so." Nate put the container on the prep table, then reached for a storage bag.

Bobby propped his hip against the table, watching Nate spoon cheese into the bag. "Heard you won that contest."

"Dessert." Nate shrugged. "High Country took it for entrées and sides."

Bobby nodded slowly. "Mom said one of the judges came over to tell you he liked your chops."

Nate blew out a breath. "Yeah, he did. It was cool."

Bobby looked squarely at his brother. "You did good today. High Country's a big time, upscale restaurant. We're comfort food, one step up from a diner. You nipped at their heels. Good for you. I'm proud of you."

"Thanks." Nate looked a little stunned.

"I'm still gonna fight you on the menu." Bobby turned to the refrigerator.

"Yep." Nate picked up his cheese. "I figured you would. See you tomorrow."

"See you."

I glanced at Nate as we turned toward my truck again. "Progress?"

"Maybe. Two steps forward, one step back." He paused to open the door for me. "At least he congratulated me. That meant a lot."

"Yeah, it did."

He climbed into the truck cab beside me. "I meant what I said—I want to buy all your rose petal jam, along with the apricot jam. And maybe some pepper peach." He sighed. "Hell, I'd buy your entire production if I could. It's that good."

"Actually, I'm thinking of increasing my production. I've got a possible assistant for the fall. And, hey, I'm going to be on TV."

"Yeah, you are. What are you going to show them?"

"Oh, God." I hadn't even thought about that. And now that I did, I was faintly terrified. "They said August. We'll still have peaches, maybe a few apricots, raspberries. I could do pear conserve with vanilla bean. People like that. But we may not have any pears yet. And there'll be blackberries. I do plum butter sometimes. I wonder how they'd feel about that?"

I pulled into Nate's driveway, biting my lip. "Maybe I should head home. I need to make some jam."

Nate reached across the seat, cupping my face in his hands so that he could kiss me. After a few moments, I decided the jam could wait. He raised his head to look at me. "You can start tomorrow. Tonight I'm going to make you cacio e pepe and we're going to kill a bottle of champagne I happen to have on hand and you're not going to worry about anything at all. Sound good?"

"Sounds terrific." All the way up the stairs to his

place, I kept telling myself to relax, to clear my mind, to get in the groove, not to think about jam. But I knew it wouldn't work.

Maybe I was going to expand my business—I hadn't decided yet. Maybe I was in love with Nate—I was around ninety percent sure I was, but I needed to cogitate a little more.

But one thing I knew for sure.

I was the jam queen of Shavano County, Colorado. And life was good.

A word about the author…

Meg Benjamin is an award-winning author of romance. Along with her Luscious Delights series for Wild Rose Press, she's also the author of the Konigsburg, Salt Box and Brewing Love series. Along with these contemporary romances, Meg is also the author of the paranormal Ramos Family trilogy and the Folk series. Meg's books have won numerous awards, including an EPIC Award, a Romantic Times Reviewers' Choice Award, the Holt Medallion from Virginia Romance Writers, the Beanpot Award from the New England Romance Writers, and the Award of Excellence from Colorado Romance Writers.